ORBITING WHAT REMAINS

Xavier Paulson

Chapter 1

○

Six Gs of gravitational pull might not sound like a lot if you've never felt it before, but it is.

On Earth, when you feel one G, one gravitational pull, you feel nothing at all. When you get up to three Gs, there isn't a significant difference, but it can become slightly more difficult to breathe, and you will likely feel uncomfortable. Four to five Gs feels like the most intense roller coaster you could ever experience. But Skye Calvert had to endure over six Gs.

The injection should have worked. Everyone taking the flight up into space was fast asleep. Everyone except her. While everyone, including Skye, wore bodysuits that allowed them to withstand the Gs without experiencing severe health effects, that didn't stop Skye from feeling any negative symptoms altogether.

Everything felt heavy, and Skye felt herself unable to even lift her hands from the armrests. She felt disoriented, her head was spinning, and she started to experience tunnel vision. Her chest was gripped with pain, and she found herself gasping for air, meekly calling for help that wouldn't come. Skye felt so lightheaded she thought she was going to die.

Skye was so engulfed in the panic attack that she hadn't the time, nor the concentration, to marvel out the window above her as the rocket launched up into space, to view the arrays of magnificent white and yellow stars that flew by as the ship ascended on a steep vertical track. Instead, her vision, dark and shimmering at the edge and slowly closing in, faded to black. That was Skye's introduction to space: passing out. It wasn't exactly a good start.

***

When Skye came to, everyone was already starting to disembark the space shuttle. That is, everyone except the single familiar face, presumably attached to the arms shaking her from her side. Skye's vision was blurry for a few moments before it settled in to see a sympathetic expression, and it finally clicked what had happened.

"Oh… Oh…" Skye was groggy but relieved that the ship finally felt stable.

"Are… you okay?" came the concerned voice of Graham, another intern.

Graham Scorsone was the only person on the ship whom she had met before, the only other student intern enrolled at the University of Michigan. Ironically, neither of them was from the area, Skye hailing from Minnesota, and Graham from South Carolina. Although Skye hadn't spent more than a few hours with Graham before, she was glad she at least knew someone on this ship. The last thing she needed to do was be left behind and wake up grounded on Earth again.

"Yes, yes, thank you," Skye lied. "I was… The injection didn't work."

"Really?"

"Yeah, I passed out during the takeoff. But not from the drug, from all the Gs."

"That's terrible," Graham said, raising his eyebrows. "Should we tell the staff?"

"No, no," Skye responded, shaking her head. "It's no big deal."

But Skye's expression made it apparent that it was, in fact, a big deal.

Graham appeared to want to say more, but he relented.

"Well, okay…"

Skye regathered her wits, hoping that if she had such a terrible commute to the International Space Hotel, she could at the very least get a glimpse into the beauty of space. But the ship apparently had other plans. The back carriage of the shuttle was almost completely enclosed by opaque metal except for a single window that ran around the top. From the angle the ship had docked, she could see nothing outside the window except for a huge metal wall running perpendicular to the ship. There were no stars in sight. Skye had missed her chance for a good view.

Skye unbuckled from her seat as Graham made his way towards the exit, realizing that now the ship must've been within the active range of the anti-gravity chambers, or otherwise simulated an artificial gravity environment, because her own feet were planted firmly to the ground, and jumping up didn't shoot her high into the air, much to her disappointment. She was glad no one seemed to notice her hopping.

Skye took her cargo out of the overhead storage space. She then followed Graham to the lobby of the docking bay. As they did so, they passed the smiling flight attendants and the pilots, who stood up near the exit and watched, proud that the fifth-ever year of interns had been delivered without any issues. Skye imagined it hadn't been too difficult, considering the ship was probably at least partially operated autonomously.

"Have a good stay at the International Space Hotel," one of the flight attendants, a blonde woman who resembled a supermodel far more than a woman who made frequent trips to space said. Skye managed a slight smile back.

Graham and Skye filed out of the ship, not knowing what to expect. They were presented with a giant security checkpoint up ahead at the entryway of the International Space Hotel, ISH for short, in a zone that resembled the security area of a regular airport down on Earth.

Graham and Skye found themselves at the back of the line, due to their tardiness in exiting the ship. However, from where they stood, they could still see past the security checkpoint to a giant lobby bustling with strolling pedestrians. Before their destination, however, there were a few armed guards. They all wore dark, bulky armored uniforms, with abnormally large shoulder pads that almost jutted out in spikes and layered plates that covered much of their torso, presumably providing some sort of bulletproof defense for the wearer. The goofy sight faintly resembled something you would see from an anime antagonist in the 1980s: Skye didn't watch anime herself, but her brother was very into it.

"TSA flashbacks," Skye whispered.

"I hope this moves faster than that," Graham murmured. "It's 2048 and my father says TSA is just as bad as it was twenty years ago."

"You can say that again," Skye replied, "and how about this gravity? I don't feel a thing."

"I suppose the antigravity chamber is doing its job, huh?" Graham asked, a smirk on his face. "Almost as if they don't need me for the engineering internship. Almost like they could just let me, I don't know, hang out in the rec room."

"You wish!" Skye said. "I thought you had some repair duties, right?"

"Yes, that's what I'm going to primarily be doing, I'd guess," Graham said, nodding. "I mean, I'm not going to be developing any hotel modifications soon. I'm no Einstein. Not that Einstein could've ever envisioned this masterpiece."

The line through security moved relatively quickly, and Skye looked ahead to anticipate the next steps. First, everyone had to set their suitcase in a receptacle in a strange egg-looking machine that scanned the inner contents of the suitcase. Skye had never seen anything quite like it. When it flashed green, that meant the passenger could move on to the second stage. If it flashed red then that meant an android TSA inspector would clank over to search the bag. Any further issues would lead to human employees having to step in and intervene. She knew this part from the repeated annoying message that played over a nearby intercom. Skye had a feeling something would go wrong: technology always seemed to break around her.

Luckily for everyone involved, there were no issues at all for the new guests ahead of Skye, save for a couple of flashing red lights. Graham and Skye passed the receptacle test without a hitch. Before Skye knew it, she was stepping through a scanner that checked her person for any potential weapons or metal items. As if they hadn't already passed through security back on Earth before boarding the shuttle.

After this, there was one more stage of security remaining. In each line, there was a pole a few feet tall, on top of which, there was an orange-looking gel. A robotic voice instructed Skye to insert her fingers into the gel, which she did. It was not as sticky as she expected but it perfectly molded to fit her fingers and lock in her fingerprints. The same robotic voice told her to pull her hand away, which she did, and her hand was surprisingly completely dry after the entire process. A grid of green lasers scanned over the orange gel before the robotic voice played again.

"Fingerprint scanned, and photo captured. Thank you."

The gel immediately reconstituted into a single, smooth solid.

Skye stepped forwards, waiting for Graham to pass the fingerprint scanner test before proceeding to the other side, where another humanoid robot, identical to the other one from earlier, stood, arms straight by its side. Graham passed by it, sizing it up a little bit, his face falling with disappointment that all of the humanoid robots were at an identical height at six feet flat, and had at least a good two inches on him.

"Please deposit your bodysuits into the chute, and then you may exit," the robot said, and he moved on, turning around and waiting for Skye to pass through.

Skye unzipped her bodysuit (she had a full layer of clothes underneath) and tossed her bodysuit into the chute. Graham did the same once he passed by, and then they were finally finished, free to roam the hotel as they desired.

As they exited into the lobby, Graham and Skye noticed a couple of water fountains. The fountains were located near a small crowd of men and women who were gathering near the exit to the security area. Skye stepped over to them, desperate to quench her thirst. It looked like each fountain contained a slot for a keycard that you'd have to swipe in order to receive water, but a message in bright yellow letters was emblazoned on the screen on top of each fountain.

Please enjoy this complimentary water, new arrivals.

While Graham and Skye both drank the odd tasting water, Skye looked at the group nearby. Judging by the way they all faced the docking area they'd just left it appeared like all of them were just waiting to fill up the shuttle once everyone had left. A few security guards (or so Skye guessed based on their black armored outfits she'd seen earlier) stood near them, murmuring.

"Twenty-one guards, gone today," one of the nearby guards was saying. "I can't believe it. What a waste."

A tall, older looking guard who looked like he commanded the attention and respect of the others smirked.

"That's how it is," The tall man said. "Our CEO is cutting costs, and people want to pursue higher-paying opportunities with security firms where they can live with their family. Everyone poaches our guys."

"Whatever you say, Fritz."

"Relax," The man replied. "Just wait two more weeks and we'll have thirty replacements… We'll only be understaffed for a short while."

Skye and Graham finished drinking, Skye feeling oddly refreshed by the water despite its slightly off-putting taste. The two made their way past the crowd and towards the main lobby, at which point Skye spoke up.

"How about that discussion back there, huh?" Skye asked. "CEO cutting costs? I hope they didn't cut any corners on the technology here."

"What're you talking about?" Graham asked. "That's impolite to eavesdrop on strangers."

"Never mind," Skye said, rolling her eyes at his prudishness, and the two fell silent, observing their surroundings until Graham piped up again.

"Do you know where to go? I'm directionally challenged."

"Good thing you're not a pilot," Skye replied. "Just follow where everyone else is going."

Skye was right. There were a few dozen interns aboard that shuttle, and all of them were headed in the same direction. They entered the giant spacious lobby, and here, an electronic sign displayed the words *INTERNS, report here for check-in.* A few tables were positioned in place for interns to line up and check in with the human staff. But Skye was distracted looking at the other wall.

"Look at that," Skye whispered to herself with amazement.

Skye marveled at the breathtaking view of the Earth through the glass alloy of the wall which provided an unobstructed view of the vast expanse of the ocean below. The sky was a deep shade of glowing blue, unblemished apart from strands of white clouds that resembled delicate strings of cotton candy drifting far below them. The water, a sparkling blue under the sun's rays, was nothing short of astounding. The land below on Earth looked so small that it seemed unreal, the simultaneous vastness and smallness of the blue and green sphere baffling her. It was so surreal; she could hardly put it into words.

"That might be the most beautiful thing I've ever seen," Skye said.

"Wow," Graham said, nodding. "That is… fantastic."

Skye turned her attention over to the line. The growing line stood in front of a table, where a man and a woman wearing navy blue polo shirts were handing out key cards and itineraries, as well as checking in the new guests using a touch screen of some kind that was propped up on a swivel.

With each new arrival, the welcoming committee opened a new crisp white envelope to pull out a keycard and present it to the oncoming intern. It had been a long while since Skye had seen a paper envelope (everything was digital now), and she was taken aback by the sight.

Despite the manual process and notable lack of androids involved here, the line moved quickly. Within a couple of minutes, Skye and Graham were standing in front of the man and the woman, respectively.

"First things first," the man told Skye, "What's your name?"

"Skye. Skye Calvert."

"All right, all right," the man said, swiping down on his surface with his finger and scrunching his eyes. "Communications intern?"

"That's right. I'll be an assistant with the announcement coordinator."

"Okay, good." The man reached over onto the table for the last unopened envelope and opened it up before handing over the keycard.

"Here's the keycard. You will be residing in a single staff room, which is comfortably large. Not as large as the single hotel room, but not bad, trust me. The room number is on the keycard. I'm assuming you're aware of what amenities we have to offer, but in the event you don't, you will find a pamphlet on the nightstand next to your bed. Also included will be the log-in information for the staff's Wi-Fi network."

Skye grabbed the keycard. Prominently displayed on the side was the number 032.

"Thanks."

"You will have orientation for a couple of days, starting tomorrow. First thing's first, however, there will be an intern party tonight at 8 p.m. in the Entertainment Hall. Dinner will be provided."

"Thank you. What's the space-time right now? Being as I'm not connected to the Wi-Fi yet and all."

"It's 4:41 p.m. right now. You have a couple of hours to unpack and make yourself at home."

"Okay, thank you… And, if I may ask, how should I find these rooms?"

"Just follow the crowds, and every couple of hundred feet there's a directory with a map of the ship, which you can use."

Skye pocketed the keycard before turning to Graham, who had been waiting off the side, having already checked in.

"Thanks for waiting for me," Skye said when she walked over to him.

"No problem. I don't want to get lost," Graham replied, smiling. "It wasn't that long."

"Well, okay, Mr. Directionally Challenged, let's go," Skye said. "Oh, what's your room number?"

"Umm… Let me look. 33. Why?"

"32!" Skye cheered. "We're roommates. Well, almost roommates."

"That's great," Graham responded without an ounce of excitement. "Let's go find our rooms."

Skye was first and foremost surprised by how large the space station was. After passing through the area of the docking bay, they passed through a couple of vast carpeted hallways. They did so by standing on a central escalator platform which automatically propelled the pair of them forwards, past a couple of restaurants, a small souvenir shop, some bathrooms, and the Entertainment Hall. She could see glimpses of space through the windows towards Earth (she knew there was some sort of system in place to significantly dim the windows that faced the Sun, which already were specially designed to minimize radiation). It also appeared that every fifty feet or so, there was some sort of metal arch spanning the walls and the ceiling. She soon realized was a sort of emergency airlock that could seal off if there was a breach in the roof or the window. She hoped none would ever have to be used for her sake.

Even though this entire experience seemed otherworldly, there were still parts that reminded them of home. There were billboards on some of the walls. One of them flashed with advertisements from a popular fast-food chain that had opened the first fast-food franchise in space in history (the *Famous Foodstack*), a souvenir shop played an ad featuring its various items (which were, of course, extremely overpriced), and a giant blue logo over a white background was projected onto a screen that read *Ascendant*

Technologies, purporting to be the "Sponsor of the International Space Hotel."

Skye and Graham were so absorbed in taking in all of the sights of this new environment that they didn't talk until they had reached the Entertainment Hall a few minutes later. Skye could only tell the location based upon the sign hanging from the ceiling.

"That's where our party should be tonight," Graham said, pointing it out.

"Sounds fun," Skye replied. "I hope we get along with the other interns."

Skye couldn't look into the Entertainment Hall, and only saw a big black pair of doors out front, but she had heard online that it was huge inside, with some sort of theater and space for dozens of tables. They hardly needed so much space. The emails she'd been sent had told her there were only thirty-three interns, selected from across the country. She'd had a one in a thousand, no, maybe a ten-thousand chance of being selected, and as she stood there, slowly proceeding towards the main hotel area, peering through the windows and into the beauty that was the cosmos of space, of stars glowing from perhaps millions of light years away, it started to hit her.

I'm doing this, she realized, her hands clenching on the handrail, *I've gone to space and I'm about to stay here for literally months*. She was the first person in her entire town in Minnesota, and possibly her entire county, to ever go to space.

It was only a couple of minutes later that Graham and Skye were in line waiting to check in at the receptionist's desks, behind some of the other guests. The receptionists were, of course, robots, robots of the same nature and appearance as the human-like robots that had been screening them at the security checkpoint.

The check-in process was smooth. Skye gave them her name and an ID that had been provided, before showing them her keycard. When she did, a flap on its metallic eyes opened up and a laser went down and scanned the ID.

"Keycard accepted," the robot hummed in its distinct animatronic voice, "I hope you enjoy your stay at the International Space Hotel."

Skye followed Graham, realizing that this hotel was, like her college dormitory, a new home away from home. She truly did hope she would enjoy her stay, because there would be no going home until the allotted time was up, barring some sort of massive emergency in the hotel.

Chapter 2

Skye's hotel room was not overly decorated, but it was also surprisingly luxurious and well-stocked. The room contained a giant desk, like most of the other hotels Skye visited back down on Earth, a safe, and a do-it-all Cold-Zone™ machine, a joint machine that comprised of a mini-fridge, freezer, and coffee-maker all in one. Skye had just wished it'd come with a juice dispenser, but she figured that those models were probably reserved for the VIP rooms.

There was also a small sofa on the side of the room, as well as a decent-sized bed that appeared to be a Queen size. A couple of printed paintings were hung up around the room, and in the corner, an ornate, twisty glass light several feet tall. It reminded Skye of everything she'd ever found wrong with modern art, but a press of the button on its side confirmed that it at least functioned well. There was also a nightstand next to the bed, and, like the one staff back in the docking lobby area had promised, a pamphlet and log-in information.

She first checked the Wi-Fi info, and connected to the Wi-Fi for the staff, plainly called "ISH Staff." Skye would not be able to call anyone on Earth with her phone, neither by audio or video. The restriction, unfortunately, extended to pretty much all forms of social media, meaning that the Wi-Fi network would only pretty much handle phone calls and texts to others on board the ship. It was her understanding that most of the internet was blocked, save for a few approved websites. Any access to further required a higher clearance level, or probably a lot of money.

Skye's phone automatically synced to the space-time. The ISH orbited around Earth in every direction, meaning that the time zones they passed through would otherwise be rapidly changing, so the International Space Hotel always remained synced with the same time zone.

Skye then turned her attention over to the itinerary. Orientation looked to be two complete days, and the next day after that was a Friday, meaning she would work one day before the weekend. But she couldn't even start to think what she'd be doing on the off days; there was a giant television monitor in the room (it seemed as if only the VIP guests, and perhaps the high-level execs, had access to the holo-gram TVs), meaning she could sit back and lounge all day. But she was in space. There was no point to Skye sitting back and doing nothing when she could quite literally have the whole world in her hand when she looked out some of the windows.

Skye checked behind the lamp and found another small placard, as well as a red button with the word 'emergency' plastered on it. The button itself was encased in a little plastic box that covered the button and flipped open upon pulling, reminding her of what she'd always seen the president's nuclear launch buttons look like in the movies. Skye first checked out the placard. This placard included instructions on how to activate the tv with voice controls, and was accompanied with a remote for those who didn't want to use it. She grabbed the remote, and a light appeared on the television monitor, presenting a silent message.

Greetings, Skye Calvert. Welcome to the International Space Hotel.

Skye sat up on her bed. A line of text formed on the blank white canvas that was the powered TV, and more and more words appeared.

Would you like a guided audio tour of your room? Say "yes", or hit the "OK" button on your remote to proceed. If not, please say "no" or hit the "BACK" button on your remote. Please note that you can access the virtual tour at any point by saying "ROB, play the tour." You can also hit "options" on the remote to cycle through my personalities as I deliver the tour to randomize my A.I. driven personality.

"Yes," Skye said. She grabbed the remote tighter.

The previous message disappeared, and a face appeared on the screen. It was a woman, with a tan face and dark brown hair. But the face looked extremely smooth, so clean it almost sparkled like a diamond, and Skye knew the woman wasn't real. Then, all at once, she opened her mouth and began to speak: ROB's robotic voice was enough to let Skye know this was an A.I.

Thank you for choosing to stay here at the International Hotel. Welcome to Room 32. Here you will find your itinerary in the drawer of your nightstand as well as a guide on operating the television. As you are aware, this room will be your residence over the next few months over the summer of 2048.

You may be wondering about your amenities. Alan Lusky, the CEO of the International Space Hotel, has ensured that you have a wide variety of resources and magnificent furniture to best optimize your stay in space. Firstly, you have your 60x80 Queen-size bed, with fine sheets and pillows printed in America.

The image quickly transformed into the bed, and a graphic pointing out the various sections of the room as the A.I. spoke appeared.

On the side of the bed, you can access two sliders. One of them can raise or lower the bed to your preferred elevation, while the other one adjusts the bed to be as soft, or firm, as you desire.

Skye hadn't even noticed it yet, somehow. She reached to the side and raised the bed on an incline, and adjusted the other setting to make the bed super soft. She grinned. She was truly living a life of luxury. Now it was just time to try out the remote and spice things up. Skye hit the "options" button.

ROB's face appeared in the corner of the screen, and was altered all of a sudden into something different entirely. It was now taking on the form of a man, with an old-fashioned red bandana covering its head, a deep black beard, an eyepatch, covering about a quarter of the screen. Skye could guess who it was as ROB's voice dropped an octave or two lower.

Ahoy matey! Ye also have your very own comfortable two-person sofa on the side of the room. Much more comfortable than the poop deck! You also have access to our lighting panel, in which you can change the color of the lights, as well as adjust how light, or dark, you want the room to be lit!

Please, turn the lights in your room off whenever you do not need them on. Lights will automatically turn off within five minutes if no individual is detected inside. Don't ya forget it, or you will walk the plank!

Skye found the personality a little bit too obnoxious, and the one-liners a bit predictable, so she hit options again.

Once again, the icon in the corner of the screen flashed with ROB's generated face, this time taking on a cool-looking man in a fedora and, judging by the cut-off top of their shirt collar, a suit. It was a mobster with a slower pace of speaking and the swag and Jersey accent to match it.

As you can see behind the lamp on a metal strip, there are two buttons. In order that you do not accidentally confuse the buttons with that of the lamp and accidentally press them at night, both are encased in plastic boxes which must be lifted before you press them, like so. Two buttons, like the two families of the city. Never betray us, our blood oath.

The television switched from the A.I's face to a rugged animation of a hand grabbing and opening the box, with arrows showing how to open up it. Skye smirked at how campy the animations were. It reminded her of those old videos her elementary and middle school used to make her watch that were from the beginning of the century, or even before. The mobster's icon evaporated from the screen.

The red emergency button is reserved in the event of an immediate emergency. Don't play pranks with that, or you'll sleep with the fishes.

Skye hit options again, and this time, the top half of a far different avatar popped up into the screen.

She had long magenta hair, a bust far too large for her body, and a ridiculous colorful tight-fitting maid-like outfit: Skye knew what it was, a so-called *waifu,* and she wanted out before it had even spoken.

"Oh no…" Skye sputtered. She aimed for the options button, pressed it. Nothing.

In the instance that they are pressed, security guards, as well as medical personnel, will arrive on the scene as fast as they can. Please only call emergencies in a major event such as a health emergency, robbery, or active shooter situation.

The face took up more of the screen now, almost half of it, so much so that Skye could hardly focus on the virtual tour's animations of the room at all.

Do you want to shoot something with me, senpai? You make me so horny!

"Oh no! Please, no! *God* no!" Skye mashed the options button, but nothing seemed to be happening.

In the event you need room service to come and clean the sheets or clean up a spill, you can reach the number within your itinerary, and save it onto your phone. The number should be available 24/7 from anywhere within the ISH. I'll come and get you cleaned in my maid suit! ♡

"Stop! Stop it ROB! Now!" Skye called out, but there was no response at all, the avatar winking at her, as if it knew what Skye wanted and was doing exactly the opposite.

Towards the front of the room, you also have the front desk, equipped with a chair, as well as numerous drawers. This is located directly underneath the TV and provides a space for doing productive work without any distraction. You can be my chair any day of the week!

"Please! Shit! Fuck! Switch!"

The screen transitioned to showing a 3D model of the bathroom that appeared to be identical to hers, and finally, ROB's face appeared to have restored back to its default. Fourth time was the charm, apparently.

"Oh, thank God! Thank you, Lord!" Skye cried out, and she slammed her remote down on the nightstand, and returned to focus on the virtual tour as ROB returned to its deadpan, monotonic delivery.

You also have access to your bathroom, equipped with your very own sink, toilet, bidet, and shower. Please note that all showers are limited to five minutes before they automatically turn off for conservation purposes. Likewise, sinks will automatically turn off after 1 minute of running continuously. For items such as diapers, condoms, and menstrual products, please do not flush them down the toilet. Instead, use a disposal chute embedded in the wall located next to the toilet. To open, simply yank the handle and put whatever bathroom products are needed to be disposed of before *closing it. Note that this disposal chute is essential to remember as water is recycled in the operation of the ISH, and contaminating it with any other unwanted objects may result in fines upwards of $1,000.*

"The poop chute," Skye stated aloud, giggling at her remark. "Literally."

The animation switched back to ROB's face.

I'm sorry, I didn't get that. Was that a question?

"Uhhh, no!" Skye exclaimed, panicking. "Resume virtual tour."

Very well. Resuming your virtual tour.

The face stared blankly for a few moments until it continued right where it left off.

That concludes your virtual tour. However, there are also a few other key important rules to keep in mind when living in the International Space Hotel. Violations of said rules can lead to discretionary punishments on a case-by-case basis. Firstly, do not go over the max capacity limit of 10 individuals per single hotel room at any time. Secondly, while you are welcome to visit other individuals' rooms, unauthorized access to any other room is strictly forbidden. Thirdly-

"Yes, mom," Skye mumbled very quietly.

I'm sorry, I didn't get that. Was that a question?

"No," Skye replied firmly. "That's good enough for now, ROB, thank you. Power off."

And with that, the television flickered off, allowing Skye to finally settle down.

Skye took her sweet time unpacking everything in a good place and tidying up the room to the best of her ability. The room itself was extremely clean, which made sense given they were in space, save for an ambiguous brownish stain on the carpet next to the bed. Skye made a mental note to always climb onto the bed from the left side and not the right side. She thought about calling cleaning services, but she didn't even remember how due to the debacle with the virtual tour.

After Skye was finished unpacking, she checked the clock and saw that it was only 5:36 space-time. Skye knew she'd sleep like a rock at night.

Skye headed over to the mirror to get herself ready for the evening. She spent most of the time staring at her reflection as she did her hair and makeup. Her long, blonde hair, usually neatly brushed or tied into a ponytail, currently looked wild as if she'd had a bad hair day (she supposed traveling to space did that to one's own hair), and she struggled to get all of the knots out. Skye was at least relieved that the red streak in her hair, which she'd always dyed for the past seven years, still looked beautiful and deep. Skye thought she looked pretty good in the mirror, and she hoped this whole lower gravity thing wouldn't distend her stomach and make her gain weight – she'd heard stories how space could affect your physique in the long-term, compress your skin and make you fat. After finishing up her self-care routine a while later, Skye lay down on the bed, deep in thought.

That first day felt so surreal. Only several hours ago she'd been in Florida, at the launch site, and had bid farewell to her family. She'd gotten to say goodbye to her father, her mother, and even her little sister and brother. Her little sister, Emily, was a junior in high school while her brother, Braydon, was in the eighth grade, and even though they sometimes got on her nerves, the thought of not seeing them again for the entire summer, when they usually got to hang out, was sad. During fall break, winter break, and spring break the past two years of college she'd always gone home. But now she was set to stay here for three months, with no realistic chance of going back home.

***

Meeting the other interns in the Entertainment Hall started a bit stranger than she expected.

"My name's Minnie. Don't get on my bad side."

Skye didn't know why she had thought this was a good way to open up, but she had. This woman, a regular looking blonde who she wouldn't have batted an eye at back on Earth, was clearly not best friend material.

"Oh," Skye said shyly, not knowing what to make of the response. The fact that people like this existed was almost comical to her.

"Oh dear," Skye said. "I'm just here to make friends."

"I don't know if that's a good idea," Minnie responded. "Y'know, this is a competition? I heard the selection process is extremely selective. Apparently, less than half of interns convert to full-time hires. So, I don't want anyone to get in my way."

"Doesn't mean you need to be mean to everyone you encounter," Skye managed, not usually a fan of conflict but wanting to put this insufferable girl in her place.

"Mean? Who says I'm mean?" Minnie said, frowning. "Did you just call me mean?"

"Uh... No? Wrong word, I meant independent."

"Well good. Because if you did call me mean, then I'd have to make you my primary rival. That would go bad for you. It always does."

"Noted," Skye said. She took a sip of her non-alcoholic fruit punch before walking away, her eyebrows raised the entire time. Minnie didn't tell her to stop so she moved on.

Minnie seemed so like a not-like-the-other-girls type, so unbelievably brazen and odd that Skye was certain someone like her couldn't exist outside of a campy movie or some YA book. But she was certain she was bound to find some *normal* people, so she turned her attention to the few dozen interns milling about in the Entertainment Hall now, who were all waiting for the dinner to be served. Right now, everyone stood near the snack bar, interacting with each other. It struck Skye that she would see these people often, as she would routinely meet at intern events over the next few months, and she realized she had to get along.

Still, Skye gritted her teeth a little bit, squeamish. She never was prolific in these types of social situations. She much preferred individual one-on-one talks, but that wasn't exactly going to be easy in this setting.

Skye walked towards a man and woman who looked to be a little bit more welcoming, and the pair engaged in some kind of energetic conversation.

"No, no, that's bonkers," the woman said, shaking her head. She looked biracial, or otherwise of indistinguishable race, perhaps half-white and half-Hispanic, or half-white and half-Asian; Skye couldn't quite tell. She wore a knee-length blue dress and wore a gold chain with a cross on the end around her neck.

The man laughed before turning to Skye and freezing in place.

"Well, hello," the man said, his voice laced with a hint of nonchalance that betrayed his entranced exterior.

"Um, hi," Skye replied meekly. "I'm Skye."

"Nice to meet you," the woman replied, offering her hand. "I'm Madison, Madison Flores, but you can call me Maddie."

Skye shook her hand before shaking the hand of the other man, his grip tightening around her hand stronger than he needed to. He was staring at her while he did so, his eyes scanning Skye as he checked her out.

"I'm Drake Johnston," he said. "Skye. That's a pretty name."

"Thank you," Skye managed. "It's nice to meet you. Where are both of you from?"

"I'm from Allentown, Pennsylvania," Drake replied. "Well, near Allentown. You know it?"

"I can't say I do," Skye answered.

"It gets overshadowed by Pittsburgh and Philadelphia because of sports. I go to Penn State. I'm going to be a senior, and I'm interning in finance."

"I'm a rising junior at the University of Michigan," Skye replied. "I'm originally from Minnesota, though. I study communications, and I'll be working with the announcements team."

Drake frowned, evidently displeased by her position or area of study. Madison jumped in before either of them could say anything else.

"At school, I study bio and chemistry," Madison said. "Want to go to med school. Figure this should look good on my resumé."

"That's great!" Skye chimed. "Where at?"

"Bates College in Maine."

"Ooh," Skye replied. "That's a good school, isn't it?"

"I think so," Madison responded, nodding. "I'm from California, so the weather isn't exactly nice for me, and it's Maine, so that lets you know about how interesting the area is, but the school is pretty much Ivy level so I'm not complaining."

"Well, it sounds miserable," Drake interjected rudely. "Going to a school that small- I mean, that like defeats the purpose of college, doesn't it?"

"No one asked for your input," Madison snapped back. Skye had to restrain herself from grinning at the remark, and Drake's eyes widened before he turned to Skye once again.

"I love the hair," Drake blurted, gesturing to Skye's hair. Skye's hair was long and curly, and Skye reflexively touched it. "That red highlight is a nice touch."

"Is it now? My sister always jokes that it makes me look like a rejected girl band wannabe."

"Nonsense, it fits you well," Drake replied. "Got a whole Eva look going on."

"Eva? The one who almost died of a drug overdose a week ago, that Eva?"

"Yeah, she's one of my favorite artists, I'm glad she's okay," Drake responded.

Nearby, one of the robots had delivered a new tray of cold appetizers onto the giant long tables. Drake looked like he wanted to lick his lips, and he raised his hand in the air to motion goodbye.

"I'm going to go get apps, but talk to you both later?" Drake asked.

"Sure," Skye replied.

Drake strode off, looking back to catch one more glance at Skye.

"How about that guy, huh?"

"What?"

"He was ogling at you. Dude has zero game."

"I guess you're right," Skye said, smiling. "You should've seen the last chick I had a conversation with. She said she thought I could be her rival, or something."

"What the hell?"

"Yeah… But it's good to know some people here are reasonable. We should get to know each other."

"Totally," Madison replied. "I think my trip would be a lot more enjoyable knowing I got someone to watch my back. Us women got to watch each other's back, especially with guys like Drake coming onto you."

Dinner is now served. Please form a single-file line.

All the interns rushed to form a single file line. Skye found herself lined up in the middle, a couple of people behind Graham but right behind Madison. Drake lined up towards the very front of the line.

A couple of robot waiters brought out pans of food covered by metal food domes onto the long tables before lifting the lids to reveal the food below. It all looked surprisingly okay, since Skye had heard some horror stories about bad food in space, and apparently, the only really good restaurant cost an arm and a leg.

There were four containers total: the first contained spaghetti and marinara sauce, the second meatballs, the third garlic bread, and the fourth a Caesar salad. There were also separate shakers for parmesan and red pepper flakes.

"It's our first space food," Madison whispered excitedly. "If only it was something a tad more interesting than the most generic food in the universe."

In the frenzy to line up for food, someone bumped into her, as she vied for position in the line. Madison, of course, let the woman go ahead of her.

"Ope, go ahead," Skye said, as Madison chuckled.

"You're Minnesota nice," Madison said.

"Oh yeah?" Skye asked. "Thank you. You're Hollywood hot."

Madison laughed.

"Thanks, I may be from LA, but not Hollywood," Madison said. "I grew up in Boyle Heights, and then moved to the suburbs after my mom passed when I was six. You can call me Boyle Heights Baddie, if you desire. I'd say Boyle Heights bitch, but I don't think that kind of language is going to be appropriate in a professional setting."

"Uh… I'll stick with Maddie," Skye responded, and Madison shrugged, shoveling a large pile of spaghetti onto her plate.

"Suit yourself."

Once Madison and Skye served themselves, they were presented with an awful sight: Drake was standing around near the beverages and snack bar with a full plate of food, as if waiting for the perfect moment to strike and slip into the chair right next to Skye. It appeared he had waited for a minute under the pretense of sitting in the right place.

Skye was lucky, however. Skye and Madison quickly claimed the remaining two spots on one of the circle tables, which looked to seat around eight or nine people total, meaning Drake had no choice but to sit down at a separate table.

Skye thought she could feel Drake's eyes baring into the back of her head for a while, but she figured she was being a tad bit paranoid, and she soon became distracted by talking to some of the other interns who she'd never met before. Unlike Minnie and Drake, most of the people there came across as relatively normal people. Soon after she sat down, Graham walked over to the person to ask someone else at the table.

"Can I sit here? I'm friends with this person and I'd appreciate it if we swapped seats."

"Sure," they said, and before Skye knew it, she was seated between Madison and Graham, who she felt were her new friends.

She noticed that Graham was staring downwards a lot, and appeared to be massaging his head.

"How are you feeling, Graham?" Skye asked.

"A bit space sick, you know, lightheaded adjusting to this," Graham admitted. "It's nothing I can't handle."

"Well, I hope you feel better," Skye answered. "How about you, Maddie?"

"Fit as a fiddle, as they say," Madison replied.

"Yeah," Skye said, thinking back. "Did you get a virtual tour of your hotel room? I did. Wow, what a trip with those personalities. It was... strange."

"Yes," Madison replied. "I got a superhero, a goth girl, and some British queen. I was about to get to a fourth, but then it ended. How about you?"

"Uh, a pirate, a mobster. Some anime girl. It was... weird," Skye managed, not wanting to divulge all the details of what had happened.

"Yo, Graham cracker," Madison called over to her side. "How about you?"

Graham was silent for a few moments, reluctant to engage in this conversation. "I don't want to talk about it. Please don't call me that."

"He probably had cybersex with ROB," Madison whispered, snorting. Skye smiled but felt bad for Maddie making jokes at Graham's expense.

"I can hear you," Graham bit back. "Don't make fun of me."

The three (or to be more accurate, Madison, Skye partially, and Graham hardly whatsoever) soon engaged in the conversation with the rest of the table, which naturally gravitated from topics of health (for a few of them, but fortunately not Skye, felt the minor symptoms of space sickness), before shifting to everyone's particular internships.

Skye quickly felt intimidated as Graham talked about his upcoming internship with the Engineering team, shadowing with the crew on the engines and thrusters throughout the summer. Madison shared how she would get to work with the nurses in the pharmacy and assist the three doctors on board the ship in the event there were any medical emergencies. Skye hoped for her sake nothing would go wrong, as she could imagine just how awkward it would be to look past the doctors and nurses in a vulnerable medical situation to see Madison. When it was her turn to share, Skye felt like an imposter among these accomplished individuals, stumbling over her words and feeling like a mere child among gods and goddesses.

"Nothing crazy, you know. I'll be sending some emails, ah, you know, help supervise some meetings," she said. She'd read it in the job description, and she frankly had no idea what that would look like.

"You're an administrative assistant, then?" Someone asked from across the table, a man who appeared to be stroking his beard every other minute.

"Something like that."

The dinner passed by quickly. The food was good and everyone was allowed to line up again to get seconds. They were all talking a little bit more about what they thought was going to happen when, suddenly, the lights to the entire room flickered off.

There were a few gasps and intermittent screams from the bunch, and Skye tensed up, grabbing for her phone, but then another light flickered on, a spotlight on the stage, and everyone almost instantly fell silent.

A man in a suit walked over to a microphone, a large, slitted one that might've been straight out of the mid-20th century, basking in the center of the spotlight. The man in question was bald, with blue eyes and a square jawline that gave him an intimidating yet inexplicably attractive appearance. Skye estimated him to be in his late thirties or early forties, but his skin looked surprisingly smooth for a man of his age, his face glistening like a recently polished piece of silverware. She knew that billionaires lived differently, with their fancy medical treatments and plastic surgeries, and there was something about his whole aura screamed he made the big bucks.

Skye was pretty sure she'd seen his face on one of the popular magazines sometimes, with his extraordinarily pretty wife and young pampered daughter, who might've been seven or so now. Skye wished she'd been born with a silver spoon in her mouth. In her milquetoast middle class upbringing, it was more like she'd been dealt a steel spoon.

"Hello! Hello!" The man greeted them. "Apologies, the lights were supposed to be dimmed, and not turned off completely, but I can assure you that I will take the steps necessary to rectify this issue so it doesn't occur in the future."

The room fell absolutely silent, the faint chattering in the background stopping.

"Now, I will make this short and sweet. My name is Alan Lusky. Perhaps you've heard of me. I am the CEO and chairman of the International Space Station. I've been running this operation for five years, ever since it was first opened to the public in 2043, and I hope to be here for longer.

"Now you may or may not know it, but you can consider yourself one of the most privileged people in the world. It is estimated that slightly less than 100,000 people over the course of human history have ever been to space. You are one of them. There are nine billion people alive. Those are astonishing odds. But you weren't here because you were lucky. You were chosen because you were the best. The best and brightest of what America has to offer. Over the next few months, you will have a chance to not only make an impact on this organization, or to bolster your resume to the crème de la crème of any young professional, but to better yourself significantly as a human being, and to gain an experience you will never forget.

"These next few months will not be easy. Even though we do what we can to ease you into your role, and much of our program revolves around tapping into your inner potential, these will be trying times. You will be away from your family, and will only be allowed surface calls once a week. And unlike any other internship you may have ever worked, at the end of the day, there's no going back home, to your apartment, where you can relax and decompress. Sure, you may have free time, but everything out there-" Alan motioned out to the windows behind him. "serves as a stark reminder of where we are, and where you are along your journey."

"Now I know you came here to meet other interns, and not be lectured. This is not the last time you will see me. You will have ample opportunity over our monthly lecture series to hear from me. But now I think it's time for some festivities. Tomorrow at 9 a.m., after all, orientation will commence. We will be letting in some of the guests now, in order to have a chance to listen."

Skye looked behind with a frown as the back doors flew open, and a crowd of guests rushed in towards the well in front of the stage, chattering excitedly. Some of them were practically leaping for joy.

"What...?" Skye managed amid the murmurs and gasps of her neighbors.

"She's one of the biggest pop stars of the decade. And perhaps one of our biggest named guests of the year. Please welcome pop star, Eva!"

Skye's jaw dropped, and there were screams of happiness and surprise from throughout the audience as Madison shook Skye excitedly. A figure stepped out from the shadows to step on the stage and shake Alan Lusky's hand before he walked off. She wore a flamboyant gold blazer and dress pants, and her hair, knotted, was blonde, much like Skye. The crowd broke into uproarious applause.

"Hello, International Space Hotel!" Eva exclaimed, grinning. "It turns out that news of my overdose was greatly exaggerated."

Chapter 3

The next few hours were a blur for Skye.

The rules for drinking were rather strict in the Entertainment Hall. There was only one open bar, which was reserved completely for guests. It was company policy for any temp employees to not drink except on the weekends. This meant that as an intern, she was prohibited from purchasing any alcohol drinks. Still, that wouldn't stop her.

The hall boomed with Eva's alto voice as she danced on the stage. A light show projected various colors and shapes onto the ceiling, and her voice complemented the blaring synthesizers well with each pulsing rhythm. Her voice was fast, so fast that Skye could hardly make out any of her words. But it upbeat and sounded catchy, so Skye didn't mind the fact. Even if Skye had heard the lyrics more clearly, then she likely would've realized the entire song was about an acid trip, and probably wouldn't have thought it better for its philosophical depth or relatability.

Skye danced for a good fifteen minutes on the dance floor, lost in the crowd and working up a good sweat, until she heard a loud voice calling out from behind her, and someone else drawing nearer.

"Mind if I dance with you?"

Skye whipped around, her heart racing. She was almost ready to deliver a hefty slap to the face, expecting it to be Drake from earlier, trying to make a move on her. But no, it was Graham.

"Of course!" Skye smiled.

"You seem pumped," Graham said. He bobbed a head to the music in a way that let Skye know he probably only danced every once in a blue moon.

"Heck yeah, we are!" Madison exclaimed, bumping into Graham with such force that Graham was almost knocked off his feet. She was bouncing up with the song, a grin plastered on her face, and from Skye's perspective

"Not my genre, to be honest!" Graham admitted. "I guess I like the oldies more. But this is still a vibe."

"Oh, into the classics, huh? You quirky dog," Madison jaunted.

"No, I'm not quirky, nor am I a dog," Graham said, laughing out loud. "God, I would probably be more into this whole dancing thing with a drink."

"You 21?" Madison asked.

"Nope," Graham said. At that, he recoiled a little bit, as if Madison was a probing federal agent. "I'm 20, going into my junior year, just like Skye."

"Do the rules even apply though?" Skye asked. "Because I thought technically, we're under the jurisdiction of the U.S. government, but the laws aren't exactly the same."

"I think so," Madison agreed. "I'm pretty sure the drinking age is 18, to appeal to international guests."

"So we can drink?" Graham asked, excited, as if he'd been wound up tight for a while and was looking to take it easy for once.

"No," Madison replied.

"What? How come!?"

Skye was finding it enjoyable to see Graham loosen up a bit.

"Oh, well, I tried going to the bar, but they didn't let me," Madison explained. "They said us temp employees are only permitted to drink on the weekends, and not until orientation is complete. Something about us needing to stay focused, and it being company policy.”

“Wow,” Skye replied. “I am disappointed.”

“I notice you seem to know each other,” Madison said, changing the topic, “How’s that? He your boyfriend?”

“No, stop it,” Skye replied, shaking her head rapidly.

“You’re blushing!”

“Am not!”

“Am too!”

“Okay, okay, come on, now, ladies,” Graham said awkwardly. “Y’all are acting too wild.”

Skye stood and observed Graham’s features: a plain-ish face, with a light spattering of pimples on his chin, straight brown hair, and crisp brown eyes. He may have been rather average as far as stature and appearances went, but he seemed intelligent and genuine. Still, she hardly knew him. Madison’s probing eyes caused her to only blush more.

“We just know each other from school,” Skye managed. “We both go to the University of Michigan.”

“Ooh, so you two have past history?” Madison asked excitedly. “I never would’ve guessed you went to the same school, what with his accent and all.”

“Appearances can be deceiving,” Skye quipped.

“That’s right,” Graham agreed. “Everyone hears my accent and assumes I’m going to wrangle a gator or watch some football – when I just like reading a good novel and studying up on engineering. Trust me, I mask my accent more than most.”

“Well, you look like you’re enjoying dancing,” Madison replied, “so you can’t be that introverted.”

Graham smiled.

"I guess so."

"Excuse me," another voice said. A man, looking to be perhaps a couple of years older than them, tall at six foot one, bulky, and dark-skinned, interrupted the conversation.

"Yeah?" Madison asked. "What's up?"

"I promise I wasn't eavesdropping on your conversation, but I overheard you say something about not being able to drink. Want to change that? I might be able to set you up."

"Uhh… Who are you?" Skye asked.

"I'm Marcell," the man said, extending his hand. After a couple of seconds of staring at it, they shook it one by one. "I'm a security guard here, but between you and me, I kind of got out of my shift so I could watch the concert."

"Spoken like a true Eva-sive," Madison observed. "You an Evasive?"

"That's an understatement," Marcell said. "I'm probably her biggest fan on board this entire space station."

"Doubtful," Madison answered. "Not so long as I am on board."

"I can't believe she's perfectly okay though," Skye said. "I thought they said she almost died within the past week, and she's already in space? Even if medicine has advanced so much in the past century, that doesn't seem like a smart or safe move."

"Media," Madison said, shrugging. "Everything's always sensationalized, media's always overhyping and coming up with some fake stories. I guess that's how it is!"

"Yeah," Marcell agreed. "I'm assuming you lot are all interns, then?"

"That's right," Graham answered. "What about you?"

"No, no," Marcell said, shaking his head. "Although believe it or not, I was on the first batch of interns ever for this ship, five years ago."

"No, that's crazy!" Skye said. "That's actually amazing. You've been here this whole time?"

"Well, I had a couple of internships here. Then they gave me a full-time offer. Speaking of which…" He looked over to the bar. "You hold it right there; I can get you what you want."

For a few minutes, they stood there, talking and dancing as Eva moved onto the next song, wondering if this guy was actually going to follow through with his promise. Then they saw him carrying the bottle of champagne from the bar and blending in the crowd, and Skye grinned. He was walking towards them.

***

And that was how Skye, Graham, and Madison got wasted together. They were first in the crowd, and then, by the time they were through the bottle, Eva was wrapping up in her last song or two. Marcell got another bottle for the road, and, once they were done, the four moved together into the hallways, trying to blend in the crowd. As much as a meet and greet with the famous celebrity would've pleasured them greatly, arguably none more than Madison, Eva was quickly whisked away, escorted by a couple of security guards, and Marcell gave a suggestion as they walked out with the crowd.

"I know the perfect place to hang out and gaze at the Earth. You'll love it. It's one of the gazing lobbies."

"Pfft," Madison spat out, laughing.

"What?" Marcell asked, confused. "What's funny about that?"

"Huh. Gazing lobby. Sounds kinda sleazy to me too," Skye laughed. There was something about the drinks and the movement of dancing that had left her feeling quite buzzed.

"Geez, you two are really drunk right now, aren't you?" Graham asked.

"Are you not?" Madison asked, raising her eyebrows, and Graham shrugged.

"Ain't my first rodeo," he admitted, and the others laughed.

"Look at you! I thought you were so uptight, and yet you are like a crazy party animal!" Madison laughed.

"Hey guys," Marcell said, "not to change the topic, but gazing lobby? Are you all up for it?"

"Let's do it!" Skye exclaimed. "I-I'm not tired at all."

***

The four of them stared out the sky straight on Earth. Skye's jaw dropped, but she forgot that it did.

"Look at her," Madison whispered, gawking at her, and Graham giggled. "You can tell she's not used to drinking. She isn't a bona fide experienced substance user, like myself."

"You say that like you're proud," Graham observed, and Madison shrugged.

"I've stared up here almost every evening for years," Marcell explained. "And I guess every day it's so beautiful. Reminds me that we're a part of something bigger… Much bigger… And yet we can still escape it if we want."

There were a few dozen total seated on the soft cushioned chairs that all faced one wall. The wall was made entirely of opaque and thick synthesized glass which allowed them to stare directly at Earth below.

Even though it was around midnight according to space-time and hence, which meant that many people on board the ship were in bed or about to retire for the night, a bright sunlight illuminated the current landmass that they orbited. The light exposed its slightly bumpy terrain and several long islands. Skye would have likely been fast asleep a couple of hours before, if this whole social booze event hadn't energized her, and in that moment she was glad she was awake.

"This is familiar," Madison said.

"Japan," Skye muttered, and Marcell nodded to the affirmative.

"Japan? I thought it was Florida island," Madison said, and they burst out laughing, so much so that they got some negative annoyed glances from some of the guests who wanted to admire the sights in a more peaceful and tranquil environment.

The guests here were bougie, wealthy beyond Skye's wildest dreams, and she would have guessed that they didn't expect their trip to be bothered by college-aged rabble rousers. One of them, a man with a golden watch sipping what appeared to be some sort of blue fruity cocktail from his seat, was so annoyed by the commotion that he stood up and exited the room outright.

"I forget how many islands there are in Japan," Graham said in amazement. "I guess I never sat down and studied geography so much… I oughtta."

The four of them Earth-gazed for a good twenty minutes before Marcell decided that they should all return to their rooms for the night.

"I don't want you all to get in trouble and oversleep because of me," Marcell explained. "Although if everything's the same, you can set alarms automatically in the rooms themselves which'll wake you up so you shouldn't worry about that unless you fall back asleep."

"Of course," Skye replied. "Thanks for showing us around. And… you know."

"Of course," Marcell replied. "It was my pleasure."

"We should stay in touch," Madison said, nodding at Marcell. "That wasn't an invitation to touch me, but for you, I might make an exception."

"I'm gay," Marcell replied, laughing. "So don't feel like you need to hit on me."

"Dammit," Madison muttered, and Skye snorted. Madison sighed. "I have a boyfriend to be faithful to, anyway, so that's probably the best that I, you know, keep my fidelity."

The four of them parted ways, but not until they made it clear where each of them roomed, with each of them typing down each other's room number down on their phone. Graham stayed in Room 33, Skye in Room 32, Madison in Room 115, and Marcell stayed full-time in Room 248.

"Catch you all later," Marcell said.

They all parted ways, waving goodbye.

Chapter 4

"Ma, I'm here, I'm here." Marcell grabbed the receiver of the phone in the call center so tightly that his knuckles turned white. He felt down, and it was no wonder why; the previous day, he'd gotten shitfaced with a bunch of 20-year-olds.

"It's been three months! Three months!" Her mother howled. "You should be ashamed of yourself!"

"I know, I know," Marcell said. "It's just, I've been so tied up with work lately, and things have been busier than ever this past year. I did find time to shoot a couple of emails just to update you, though, if you checked."

"Email! You think we wanna sit around typing our emails, like a corporate shmuck kissin' ass! You are out of your damn mind if you think I want to have a long conversation over *email*!"

"Okay, okay," Marcell said. "It was a little bit irresponsible of me, sorry. I…" Marcell was about to say more, but he bit down on his tongue. "Okay, you're right. I'll call you more often. Every six weeks."

"Two weeks. Every other Friday!"

"Let's make that every month."

"You're trying to treat this like a job negotiation. No, no, I'm your mother. I'm your boss, you hear me? You do what I say."

"Every month. Best I can do."

"Sheesh. Fine, fine. I'd whoop your ass if you weren't 300 miles in the air. I brought you into this world… If only I could bring you back to it again."

Marcell exhaled. *Here we go again.*

"Now why'd you call me?"

"I just wanted to check in. It's been a while, and I wanted to say hi to Reese," Marcell said, smiling.

"Reese. Huh. Huh. Ha! Ha! Ha!" The laughter was stilted and forced, and the smile that had been on Marcell's face quickly evaporated.

"What's up? Ma? Why are you laughing like that? Did something happen?"

"Yes, something happened. Dumbass got himself busted with Chris. He's rotting in a jail cell."

"You're joking."

"No, Marcell, I'm not joking! You should've been there. He always looked up to you, you know. Ever since you left, he's gone off the rails. Off the rails like a maniac."

"W-what did he do? Is he okay? How long are we talking about?"

"Yes, he's fine! He got ten months. Helped steal a car. You know how them kids are. But he wasn't the driver! Chris got them in an accident. He got 3 years, and it ain't looking good."

Marcell breathed out. He wasn't sure if it was in relief, or exasperation. But what he did know was that he was pissed.

"Why didn't you tell me earlier? Why the *hell* didn't you email me back?"

"Because I'm not writing you no encyclopedia, especially if your contract's finishing up in the next month."

"Okay, okay," Marcell said. "About that… I got my contract renewed. Another twelve months."

"You *what*?"

"I know, I know! But I got a good pay bump, since I'll be onboarding and training a bunch of new security guards these next few weeks. A really good pay bump. We're talking, I'm about to crack six figures big. Just think. With the money being tax-exempt and all, I'll even double what I send back. Two thousand a month. How's that sound?"

Marcell's mother was silent for a few moments. "You really hate us that much?"

"No. That isn't true at all."

"Really? What about the thousand I wire back every month? Does that count for nothing?"

"Love ain't measured in money. Love is measured in the time you spend with those you love. Love is measured in the hugs you give your family and the effort you do to be a real man. Not like the scum that is your father. Bradley doesn't know the first thing about love."

"I have my own life," Marcell fired back. "I love you more than the world, but God sometimes do I wish I had *just* a bit of gratitude for what I do. Like this isn't tough on me too."

"Reese needs a father. Your father was never there. Now his big bro ain't there. What did you think would happen?"

"I'm 24, ma! Just cause I'm not like the rest of them, don't have any babies of my own, and didn't make any stupid financial decisions, doesn't make me beholden to you my entire life! Stop gaslighting me."

"Really? Is that it? You think you're better than us because you got through college? Because you, unlike all of us, got out of town, and into that fancy hotel?"

"No. I am your son. Nothing ever changes that."

"Well, you seem to no longer want any part of this family. Because I haven't spoken to you face to face in *years*."

"Please don't say that, ma. It really hurts me."

"Arianna. She's infertile, you know."

"What? What are you talking about?"

"She's absolutely devastated. Finally settled down with a good boyfriend the past year. The man's making okay money too, and he seems to be a decent man. More decent than Bradley. She's only twenty-three, but she's got the news there's no chance she can ever be pregnant. Something about how her fallopian tubes are all messed up. It's enough to make a grown woman like me cry."

"That's horrible. Has she considered adoption? With the food shortages all across the world there's a lot of orphans in need of a home, you know."

"Adoption!" His mother scoffed. "Don't make me laugh. That isn't real flesh and bones: nothing compares to producing offspring of your own. Miss me with that adoption nonsense. You know what sucks about it, though? Nothing I ever could do will change it. Reese will probably be dead before he's twenty, the way he's been doing things. Arianna can never have grandkids. But you... You could."

"That isn't happening, ever," Marcell said. "We've gone over this. I'm gay. You don't have to agree with it, but you have to accept it. It's not that wild of a concept, especially considering how times are nowadays."

"You had girlfriends in high school," She insisted. "You had quite a few of them too, because you were popular."

"Stop it. I'm warning you."

"Don't tell me you didn't sleep with all of them either? You liked it! You totally did! Maybe if you'd stop being *selfish*, just sleeping with those other men and pretending like they're all clones of yourself, then you could leave a legacy. Instead of leaving us like Bradley and pretending like somehow, you're all doing us a huge favor-"

Marcell slammed the phone down, before instantly regretting it and grabbing for the receiver. But the call had automatically disconnected, and that was that. He contemplated calling her again. But he checked the clock and saw there were only a couple of minutes left anyway. So instead, he walked out of the room, greeted by the voice of a robot bidding him farewell.

I hope you had a good call, and have a good rest of your day.

Marcell held a middle finger behind his back as he walked out of that room and reported back to work.

Chapter 5

Orientation was, somehow, more boring than Skye had expected.

The front of the Entertainment Hall, which only yesterday had been an open-floor venue with an expansive dance floor littered with crumbs of food, was now an immaculately cleaned patch of carpet where several rows of chairs faced the stage. On the stage, a hologram projected into the air and played videos that all were required to watch.

At the start, there were a lot of videos and a couple of lectures about the spaceship. They demonstrated the ship's layout through a holographic map and showed where the emergency escape pods were located. The videos also explained how they were generally locked unless an emergency alarm (found at several points in different hallways) was activated. Videos explained how everyone was explicitly restricted from any areas with a security level 2 or 3, unless they either worked there or otherwise received special clearance. HR representatives informed everyone about the general meal schedule and explained that they could have a free meal in the cafeteria, but had to pay for their meals at restaurants. They also highlighted specific guidelines and warned that violating them would result in disciplinary action including a one-day suspension or write-up. Those who were fired would be confined to their room for the rest of the trip, only able to go out for meals at the cafeteria. Those who committed any crimes would be held in the prison wing until the next shuttle to Earth was available, at which point they would be sent back down to Earth and charged in an American court of law. Skye was surprised that they even had prison cells in space, but she figured it was mainly for show. She couldn't imagine anyone being reckless enough to commit a crime in space.

The entire time orientation continued, Madison sat in the chair next to Skye, whispering comments in her ear which made her smile. There was her feedback for the layout: "I don't know where any of these things are, let alone where we are. Are we even sure this is the ISH?" Her feedback to the cafeteria was equally hilarious. "All I want to do is eat at a six-star restaurant before I die, and for it to not cost $300." And then there was her comment about the prison, in which Skye had to cover her mouth so as to not audibly guffaw and draw the ire of any nearby audience members. "Do you think the prisons are nice like everywhere else on this ship, like a Swedish prison? Because if so, I might do something I will regret."

This orientation part took up most of the first day. Skye also got the chance to meet with her reporting manager at this time, the very person who had conducted her interview when she was down on Earth. The reception during the interview had been, surprisingly, not as spotty as she expected, probably because there were only apparently three different places outside of the cabin of the spaceship, both of which were booked multiple days ahead of time. At least the interns were reserved to have a check-in with their family at the midpoint.

"Why, hello again, Skye," the PA announcer introduced themselves. Their name was Lex. Non-binary, red-headed and with a pair of large black spectacles, they were one of the more androgynous people Skye had encountered in her life. They stood up and shook Skye with hands that were surprisingly more tough than she expected.

"Hello, Mx. Groves," Skye said, smiling. "Thank you again for providing me this opportunity. Truly, I am lucky."

"Please, call me Lex," Lex responded, "and the honor is all mine."

Lex proceeded to walk Skye through some of the fundamentals of what Skye's responsibilities would look like for this summer. Despite working with them on the P.A. announcement, Skye would not be making any announcements herself, as there were already two people on that job. However, Skye would be responsible as a personal aid during important meetings, and would be sent around to communicate important information at times, delivering messages, recordings and documents. This was, Lex explained, because there were questions about the security of any of the radio channels on board, and one of the last things Alan Lusky and the ship's management wanted was the Chinese or Russians to glean some important information by having one of their agents on board eavesdrop or intercept on the proper frequency.

"I don't know why this would be such an issue," Skye said at one point. "I mean, this is a hotel. Just why is this all so important?"

"Yes," Lex replied. "I understand why you would feel this way. However, I can assure you that there are many important guests, including government officials, on board at any given time, who often conduct business on the ship. There's nowhere more neutral, you have to understand, to do anything like that than in space. Here, you can rest assured there's no way ever anyone could realistically plan an assassination, no way someone could commit any crime without serious consequences. Likewise, if there's any place to have a secure conversation without a large risk of anyone eavesdropping on it, then it's 300 miles above the surface like we are."

"I see."

"One of the most essential components to remember about this job is the confidentiality of information. You will be privy to information no one else will in the entire ship. It's a part of your job. It will be your job at times to communicate these messages or act as a sort of hostess during these meetings. If they ask for you to fetch some drink or food, then you will do so."

"They won't…" Skye said, her voice drawing off. "Hold on, this isn't like what I think you're talking about. I mean, they're not going to ask for you know… Favors." She grew pale.

"No, no," Lex said, shaking their head. "No, Skye, honey, don't you worry about that. I will train you, however, on how to approach various different scenarios."

"This wasn't exactly in the job description. I mean, I figured it was an admin assistant job, but I didn't think I'd have to be a server. I have to admit that I'm a little bit flustered." And Skye couldn't help but feel a bit light-headed, and a bit anxious. Her heart raced.

This wasn't what she'd expected at all. It wasn't supposed to be like this. Although Skye had worked as a waitress back her freshman year, it was not like that had been a very pleasant experience overall. Being a waitress for the famous and wealthy sounded even more stressful. If her experience in the food industry had shown her anything, it was that the richer the customer was, the less generous they were with their tips.

"Yes, we tend to keep that part of your job description vague," Lex admitted. "But your experience worked to your advantage. Your coursework, your background… We thought you would make the perfect fit for this job. You're versatile, Skye, and we have the utmost confidence in your abilities."

"But I'm 20 years old. Why would you hire me to do something like this? Couldn't you hire someone better, more experienced… Someone more trusted? You said I'd be standing there during people's important conversations. That honestly sounds intrusive."

"We think you're the woman for the job, so that's why I asked you," Lex said. "Assuming you're up for it? If not, I can probably reassign you somewhere else."

Skye paused for a few seconds before her heart sank. Why would they ever hire a college-aged intern for a job like this? Probably because they never planned to retain her at all. Skye guessed that they would continue hiring attractive-looking interns every year just to check a box before moving onto the next one. She'd certainly never hear enough to be considered dangerous to the U.S. government, but she wouldn't be back anyway. That was the conclusion that Skye made, and it made her upset. She'd fought so hard to win this internship, only for this to be the result. For this position to be nothing more than a phony job which likely involved a bunch of men staring at her cleavage.

"Is that a yes? Are you all right?" Lex asked, concerned.

"I'm fine, I'm fine, and yes, I'm ready," Skye replied. "But what about my clothes? I was never instructed to pack any sort of formal clothes. I packed a little bit, but not enough, and maybe not what you want."

"Yes. Speaking of which, I hope you don't mind, room service will be showing up to your place in the next couple of hours while you work. They will provide the outfits. As you know, we've already received your measurements during onboarding. You will try them on and see to it that anything that fits stays up in the closet, and anything else, you can leave it on the ground. Room service will get the hint. Do you understand? You can try them out tonight."

"Yes." Skye was silent for a few minutes, baffled and full of questions. "Is that my entire duty, then? To just be this... hostess?"

"No. You will shadow us. Oh, and occasionally... There are certain emergencies on board," Lex explained. "What I mean to say, is that people die, just like people occasionally die during flights, or on cruises. When this happens, you will make a recording of it and log it into our system."

"So, what do I do then?"

"You'll simply read off a placard containing information such as name, date of birth, time of death, place of death, cause of death. It's pretty straightforward. Obviously, you don't have to deal with the body. That'll be security or the medical team's job, and they have a whole protocol for that sort of thing."

"How often does this happen?" Skye asked, eyes opening. "How often do people die?"

"Not very often. I'd say a couple times a month. Mainly old folks. Fortunately, we haven't had any bad incidents in the past couple of years."

"Is that all I'll be recording?"

"That should be all, although if anything else comes up, we'll let you know. Much of the time, you will be able to sit in and watch me and my colleague Franco work as the announcers. Are you ready to complete your training?"

Skye nodded, although internally, she didn't feel like she was ready. Not at all.

***

"That goes right there… And perfect."

Madison looked up at the pharmacist, before turning back to the shelves. There were rows upon rows of medication of many different types. The supply was so large that it looked like it would be sufficient to support a small country.

"You got the hang of this," the pharmacist continued. "That's what matters."

"I mean, it makes sense," Madison replied. She stood up, and shook her hand again. "Thank you, doctor."

"Remember, call me Sarah."

"Sorry, sorry- it's just, technically you're a doctor, so."

"That's true. But I'm not an actual doctor."

"I'm sure you've saved many lives."

Sarah checked her phone, before looking back at the front counter. Today's service was slow, as it seemed no one was going to the pharmacy at all, and she struggled to conceal a yawn.

"Tomorrow, you should shadow Dr. Chetana. Maybe you can get a little bit of experience there."

"Of course, of course," Madison said, nodding. "And in the meantime? What should I do, go complete those training modules?"

"Did you get that spreadsheet completed?"

"Yes, it was completed," Madison said. "I excel with… never mind."

"You can go ahead and do that. Although, now that I think about it, you've done a lot of work. So, you can just hang out until five and then I'll let you loose."

"Thanks," Madison said. "If you have anything else you need me to do, let me know."

"No, don't sweat it. Most of the patients who visit the pharmacy come for basic treatments to alleviate the symptoms of space sickness. It's no problem."

Madison moved over to the computer. For a few minutes, she switched between tabs and double-checked her work. Eventually, she heard walking and murmuring, and she moved out of the office to see Sarah move over to the back room. She followed her into the pharmacy and watched her move over to the back corner, where a giant locked metal cabinet was. Sarah turned around after noticing that she was being followed.

"Oh, hi," Sarah greeted her.

"Need me to fetch something?"

"Oh, I got it," Sarah said. She slipped her keys into the locker and unlocked the cabinet before opening up the door.

"What's this?"

"The strong stuff," Sarah explained. "Most of our opioids and narcotics are stored here."

Madison stepped closer. Madison's hands quivered a little bit in excitement as her eyes scanned the rows, observing the various medications that were there. Oxycodone. Morphine. Codeine. And her eyes were caught off guard by what looked to be even behind the main rows, behind a second lock and a metal grate. There were pale yellow containers, and she had to squeeze her eyes to read what the labels said.

Noxium. That word was familiar, but she didn't know why.

"Noxium, huh?"

"Oh, that," Sarah said, grabbing a vial of codeine before looking at them for a second. Then she locked up the cabinet. "Yeah, Noxium is some of the top-notch experimental stuff. It's practically military-grade."

"Let me guess, we store tear gas too?"

"Tear gas? Well, it wouldn't surprise me if Security somehow stored them, since they have an arsenal, but there are no medical applications, so there's nothing here."

"I'm struggling to see the purpose of experimental gas on board."

"It's knock-out gas. You know, when you're asleep you consume less oxygen. If there are any issues, this can be used to knock people out and to better control our oxygen supply."

"That… makes sense. And the other stuff there? I mean those are some hard drugs, why would we need some of them? The painkillers I understand, but it's not like we're going to perform a heart transplant here."

Madison followed Sarah up to the front desk as she bagged the medicine and completed the transaction with the customer. She stood back for a few minutes. Only after Sarah was finished with this did they resume the conversation.

"They have everything they need in the event of a major emergency or potentially, even a surgery," Sarah explained. "This hotel is huge. There can be up to 1,000 people at any given time. And accidents *do* happen. Not a lot, but they do happen. You'll find that out when you meet our resident surgeon, Dr. Silva."

"Okay," Madison replied. "Sorry for asking so many questions."

"That kind of drive is important. It separates the real go-getters from those who're just trying to make a quick buck. So, there's no need to apologize at all," Sarah said, and Madison smiled. "You can clock out now if you want. You've done good work today."

Madison slowly backed away, looking back every several seconds to see if Sarah had stashed the keys to the cabinet anywhere. But she didn't. It looked like she carried the keys on it herself, and Madison walked away, deep in thought.

***

Graham's first-ever official shift on the job at the International Space Hotel wasn't what he expected.

It started out regular enough. Graham reported to the Engineering Facility in a timely fashion. At the door, he had to scan his own personal ID necklace before the door clicked open and he passed through into the engineering facility.

The Engineering Facility was a term that could hardly capture the grandeur of the room. Prior to entering the main facility,

Graham passed by a few offices and couldn't resist peering through a window to catch a glimpse of what was inside. What he saw was nothing short of awe-inspiring.

The room was packed with an impressive range of laboratory equipment and a dizzying array of machines that appeared so expensive that Graham could only imagine the cost of the entire room being equivalent to the GDP of a small country. At the back of the room, towering metal conveyor belts and giant robotic arms whirred into motion, seamlessly assembling metal parts together. And then there were the engineers, each sporting the proper safety gear of hard hats and goggles, who moved about with purpose. Some gathered in small groups, huddled over schematics on a table, while others walked around, observing and monitoring the machines or some computer screens likely displaying key information. The sounds that filled the space were music to Graham's ears: the rhythmic clang of metal, the smooth hum of machinery, and the chatter of the engineers. He felt a sense of belonging and couldn't help but imagine this place becoming his second home.

This job was becoming all the more real for Graham. And with it, the real possibility of being eventually hired to be one of these engineers. Graham was so excited that he could just run out and network with them.

Another guy who looked around his age was milling in the area, and when he saw Graham, he walked over to him, greeting him.

"Hey, are you an intern too?"

"Indeed, I am," Graham said.

"Cool. With Mr. Xiong?"

"Yeah. Is anyone else here?"

But the other man looked around and shrugged. "Not from what I can tell. I'm Yusef, by the way."

"Graham."

"I've been here for like twenty minutes. Not a peep from anyone. I wonder if our manager forgot about us."

"He said he'd meet us here at nine o' clock, so I don't know. Maybe we should wait a little bit? I'm not trying to make a bad impression by running off looking for him."

"Good call."

A few minutes passed and the man they were waiting for did show. Little did Graham know that this would be a general pattern for his manager.

"Apologies for being late," the man said. "I got a little bit tied up, and then I knew I was forgetting something. My name is Mr. Xiong. You can call me Mr. X. I will be your manager over the next few months."

"Hello," Graham and the other intern said in tandem.

Mr. Xiong chuckled. "It looks like you two have chemistry already. What are your first names?"

"Yusef."

"I'm Graham."

"Okay, good. You don't have the same names. You see, last year, I had two interns. Both were called Alex. One of them was male, the other one was female, yet every time I said one of their names, they both answered 'yes'."

"What happened to them?" Yusef blurted.

"They are no longer with us," Mr. Xiong replied, and Graham raised his eyebrows.

"W-what?" Graham asked, slightly exasperated. "They… passed away?"

"Oh, no, we didn't retain them. Come on, already. I want to show you the ropes."

"Is there anyone else we're waiting for?" Yusef asked.

"No," Mr. Xiong said. "There's only nine engineering interns total, and only two working for me. You were sorted due to your concentration and application."

"Electrical," Yusef asserted.

"Yes, both of you. Oh, and I should say the line. Welcome to the Engineering Facility of the International Space Hotel."

"Thank you," Graham and Yusef replied together.

"Follow me to the electrical room, and I will show you," Mr. Xiong said.

It was a short walk to the electrical room, where they were provided an in-depth tour by Mr. Xiong. Over the course of it, Yusef repeatedly asked thoughtful questions. Graham didn't know why, but he felt a little bit threatened by Yusef. He was, by the looks of things, a sort of intellectual rival, and Graham was determined to not let himself be overshadowed.

"Here," Mr. Xiong said at one point, throwing open the metal doors to an electrical box. "Right now, there is an issue here for one of the rooms. Lights went out. Tell me what's wrong with this."

Is this a joke? Graham asked himself in his mind. *Who does he think we are, basic electricians?*

Graham and Yusef inspected the contents of the electrical box thoroughly over the next few seconds. Graham scanned the area like a hawk.

"Faulty wiring here," Graham barked before Yusef could get a word in edgewise. "You can tell by the frays there."

"Yes," Mr. Xiong replied.

"Well, why don't you call the electrician?" Yusef asked like a smart-aleck. "After all, this is their job, right?"

"Well, lucky you, it turns out that I have equipment," Mr. Xiong replied. "First things first, put these gloves on. Safety is our number one priority here, especially in this line of work."

He slammed a toolbox which he must have hidden behind some machinery down onto the ground in front of them. He also tossed a couple of gloves on the ground, providing a line of wire and electrical tape. Yusef and Graham turned to face each other before diving down to the ground like football players trying to recover a fumble.

"Lesson number one," Mr. Xiong told them as they rushed to slip on their gloves and replace the wiring. "Here at the International Space Hotel, you have to step up sometimes and do things you aren't comfortable with. Including grunt work, like this. It could save a life."

Chapter 6

Graham sat on his desk, unable to believe what he was seeing. Hours before he'd been introduced to his internship by Mr. Xiong, and now he was looking at some fascinating documentation to get a better understanding of the ship.

The schematics for the ship were unbelievable: truly the International Space Hotel was one of the biggest wonders of the whole world. Or the whole solar system, you might have to say, since technically you couldn't really count it as being on the world anymore.

Graham was caught up in wonderment, flipping through these schematics, when he first noticed something unusual. The first discrepancy he noticed was that it was on a smaller page, as well as gray, rather than blue. Then he saw the strange shape on the schematics and was flabbergasted.

"The heck is this?" Graham mumbled.

The shape was unlike anything he'd ever seen onboard the ship. It certainly wasn't any of the escape pods which he'd taken a look at earlier. It looked conic. Almost like an ice cream cone. But there was a barrel underneath it, faintly resembling the barrel of a gun. He looked at the machinery and assessed the dimensions, and realized that whatever this was, it was substantially larger than any escape pod. No, significantly. The dimensions along the side indicated that this thing was as large as a building, when you considered the length from the small compartment on top to the bottom tip of it, although it was nothing compared to the sheer size of the ISH. From this particular viewpoint he was looking at, he could make out the words "Ascendant" stenciled into the side of the station. He wondered briefly if this was research vessel, or a mobile laboratory. But then another thought, more sinister, flashed across his mind.

This looks like a weapon, Graham thought. *Judging by the dimensions, a superweapon, really.*

It looked like it was powered off what looked like a line of fuel cells. It seemed like there also were some sort of odd glass panels that looked like they almost routed solar energy down into the main cone. Judging by the way the barrel narrowed, then, that could mean…

It's a laser.

Graham could see the fine print now in the corner of the page. The *Space Armament Station 1*. And in quotation marks, the phrase *"The Good Boy"* which he imagined was quite the oxymoron.

Graham's eyes narrowed. He vaguely remembered something about Ascendant, but wasn't quite sure what. Regardless, his time with the document was over.

Graham's perusal session was quickly interrupted by the sound of footsteps approaching, and he quickly buried the schematics a few pages underneath some of the other documents he was looking at. He turned to Mr. Xiong, trying to adapt as normal of a façade as he possibly could. But the only class in which Graham hadn't gotten a straight A in high school had been Acting, and he prayed he didn't look as nervous as he felt.

"How are you?" Mr. Xiong asked.

"I'm, well, uh, I'm good, Mr. X," Graham stammered. "I-I, well, I looked through it, and this is all unbelievable."

"That's good," Mr. Xiong responded. "I'm going to have you sit in on one of our meetings."

Mr. Xiong frowned, and slowly walked toward the table. Graham sat back and turned around so that his legs spread out in a way that he just knew Madison would call manspreading.

Mr. Xiong began sifting through the pages. Soon his fingers closed down on the gray page, and he pulled the gray page out. It looked like his face flashed with relief, and then he turned around to Graham, frowning.

"You didn't happen to see anything weird, did you?"

"No," Graham replied. "What are you referring to?"

"Well, that's good," Mr. Xiong said, dodging the question and folding the schematics up close. "I'd have to kill you if you'd have seen this page."

Graham could feel his face turning beet red.

"That's a joke," Mr. Xiong said, and he broke out laughing.

"Oh! Aha!" Graham said, forcing a laugh that sounded like a dying animal.

"Meeting in ten minutes," Mr. Xiong offered as he walked out of the room. He peered back to look at Graham one last time. "Over in one of the Engineering meeting rooms. You'll find it."

"Gotcha," Graham rasped, and then Mr. Xiong disappeared out the door and to wherever he was bringing the schematic.

Graham breathed out deeply. He didn't know what the significance was of what he saw, but he knew he wasn't supposed to have seen it, and that scared him.

Chapter 7

The training flew by quickly for Skye. As did the first few days aboard the ISH.

Skye settled into her new role as intern quickly. Not much at all actually occurred during the first day of orientation, nor did it the second day, when interns were prepared on what to do in the event of malfunctions with the oxygen generators or if one of the engines exploded. In any case, most of the extreme scenarios involved one of two solutions: running to the escape pods and launching back down to Earth (Skye was relieved to know there was a surplus of escape pods) or hunkering down and hoping that the engineers would fix any possible issues, lest they all die a terrible death. Although that part wasn't really touched on, Skye shuddered when she was reminded of how if anything truly went wrong and the ship lost its power and back-up power, they would all die a horrible death within minutes due to suffocation.

The Hotel itself was different from any other orbiting space station ever assembled. Even though it remained in orbit full-time, it was supervised by a flight crew, and was capable of traveling through space at speeds up to 20,000 mph. A voice on one of the videos had said that the International Space Hotel was the greatest marvel of engineering in the history of humankind, and Skye found it difficult to contend with that claim. And even though she dwelled on all of these negative scenarios potentially happening, she knew that the chances of anything going awry were astronomically slim.

After all, there were dozens of engineers of various sorts, both mechanical and electrical, not to mention a handful of interns, among them Graham, and their presence re-assured her. Learning other factoids about just how massive the ISH put many of her worries to rest: apparently, there were multiple weeks' worth of frozen food on board, not to mention a complete gigantic, beautiful garden that could sustain around fifty individuals indefinitely. She wanted to visit this garden as soon as possible but learned that it was only open to the public during the weekend, much to her chagrin, and even then, it was only when you pay for a tour. One of the other interns, Kyra, interned in the garden and at lunch on Friday regaled Skye, Graham and Madison of descriptions of the magnificence of the garden, promising to walk them through it Saturday.

"For free," she added. "I'm an intern, but I'll run it by my manager just to make sure."

Not only were there gardens, but there were adjacent laboratories where all of the meat was grown. Identical in taste and texture to that of real meat, thirty pounds of meat could be produced at maximum capacity by the laboratory every day, which, while a lot, was not enough to create a sustainable food source for too many people.

***

Even though the internship put a lot of pressure on everyone to perform, there was plenty of time for them to decompress.

During the weekdays, Skye usually relaxed in her hotel room, while Madison went exploring around to find people to meet and talk to. Graham, on the other hand, hit up a very small, and in his mind, very awesome, gaming room in the ship, which was chock-full of all kinds of the newest gaming systems. The gaming room was usually not quite packed, but not quite empty, either, leading to

62

the ideal number of individuals to play playing co-op or versus on the ultra-realistic gaming consoles.

The weekend, however, meant much more free time for all of them, so that meant something special was planned.

Before Kyra went to show them the gardens on Saturday, the three friends joined Kyra to hit up the bowling alley. Their group initially consisted of the four of Skye, Kyra, Graham, and Madison, but there were others in the bowling alley, two of whom joined their group to complete the group of six on their bowling squad.

"Shit," Skye mumbled under her breath when she saw the last member walk over.

The first unexpected group member was a girl called Ella who was shy and invited to join their group by Madison. Skye had no issues with her at all.

The sixth member to round out their group, unfortunately, was Drake.

"Ladies," he said. Skye imagined if he was wearing a fedora, he'd quite literally have tipped his hat at them. "Graham."

"Drake, right?" Skye asked. Drake's face lit up once she recalled his name.

"That's right," Drake answered. "You don't mind if I join you all, right?"

"No, not at all," Madison replied, in a voice dripping with sarcasm, but he must've either not picked up on it, or not cared.

"Come on," Kyra replied. "We gotta have six of us for an even number."

"Isn't six an unlucky number?" Skye questioned.

"You're telling me," Kyra laughed. "I got room number 166. Satan's number. I'm shocked I didn't get room 666. I would bet there's an Ouija board and Satan's pitchfork waiting in there."

The six of them stood next to human android which spoke up after they all entered their information.

"You will be assigned in bowling lane 4," the android said. "Would you like to play in teams, or individually?"

Graham's mouth opened, as if to answer, but Madison stuck her hand out to cover his mouth.

"Teams," Madison blurted out.

"I didn't want that," Graham whined, but Madison stuck out her tongue.

"I don't want to play this individually," Madison said. "I don't want to look like a moron."

"Like you need this game to make you look like one," Graham mumbled, and Madison flipped him off, before they both laughed. They had developed quite a rapport the past few days.

"Teams are good," Ella agreed.

"Would you like to randomly or manually assign teams?" The android vocalized.

"Manually," Skye answered, and she stepped right in front of it.

"Who would you like for Team 1?"

Skye headed over to the interface in front of it, manually entering in a few names.

"She's working fast," Drake observed. "Skye, what're the teams?"

"Sorry," she said, looking back up at him when she'd finished typing. "Teams are me, Graham, and Maddie, versus you, Ella, Kyra."

"Challenge accepted," Drake said, a smirk on his face as he stared at Skye for an uncomfortably long period of time.

"Got it!" Kyra exclaimed. "You all better watch out."

Next, the six of them got their bowling shoes, and picked out the bowling balls of their choice. It was an antiquated sport and Skye had only gone bowling twice in her life, but she was still oddly excited and pumped up for this game. Their team went first, starting with Graham, who was jeered at by Madison.

"Drake's got a bigger ball than you," Madison teased.

"Shut up," Graham said, promptly rolling his fourteen-pound ball into the gutter almost immediately, leading to both Skye and Madison breaking out into hysterical laughter.

"Oh my God! You choked!" Madison called out.

"Shit!" Graham exclaimed loudly, so much so that one of only two human staff working the bowling alley issued a noise warning.

"Chill, chill," Drake told him.

The game went on for a few minutes and was extremely competitive. Their skill levels were quickly revealed: Skye was horrible, Graham mediocre, and Madison, somehow, extremely good. On the other side, Drake was leading the charge, while both Ella and Kyra were both trailing behind with underwhelming performances that were still better than Skye.

In the final round, it was team 2's turn to catch up.

"Skye, if I hit a strike on this, will you let me take you on a dinner date?" Drake asked, bending his knees enthusiastically, as if he was preparing to run a race in track.

"No," Skye answered.

"Shame," Drake said, tsking before releasing his bowling ball with a loud thud. It connected with a strike that led to him high-fiving his team and doing a little jig on the spot.

Since it was the final round, he got to roll more than once due to some convoluted rule that Skye didn't quite understand, and he ended up following up by knocking down seven pins, and then two.

The gap was closing. Ella completed a spare after hitting eight pins on her first roll and got a bonus six points on her final roll.

All that pressure led to Kyra having to score eleven points, something that, judging by her performance thus far, was doable, but probably not likely.

"You got this!" Drake said.

"Go Kyra!" Ella clapped.

Kyra hit seven bowling pins, and now needed to hit the rest to complete a spare and get the bonus points.

"That's good!" Drake cheered, whooping. "You got this!"

But Kyra didn't. She completely whiffed, barely threading the bowling ball in between the disparate three pins and going straight down the drop-off. The miss secured the victory of team 1, and Skye, Madison, and Graham high-fived each other.

"66," Kyra said, chortling as she looked up at the score board, which showed that she had achieved Satan's score. "I can't escape it."

With the game over, Skye and the others thanked Ella and said goodbye before brushing off Drake's questions of where they were going. They headed to the gardens next.

***

"It's beautiful," Skye commented as she gazed upon the gardens. And it was.

The room was, by far, the largest of any on the ship, stretching perhaps somewhere between a quarter and a half of a mile long, located in the center of the orbiting ring. The room was huge, perhaps towering a hundred or so feet tall. There were no windows in the room, but rather an assortment of various lights, some hanging down from the ceiling, otherwise plastered on the roof.

These lights focused on the various plants that allowed just the right amount of light to permeate inside.

"This over here is the trees section," Kyra said, motioning to a dozen lines of trees, each row looking different from the next. Each tree was in their own sort of pot-shaped pit below floor level, while the grounds of the walkways were made of steel, like many other parts of the ship.

"There're a lot," Madison marveled.

"We have apple trees, pear trees, oranges, peaches, and bananas," Kyra explained. "We're looking to add cherries next year."

"They're all acclimated to this weather?"

"Of course," Kyra answered. "Only the best fruits are here on board the ISH. On average, all are genetically engineered to grow ten times as fast as they would in the wild. Of course, for some plants, it still takes time for them to bud first, and there is a great variance between species."

Skye and the others followed as she weaved through different rows. There was to be the occasional small station set up with different sorts of mechanical equipment Skye couldn't recognize, as well as the monitors of a screen.

"I have to ask," Graham said, "but what exactly does your internship entail? I mean, it's clear that everything is being set to specific moisture levels and different levels of electromagnetic radiation, but what do you actually do as an intern?"

"What're you trying to say?" Madison asked defensively. "You trying to say this girl doesn't do anything? Trust me, Kyra, I'm impressed."

"No, no," Graham said, shaking his head and sighing. "I'm just curious."

"I analyze biomass production, oxygen and water contents of the soil, make sure all of the sunlight levels are up to snuff and I escalate whenever there's an issue," Kyra answered without missing a beat. "Apart from a broken sprinkler yesterday, I haven't had to do anything to be honest, and most of the time I just sit in front of a monitor. Occasionally my manager will explain some concepts for me to explain how everything's connected, although I think I have a decent grasp on how it all works."

"That sounds like the life," Graham replied. "Although I didn't mean to make it sound like you do nothing. Most of the time, I just recline and watch some of the engineers and repairmen work on blueprints or tinker with metal. They don't trust me to do more. Yet."

"I mean, we're all here because we deserve it," Skye replied. "We're here for a once-in-a-lifetime experience, hopefully a more-than-a-once-in-a-lifetime experience, if we play our cards right."

"Yes, yes, of course," Graham replied. "I dunno. I just feel like, having beaten out hundreds of applicants and having done so well in college, we all deserve to do more. Although I have learned a lot."

"It's no wonder why," Madison jested, "If you accidentally unplug the wrong thing, I'd bet you'd probably trigger a meltdown to the core of the ship."

"That's… not how it works," Graham remarked. "And there isn't even a core to the ship."

Skye was distracted by her phone loudly vibrating in her pocket.

"Woah," Skye said, pulling out her phone and scrunching her eyebrows to make sure she read the text right.

Report to the Announcements Room in no later than thirty minutes. Come dressed in appropriate attire.

Skye was glad she'd purposefully packed pants with giant pockets, because otherwise she'd hated to have lugged her purse around the entirety of the ship.

"Did you just get a phone call?" Madison asked. "Because I thought that's physically impossible."

"Oh no," Skye answered. "That's just for calls from Earth. You can still call people on the ship, if you have the proper permissions. Anyway, I got a text."

"What does it say?"

"It's from Lex, my manager. They said I have a special mission for me."

"Ooh, special mission! What're you, double-o eight?" Madison asked excitedly.

"Tell us what goes on," Graham insisted.

"I don't know, you heard what I said about confidentiality and all that," Skye said. "But I will tell you how it goes."

"Show me the outfit after, too," Madison said. "I feel cheated that you didn't let me see them when you tried them on a couple days ago."

Graham raised his eyebrows, while Kyra nodded understandingly before resuming speaking.

"I'll show them the rest of the gardens. Break a leg, Skye. Or, definitely don't."

Chapter 8

When Skye reported to the announcement room, she didn't know who or what she would see. After all, she never expected anything like this to ever happen on the weekend to begin with.

The portion of the text saying that she needed to come dressed in appropriate attire didn't exactly inspire confidence in Skye either, because at the time she received the text she was wearing nothing more than a crop-top and jeans. She looked, and felt, far more like a waitress at a nightclub in some random slightly sketchy inner suburb rather than a professional hostess likely about to deal with someone who was rich, powerful, or quite possibly, both.

Skye rushed back to her dorm. Lucky for her, she wasn't far away, and she simply stood on the fast lane of the escalator track to get back. She then put on her outfit, settling on a black and gold sequin dress with a deep neckline which showed a little bit more of her chest than she was comfortable with.

"Shit, shit," she mumbled. "Too late to change. *Fuck.*"

She hoped for her sanity's sake she would be dealing with women, and not ogling men, although, having seen the gender split of the clientele of the ISH (which seemed to be around 60% male to 40% female), that was probably a bit unlikely. Skye then looked in the mirror, quickly applying some eyeliner, deeply grateful that she'd applied lipstick and foundation earlier in the morning. Then, she checked on her time.

"Ten minutes," she said, combing a small knot out of her hair. She didn't even have time to use the restroom, and she was glad she didn't have to.

Lastly, she looked at the high heels and groaned. They looked tight, and she absolutely *knew* her feet were going to blister because of this, if her horrific track record with high heels was any indication.

Skye arrived to the announcement room to find that both Lex and Franco were there, although Franco was occupied sitting at the desk looking at a screen, while Lex leaned up against a wall, staring at the door and eagerly awaiting Skye's arrival. Judging by their slouch, and their frown, they appeared to even be anxious.

"Hello Skye," Lex said, her eyes straining as she read the hands to a glowing analog clock on the wall. "You made it in time. With 1 minute and 33 seconds left."

"Okay," Skye said, heaving for each breath.

"You look good," Franco said over from the monitor he sat behind, even though his eyes were glued to the screen he was in front of.

"Really?" Skye said. "I sure don't feel like that. I guess I didn't exactly expect to be called here on a Saturday."

"About that," Lex said. "I apologize. Usually this doesn't happen ever, let alone during your first week of your internship. But I am grateful for your timeliness."

"What do you need me to do? Why?"

"It is an urgent matter," Lex said. "Do you know who Alan Lusky is?"

"Yes, of course. He's the CEO, right?"

"Right, I figured you would be familiar. Well tell me, do you know who Grace Elliott is?"

Skye's eyes widened. "Grace Elliott… She's the speaker of the House, right? The Representative from Illinois?"

"Speaker Elliott is considered one of the frontrunners for the 2052 Presidential election, once President Chu's second term finishes up. You're going to meet her."

"Are you telling me… That I'm about to meet one of the most powerful women in the entire United States?"

"Yes."

Skye's jaw dropped.

No way. No f'in way.

"You look happy," Lex said, managing a smirk. "I know this isn't what you signed up for, but this is a tremendous opportunity."

"I'm grateful," Skye said, recollecting herself. "Where am I headed?"

"Meeting Room 01."

"01. Got it."

"I think it goes without saying, but remember to maintain your professional demeanor," Lex reminded Skye.

"Absolutely," Skye replied. "You can count on me."

Once Skye walked away, however, she felt she couldn't count on herself to count to five, let alone to successfully do the tasks for the Speaker of the House and a famous CEO.

***

The meeting room in question was located on the opposite side of the ISH. The room was arguably one of the fanciest rooms of the entire hotel, at least excluding the VIP hotel rooms. The entire décor reeked of privilege and vanity: there was an old-fashioned smooth, varnished wooden table in the center of the room, previously owned by the former president of France some two centuries ago; a

Descartes painting that had only been recently discovered and quickly bought up by Alan Lusky; and gold wallpaper. The gold wallpaper was gold, of course, not only because of the various pigments it contained, but because it was actually infused with gold dust. The cushioned chairs, threaded with gold, contained diamonds encrusted into their armrests. It was the most extreme vanity project Skye had ever seen, but with money like Alan Lusky, she supposed he had no issues flaunting his wealth.

The room was already occupied by two people, but in order to get close to them, Skye first had to pass through a few security guards in the hallway. These weren't any regular security guards from the ship, however. Whereas the security guards of the ship wore dark body armor from their feet all the way up to their head, these guards all wore a suit and tie. It was no question why. Skye figured these people were all Secret Service, although that did seem a little bit weird, because as far as she knew, Secret Service was tasked with only protecting the Presidents and former U.S. Presidents. Regardless, Skye knew that it wasn't in her place to be asking questions, or at least certainly not to these people.

One of them stepped forward, as if to block her path, but Skye rapidly showed him the ID that dangled over her neck and he quickly stepped back, uttering a quiet apology.

Skye slowly opened the door, stepping through to see two chairs inside the room occupied.

One of them was occupied by the CEO, Alan Lusky, while the other was occupied by Grace Elliott. Grace Elliott was dressed in a blazer suit and slacks and wore a necklace of pearls around her throat. Once she passed through the door, she could get a full glance of Mrs. Elliott. Seeing her determined eyes, thick eyebrows, and serious expression tantalized her: the woman had an aura of command, much like Lusky, a presence that seemed to make her occupation all the more fitting.

Both Grace Elliott and Alan Lusky turned towards the door upon their encounter with the new arrival.

"Hello," Alan Lusky greeted her.

"Greetings," Skye said. *Greetings. Who even says that? Am I some kind of alien invader trying to make first contact with the humans?*

Skye cleared her throat. "Would either of you care for any drinks, or beverages of any kind?"

"We're okay, thank you," Grace said, although Alan raised his finger.

"Actually, I could," Alan Lusky answered. "Tell the staff that Mr. Lusky wants the Lusky Classic."

"What's that?" Grace asked. "I've heard lots of rumors about your famed classic."

"Would you care to try?" Alan Lusky asked. "It's never too late to become a Lusky fan. Although the alcohol mix is a trade secret, you can probably figure out the fruit components by the taste."

"That's okay," Grace said, smiling. "A glass of iced water is all I need."

"A glass of iced water and the Classic Lusky," Skye said. "Will that be all? Is there anything else I can do for either of you?"

"Lusky Classic," Alan corrected her. "It's splitting hairs, but you want to give them the right order. And I think that's all we need."

"Ooh, sorry," Skye said, turning as red as a tomato. "I'll have that for you as soon as I can."

"Don't sweat it," Alan said, smiling.

Skye stepped out of the room. When the door closed behind her, she shook her head in frustration and embarrassment, before stepping past the posted guards and pulling out her phone.

"Call the Food Service," she commanded her phone, before being patched through to whoever was on the other side of the line.

"Hello?" The voice was a tenor one, tinged with what sounded like a French or Italian accent.

"Hello, we have an order for Meeting Room 01. It's very important."

"Meeting Room 01. Yes, I understand. What do you need?"

"An iced glass of water, and a Lusky Classic."

"Is that it?"

"Yes."

"We'll have the order ready within the next minute."

Skye walked over the distance to the closest kitchen, which was only down the length of the hallway. By the time she arrived there, the order was already sitting on a shiny metal tray to be picked up, and one of the chefs, a man with a handlebar mustache who may as well have been a living stereotype for a fancy chef, gently smiled at her before walking past her out of the room and into the hallway opposite the direction from where she had come.

Skye grabbed the tray before walking back down the hallway. Now came the difficult part. Walking in high heels was difficult enough, but now with the added pressure of delivering drinks to the CEO and the Speaker of the House of Representatives, it was challenging beyond belief. It was overall one of the hardest things which she ever had to do, and she'd taken a three-hundred level Ethics course in college.

Don't trip. Please don't trip. Don't trip. She told herself this continually as she tried her best to gracefully walk to the end of the hallway. The entire time, she felt like she was leaning over like the

Tower of Pisa. At one point, as she neared the guards, perhaps only twenty or thirty paces away from the door, she stumbled, the tray almost knocked out of her hands. The cups leaned over as the tray tilted, and it was a miracle that Skye managed to catch her footing and have the cups land perfectly back onto the tray. Only a couple of droplets of the water spilled out onto the tray, and, although glances Skye got from the suited men and women meant that she was humiliated, it wasn't as if she had to return back to the kitchen to replace the water.

Thank God, she thought when one of the guards saw her struggles and quietly opened the door for her.

"Thank you," she told the man, before stepping back into the meeting room.

"You can't be serious," Alan Lusky was saying to Grace Elliott. Skye stood there at the side of the wall. Lex had told her during training that whenever there was an important conversation going on, it was best to simply stand there with whatever you delivered until you were specifically called upon. In this case, she was as quiet as a mouse while she waited. She didn't even think they noticed her presence.

"Unfortunately, I wish I was joking," Grace said. "I know it's not the news you wanted to hear, or anyone would want to hear, but it's the cold truth."

"That's absurd," Alan Lusky said, shaking his head. His face dropped, and he sighed. "If what you're saying is true, then we could have a World War 3 situation on our hands. And we might not even be able to stop them until it's too late."

World War Three? What is he talking about? Skye thought. *Surely this has to be an exaggeration of some kind.*

"I would say, overall, the chances of that are still quite unlikely," Grace said. "But there are escalating tensions against the

Chinese and Russians, not to mention between India and Pakistan. The news hardly captures half of it. Not to mention how several of these military installations have popped up all over orbit. We do know to some extent, the sheer power of them. I heard from one of the head engineers at Lockheed Martin, he said it was like something he'd never seen before. That it's a miracle that with the technology of today we were capable of constructing such a weapon."

"Thank you for letting me into the loop, Representative Elliott," Alan Lusky responded. "Are you at liberty to tell me more?"

"Of course, of course," Grace said, chuckling. "You have the highest security clearance of any non-politician or former politician in the United States. As I was saying, there's only a few of them. It wouldn't be a problem if we owned all of them, but only one is commissioned by the United States government."

"I imagine this is much more of a different scenario than the ISH."

"Yes," Grace Elliott responded. "The International Space Hotel has treaties with over two hundred countries to orbit over, I understand."

"Yes," Lusky affirmed. "Plus, we don't even risk orbiting over North Korea or Russia."

"Yes. Well, these military installations have none. We want to disable the others, and obviously we've built up our Space Force in the past decade for a reason. But that probably isn't a viable option."

"Why? Surely our nuclear defense systems are functional?"

"Yes," Representative Elliott answered, "They are. But even then, we could face widespread nuclear retaliation, and our defenses are only capable of stopping a few at once. It's not worth taking a risk like that."

"That's understandable," Alan Lusky replied. "So why do you provide this information to me? What can I do to help?"

"Because you're our best friends in space," Grace said. "We obviously partnered together to build this station, for, well, reasons that you know, but in the event that something goes wrong… Well, the existence of the ISH is obviously critical for our survival."

"Of course, but we're only so big, and our food production only goes so far. Surely not enough to sustain ourselves."

"That's what the S.S. Washington is for. With that and the ISH… Then we're in a much better position to protect the most important," Representative Elliott answered.

Alan Lusky turned to look at Skye, and it looked almost as if he was shocked. "Oh, you're back. Please, set the tray down. You can wait outside the door, look through the window. If we need anything more, we'll let you know."

Skye stepped outside of the room, looking through the window and peering through anxiously. She saw Alan Lusky lean forward, take a sip of his Lusky Classic, and smile, as if he was engaging in a casual conversation with his friend at the bar and not the Speaker of the House.

I can't believe what they were talking about, Skye thought. *World War III? Military installations? Our survival? Just what is going on in the world?*

It all was particularly stressful because the news had seemed rather calm before she'd departed to the ISH, and she'd certainly never heard anything about global war. While there were water wars and famines occurring in much of the third world, it was her understanding that the threat of nuclear war was nothing like the Cold War, or even the failed Russian invasion of Ukraine back in the '20s.

Skye felt a little bit sick to her stomach trying to wrap her head around everything. She wanted to go and blab to Madison about what she had heard. But she remembered Lex's stern warning about confidentiality and hesitated. For now, she had to stay kaput, and wait to see if they needed anything else. She hoped the conversation wouldn't last too long.

But Skye gasped when she looked at Grace through the window. Grace was talking one minute, and then her eyes were staring blankly. Alan was looking at her from across the table confusedly, and appeared to be asking her whether she was okay. And then Grace dropped the cup of water onto the table, and it split into shards. Skye could only watch in horror as Grace collapsed onto the carpet of the floor.

"Oh no," she said, and she threw open the door and rushed inside, as security was alerted by the commotion of Alan Lusky screaming for help, and Representative Elliott fallen on the ground. She was convulsing, gasping for air. It looked like blood was rushing from her nose, from her eyes, and Skye stood to the side, hyperventilating as one of the suited women threw herself onto Grace, attempting to administer first aid. They pulled out a first aid kit, trying to treat her ailment to no avail.

"What the hell is happening! She just fell! She just fell!" Alan Lusky was exclaiming, panicking. He turned to Skye, his face turning into an expression of rage.

"You! What the *fuck* did you do?"

"M… me? What are you talking about?" Skye asked, trembling in fear.

She could hear Grace Elliott heave for breath, and then let out a gasping sigh, a final sigh that signaled the end of her life. And then there was the loud noise as the one guard who'd let her into the room started performing chest compressions in an attempt to resuscitate Elliott with CPR. Another guard seemed to be contacting the emergency services of the entire hotel, as they'd hit an emergency button and were talking to someone through an earpiece, pleading for them to send a doctor. Skye wondered if Madison would be involved in this.

"You! You did this!" Alan Lusky said, standing up and pointing at Skye. "She drank the water, it was poisoned! You'll get the electric chair for this!"

Skye collapsed to the ground, sobbing.

"I don't know what you're talking about!" She screeched, as one of the other guards seized her arms, wrapping them behind her back and throwing her onto the ground. Tears flowed freely from her eyes now, like water let loose from a broken dam. What she saw next was an image that would permanently sear itself into Skye's mind. Although her face was almost pressed against the ground, Skye saw through her blurry vision the corpse of Grace Elliott, whose face was stained with blood and whose jaw was dropped in an expression of pure shock. She noted the way her body seemed to bounce with a jolt of energy with each chest compression, until it became clear that it was already far too late.

"Take her to the hold!" Alan Lusky yelled, pointing at Skye. "*Fuck*! Why did this have to happen!? And why here!?"

Chapter 9

Contrary to whatever Madison had joked about the prison conditions were like, the cell that Skye was thrown into was nothing like a Swedish prison. When they unlocked her handcuffs and tossed her into the middle of the room, Skye felt that this was solitary confinement. There were no windows to be spoken of; only sleek metal surfaces with no sharp corners. A single light on the ceiling lit up the room just enough so that it didn't feel dark, but also not enough so that the room felt properly lit. There was a toilet in the corner of the room, a sink, and a plain, firm mattress. That was it. There wasn't even a mirror. Skye couldn't even make it over to the bed. Instead, she curled into a ball, and bawled like a baby.

The image of Grace Elliott on the ground replayed over and over in Skye's head, like a movie reel endlessly replaying.

"I want to go home!" Skye sobbed at some point. "Mom! Dad!"

When she realized the absurdity of what she had just said, and understood that no one would be coming to rescue her from Earth, Skye managed to get a grip of herself, as she re-assured herself that her name had to be cleared, since she had nothing to do with whatever the hell had just happened. She managed to catch her breath a little bit, although it was like her eyes were a leaky faucet, as she just couldn't stop herself from crying.

At one point, she could hear an alarm, one loud enough that it seemed like sirens were blaring right outside the room. Wondering if something was going on, she snapped out of her crying streak and pounded on the door, yelling for help and asking what was going on. No one paid her any visit, and, after a couple of minutes, the siren stopped. Skye slunk back to the bed in defeat, reduced to tears quickly once again.

Skye had no idea of how much time passed in that room. It felt like years, but in reality, she would've guessed it was probably only a couple of hours. When the door finally opened, Skye threw herself up from the bed.

"I'm innocent!" She proclaimed, wiping the tears from her face and jumping up from the bed with her hands raised into the air. "I'm innocent!"

"I know you are," A familiar male voice said.

Skye stepped forward, confused, until the man stepped into the room. Marcell.

Skye rushed forward as Marcell embraced her.

"It's okay, it's okay," he reassured her.

Skye tried to utter a 'thanks', an 'I'm sorry', and an 'I'm so confused' at one time, and it came out in an incomprehensible garble of words mixed with a heaving sob.

Skye pulled away from the hug after a few seconds, her eyes scanning Marcell's full black body armor. It was a little bit of a shock to see him now dressed for work and not for a night out, but it was a great relief all the same.

"What's going on?" Skye asked. She looked behind him and saw that there were a couple of other ISH guards, a man and a woman, standing back with their hands folded, and she felt incredibly awkward for making a scene.

"Your name has been cleared, and you are free to go," Marcell said. "Well, free to come with me. We need to ask you a couple of questions, and then we're going to let you free for the day. Come with me to the control room."

"I don't know anything! I didn't do anything!"

"I know," Marcell said assertively, before lowering his voice. "I know. But you just have to confirm a couple of things. The Speaker of the House just got assassinated. This is a big deal."

Skye nodded. "Let's go."

***

The front cabin of the ship had an assembly of all sorts of individuals there: there was Alan Lusky, in addition to at least a dozen or so of the ISH security guards as well as the suited governmental agents. There were plenty of other individuals milling about who Skye didn't recognize, many of them likely management for the ISH. She even saw an Indian woman in a white coat who presumably was a doctor, talking to some of the suited men and women from earlier. Meanwhile, in the very front of the control room, a few operatives were standing in front of various control boards with buttons, still at work.

Alan Lusky was standing near an employee at one of the many screens in the back of the room. It looked like they were looking at some kind of camera footage from on board the ship. Next to him, stood a clean-shaved man in a button-up shirt, much older, with white, thinning hair on his head, and narrow eyes akin to a bird of prey.

"I apologize for my... overreaction earlier," Lusky said, turning away from the screen and towards Skye. "Since you were the one delivering the drinks, I assumed that you would've been the only person who could've poisoned her... And I was wrong."

Skye looked at him. She didn't want to forgive him. Not after what she'd been through, not after crying for hours. But she still found it in her heart, anyway. Besides, this was the CEO, and she knew she should leave the impression.

I'm such a kiss-ass, she thought.

"I… understand," she said, "and I forgive you. Although what you did to me was terrible."

"What's your name?" Lusky asked. "I've been informed that you are an intern, right?"

"Skye," Skye answered, "Skye Calvert."

Alan Lusky offered her his hand, which she shook. His hands were supple and only slightly larger than hers. They were definitely the hands of a man who'd hardly done a day of physical labor in his life.

"This is Investigator McFarland," Lusky introduced, pointing to the old man beside him, and they shook hands as well. His hands were far wrinklier and calloused than Lusky.

"It's a pleasure to meet you," Skye said, although she just wanted this all to be over.

"McFarland, take it away," Lusky ordered, and McFarland nodded before clearing his throat and speaking in a baritone voice, his voice accented with either a New York or New Jersey accent, Skye couldn't be sure which.

"Yes," McFarland said. "I apologize for any misunderstanding. We brought back certain evidence to the forensics lab, and we realized the facts pointed to someone else, and not you."

"It's okay," Skye stated. "If I'd known… I'd never have brought the drinks. I swear."

"Of course, dear," McFarland responded. "Now, I need you to look at this footage, tell me if this man is familiar. Help us get to the bottom of this."

Skye's eyes narrowed as she looked at the footage. In it was a man with a handlebar mustache, wearing a chef's coat with black pants, sprinting through a hallway. The way he moved rapidly through the frame made him look like an Olympian. But there was no mistaking the familiar face.

"Why, yes," Skye explained, nodding. "I saw him in the kitchen, right as I picked up the drinks."

"Good," McFarland stated. "So, it's confirmed, then."

"That's… unfortunate," Lusky said, shaking his head. He turned to some of the staff, whispering something in one of their ears before clearing his throat and speaking loudly. "First things first, we're going to have a meeting about the camera blind spots in the ship. We thought we had ourselves covered well enough, but clearly, we didn't in the kitchen."

"Yes, sir," a woman nearby chimed.

"Mind if I ask her a couple of questions?" McFarland asked before Lusky nodded.

"You don't need my permission," Lusky insisted.

"Tell me, Ms. Calvert," McFarland said, "Do you remember anything about this man? Did he say anything strange to you, perhaps?"

"Well, no," Skye said. "I saw him walking away from the direction of the drinks, past me. But when I walked back into the hallway, he wasn't in the direction I was walking, so I'm assuming he must've headed the other way."

"What about when you placed the phone call? What was that like?"

"Some man with a foreign accent picked it up. I couldn't really tell what the accent was at the time, but now that I think about it, I think it was French. Maybe Italian. I'm not sure."

"Interesting," McFarland said. "Very interesting, indeed."

Lusky turned to the staff controlling the footage, a younger man perhaps in his mid or late-twenties.

"Can you fill her in on the current situation? I'd say after being falsely imprisoned, she deserves a little bit of an explanation."

"The man we're looking at right now, he was a recent hire, in the past two months," The man explained. "He pulled the emergency alarm, and fled the ship. He's currently on an escape pod which we are tracking, but he isn't heading towards Earth's surface, at least not yet."

So that's why I could hear an alarm, Skye reasoned. She thought back to her orientation, how escape pods could only be manually activated if an emergency alarm was triggered, and suddenly it made sense. The chef had hurriedly escaped following the assassination by probably getting as close to the escape pods as possible, yanking an emergency alarm, and fleeing the ship via the escape pods.

"His name is Jacques Morneau," McFarland added. "He's French. Or at least he claimed to be. We got his fingerprints, but interestingly, we cross-referenced his fingerprints with multiple registries and databases, and there's no matches. This is of course strange, because if you remember, we take the fingerprints of everyone who comes into this ship. I think it's safe to say that this guy altered his fingerprints, or otherwise is a literal ghost. I'd say he's been planning this for months, and he just executed his plan without a hitch."

"Didn't you vet this guy?" Skye asked. One of the people snorted nearby, and Lusky looked offended for a few moments before his face softened.

"Of course, we did, honey," Lusky answered, not without a condescending undertone. "I'd say this guy faked this identity, but he passed the culinary tests, clearly."

"We shouldn't talk about this with an intern," the man at the screen stated matter-of-factly. Lusky nodded understandingly, but McFarland rolled his eyes, as if to say, *this man doesn't know who he's dealing with.*

"You might be right," Lusky agreed. "This has been a lot. Skye… Thank you. And I apologize. As a token of my appreciation, please, accept this."

He handed her a square black card.

Premium Gift Card, the title read.

"Umm… Thank you?"

"It's a $500 gift card that's redeemable at any restaurant throughout the ship. I know that's not a lot, especially after everything you've been through. But your hiring managers track your performance closely, and I'll be sure to put a good word in for you."

"Thank you," Skye said.

Lusky was silent for a few seconds, staring off, his jaw clenching.

"What is it?" McFarland inquired.

"Nothing…" Lusky said, before sighing. "It's that, when we put in that order of drinks, I ordered a Lusky Classic, and Elliott ordered a glass of water. They clearly knew that I requested my own drink, but I even suggested it to her, too… So, who's to say that if the assassin couldn't have poisoned both of us if he couldn't have reasoned which drink was going to which of us? If she had taken my suggestion, there's a non-zero chance we'd both be dead right now."

"I see," McFarland thought, his face deep in thought, and Lusky turned away, seemingly embarrassed to appear in a vulnerable position in front of so many strangers.

"Please, assist her out of here," Lusky said, and then Marcell was at Skye's side, guiding her with a gentle touch to the shoulder out of the front cabin and back towards her hotel room.

Chapter 10

"**O**h my God! Skye! Are you okay!?" Madison asked.

Both Graham and Madison were waiting out in front of her room, anxiously waiting for Skye to come back. When they saw her and Marcell, their faces looked visibly relieved, and, each one of them hugged her, and Skye almost choked up once again. She shook her head.

"Marcell," Madison said, who smiled.

"Hello again," Marcell said. "She's okay. We're all okay."

"We didn't hear many details," Graham said. "But is it true? That Speaker Elliot was… assassinated?"

"I saw it with my own two eyes," Skye confirmed. "She's dead."

"Oh my God," Madison said, covering her mouth, her eyes widening in horror. "I can't believe you had to go through that. I'm so sorry, Skye. This world is too cruel sometimes."

"It's worse than you think," Skye said, sighing. "Alan Lusky, the CEO, was in the room. And when she dropped dead, and I'd been the one who'd delivered the drink which poisoned her. They put me in the prison hold."

Now it looked like Madison's eyes were so wide they were going to bulge and fall out of her eye sockets.

"You're kidding me," Graham said. "But how? How did this happen? I mean, we're in space, so how would it be feasible for someone to kill her, if there's no way an assassin could sneak on board past security?"

"Come on," Marcell cautioned, gesturing for Skye to stop talking. "Look, you've been through a lot, but I don't think, no, I know, you're not supposed to disclose all these details to your friends. You have a job."

"Well, you tell me, Marcell," Skye said. "Will you snitch on us if we talk about this? And if we keep it between us, will they find out?"

Marcell looked around. "As a security guard, I can say, no, they're not listening to you, although if they grow suspicious, they could plant a microphone in your room."

"They could put a microphone in the room?" Madison asked, disgusted. "That's horrible!"

"There isn't any reason to worry..." Marcell answered. "For now. Let's go inside."

"Okay," Skye said. She motioned them all to go inside her room. The timing was impeccable, as several guests scurried about this way and that from their rooms, roused by the rumors that spread like a wildfire throughout the ship, that there had been a murder on board.

"With all this stuff, I never even got to say," Madison remarked as they walked inside room 32, "That dress is beautiful."

***

Skye told all four of them everything she'd learned that night, although Marcell was there to hear about the suspected assassin. Skye told them about the assassination. How she'd simply gone to retrieve drinks, before eavesdropping on a very classified conversation. How she'd heard about the potential for a World War III brewing. She explained how Elliott had described there some

90

sorts of strange military installations in orbit, and thought that these were a significant threat to the United States. That the United States faced escalating tensions with the Chinese and Russians, and that Grace Elliott thought they were on the verge of a global war.

"What the heck," Graham said, too matter-of-factly. "Are you sure you didn't mishear anything?"

"I know what I heard," Skye said.

"Did they specify what they meant?" Madison queried, frowning. "With the installations?"

"No, not at all. I was just in the room for a couple of minutes. I don't know what they meant at all. I'm guessing they're some sort of giant weapon of mass destruction, like nukes, except we can at least defend from nukes. Oh, and they said something about the S.S. Washington. I've heard about that, of course."

"It's that one big spaceship that's set to launch soon, right? Biggest aircraft, or spacecraft, ever built, if I remember."

"Yeah, they said the ISH and the S.S. Washington would somehow work together, could sustain life or something. I don't know what that meant."

"They're just being prepared," Madison offered. "You know how it was with the Cold War, right? They had those nuclear missile drills, and bomb shelters, as if they'd make a difference in the grand scheme of things. I mean, almost everyone in the West would pretty much almost be guaranteed to die if there'd been a nuclear apocalypse."

"I think that's their plan B, if the World War hits," Graham said, brow furrowed deep in concentration. The others turned to her like he'd started speaking a foreign language. "What? Don't look at me like that, I'm just theorizing. If something's going to happen, then they're going to go into space. That's perfectly reasonable. Pack it full of politicians and their families, engineers and doctors:

and humanity survives. At least so long as the ship stays active, or until they go back down to Earth.”

“Huh,” Skye said. She’d never put that together when she’d been listening in to Lusky’s conversation. “You might be right.”

“But that still doesn’t explain the nuclear stuff,” Madison said. “That came out of left field.”

“Yes,” Graham said. “There would be talks in the news. Murmurs, warnings. But there’s been nothing. Plus, it’s only been a week since we’ve been on board.”

“Was there anything else?” Madison asked. “That they said?”

“Umm… From the talk? Not that I caught. Grace Elliott drank the water, collapsed and died, I was falsely accused, thrown in jail… And then Marcell rescued me.”

“I didn’t rescue you,” Marcell said. “I mean, I knew you were innocent, and I pushed to let you out earlier, I really did, but they didn’t let me release you until the footage vindicated you.”

“Footage?” Graham asked. “How do you mean?”

“The assassin in question,” Marcell explained, “seems to be some kind of chef. He’s the one who pulled the emergency alarm and then escaped.”

“I see,” Madison answered. “I wonder what would motivate someone to do something like that. To kill a woman, in cold blood, and then run away like a coward.”

“My guess? Fervent nationalism,” Graham said. “Sounds like this was a ploy by the Chinese to destabilize the United States.”

“But why would they undermine us that way?” Skye asked. “I thought the U.S. had better global relations with China compared to the past, although that conversation I overheard definitely made me second guess that. But if they’re going to try to weaken the U.S., weaken democracy, why would they kill the Speaker of the House? Why not the President? The Vice President? Not to mention, I’m sure they're already appointing the next Speaker of the House as we speak."

"I don't know the answer to any of those questions," Marcell admitted as he checked his phone. "But I do know that I am needed back at work. I'm going to go and see if I can learn anything about the assassin. I'll talk to you later. Oh, but there's one other thing. I'll give you all my number, and you give me yours. I know you can't normally text, but with my permissions, I'll be able to get into contact with you all if necessary, and, if I can, allow you to as well."

They all bid him farewell after exchanging their contact information. Once Marcell left the room, it was as if the conversation hit a brick wall, and Skye was absolutely drained. Madison could tell and suggested they all go to bed early, since it was around ten at night. Graham thought that was a good idea, too. But Skye remembered something first.

"Oh, and there's this," Skye said, and she pulled out the $500 gift card, and Madison practically squealed with delight.

Chapter 11

"You ready for this?"

Marcell stood beside the bed, crossing his arms and wondering if what he was experiencing was real, or not. It certainly didn't feel that way. He pondered the other's man question before answering.

"Of course I am," Marcell responded, shaking his head. "I've been ready for this my whole life. It's just…"

"What?"

"I mean, Z, I had no idea," Marcell said. "This entire time. I mean, who'd have thought a guy like you could be interested in *me*."

"A guy like me? What's that mean? You mean white men being into black men? A higher percentage of the population identifies as gay than ever before in history. Yet you're surprised?"

"Sorry Zeke, I know, I know," Marcell said. "It's just, things have moved quickly. It's tough being in security, you know? It's only been a couple of months since I've taken this space job for real."

"I should know, considering we've been on the same shift many times," Zeke replied.

"Yes, yes."

"It sounds like you're procrastinating. Are you really not willing? After everything I went through to confess my feelings to you?"

"No. No, I mean, I'm not procrastinating, I am willing. I am willing."

"Well, do me a favor, would you, and turn around to let me undress."

"Turn around?"

"Yes. You go right ahead too. Sorry, this part is always the most squeamish for me."

Marcell turned around towards the lamp. Slowly he stripped off his shirt first, then his undershirt. He breathed out deeply as he fiddled with his pants, undoing his belt. Then it was onto his final layer. His underwear was down around his knees and he was about to turn around when he heard rapid footsteps pattering behind on the carpet. He moved to turn around, to pull up his underwear again, but it was too late.

"Surprise, bitch!"

Several hands grabbed him from behind, and he could only flail desperately as the rope encircled him, tied him taut. A noose was tied around his neck, much like a cowboy trying to catch a steer, and he desperately heaved for air until the noose loosened, and he was thrown onto the bed.

"What! What!?" He sputtered out. His face was red, and he rolled around on the bed to get a clear view of his assailants.

But he couldn't see who it was, because there were three of them. All three of them wore security guard outfits with their name patch purposefully covered up with black tape, and their faces were covered with some sort of makeshift bandanas. Marcell could see their eyes, as well as skin tone, and that was it. And then there was

Zeke, who stood against the back wall, staring down at the ground in shame.

"I'm sorry Marcell!" Zeke said. "They said they'd… They'd do things if I didn't help them out! I… I had no choice. I had to!"

"Who?" Marcell said. "You can have a clear conscience. Tell me who!"

"I… I…"

But one of the armored guards was there, grabbing him roughly and dragging him out of the room before he could even make up his mind whether to snitch or not. That left Marcell alone with two of them. Marcell managed to pull his underwear back up and his pants partially up as well, and, with newfound strength, tried kicking them away, but the blows hardly affected them.

"You get a kick out of this, huh?" Marcell spat.

"Shut up, fag." The voice's electronic tone showed that the assailant even had a voice changer underneath their bandana to obscure their voice.

"Fag? Really? Fag? It's 2045 and you still use that word? Bigot."

One guard reached out and pulled the lamp out of the outlet, as the other guard held him down onto the bed. He tried kicking his legs, but the ropes constricted his movements.

"What are you going to do? Stop it! Stop it!"

The same guard with the lamp looked at the other one, nodded, and then brought the metal lamp down on Marcell's side, connecting with his ribs in a blow that sent pain shooting up his chest.

"No! Please! Oh, god!" And he knew the rooms were soundproofed, making the ordeal even more horrifying.

"Please! Please!"

And then the third security guard was there. They were hitting him with the lamp all over the torso and below, again and again.

Marcell screamed, begged for mercy as the three laughed, high-fiving each other and passing around the lamp sleek with blood as if they were friends passing around a bottle of booze.

"Do us a favor and quit!" One of them yelled over Marcell's howling.

Marcell woke up with a start, drenched in sweat, gasping for air. He paced around the room. Sometimes, he swore he could still feel the ache, and tonight was one of those nights.

"Stupid. Stupid fucking Zeke. Stupid fucking security. I..."

He stopped in front of the desk, where a picture of his family stared at him. Despite the darkness, he picked up the picture to look at the picture of his parents, straining his eyes in the almost non-existent light. Back when they had been together. Back when they had been a family. Before Bradley had left his mother for another younger woman.

"What more do I have to do? Am I never enough? And you think I abandoned you? Jesus. Jesus Christ."

Marcell paced around the room, thinking about the nightmare once again before speaking resolutely. Even though the nightmare was not a fantasy but something that had happened to him only three years prior, he was resolute when he spoke aloud to himself, to existence.

"I will never... feel love again."

Chapter 12

Skye coped well with Grace Elliott's death, considering the circumstances. That isn't to say it didn't bother her. That same night of the assassination, she only slept four or five hours, and, what little sleep she did experience was riddled with nightmares induced from what she'd seen of Grace Elliott flopping on the ground like a dying fish, with blood running down her face like red mascara. Multiple times she awoke gasping and crying, and Skye wished at multiple points that night that she'd never accepted the internship to begin with.

But there were no alternative options, and Skye somehow felt like she made peace with what she had been through over the course of that night. Still, Skye was awake and then back asleep for many hours, and by the time she decided to actually clamber out of bed and get up for good, it was past eleven in the morning. She got up before taking a long shower.

Skye was grateful that with the ship's technology she was capable of texting those on board, and she formed plans to grab lunch with Graham and Madison, the latter of whom also brought along Kyra. As it was a Sunday, the day was free for all of them. The four decided to flaunt the gift card by going to the Alpha Grille, where they all proceeded to order extremely pricy entrees for themselves. During the entire conversation, none of them ever brought up Elliott's death, not even once.

"This lamb chop is so tender," Graham commented at one point, his grin so wide it almost stretched from ear to ear. "Tastes like they just slaughtered it back in the kitchen."

"Same with my steak," Skye agreed. "It's so good. Grilled to perfection."

"It's grown in the lab," Kyra said. "Almost all of it is, at least from this place. Some of it might be shipped from Earth, but that's mainly cafeteria and grocery food."

"Then how does it taste so good? Tell me that Chemistry, Kyra!" Madison exclaimed.

But Kyra laughed and said that was above her pay grade, shaking her head.

"You know, you almost forget how many people are on board," Kyra offered.

"How so?" Madison asked.

"I mean, these meals are prepared by human chefs," Kyra said. "That's a ton of supplies you have to get shipped, and then there's the labor costs and all the other costs."

"I never thought about that," Skye replied. "This is some good stuff."

"I heard they're looking at replacing a lot of the staff with androids, soon," Graham replied. "They have them doing security, some basic catering, and operating the call center, but they're still waiting for a bellhop and janitor model."

"Of course, you'd know," Madison said, rolling her eyes a little bit. "Thank you, for expediting the inevitable automation and mass unemployment of our population into fruition."

Graham shrugged. "Just doing my job. Besides, they've said that for decades."

"Now that you mention it," Kyra said. "I struck up a conversation with a very angry janitor a couple days ago."

At this, she snorted loudly, so loudly, in fact, that a couple of other guests turned in their direction, and Kyra recoiled in embarrassment.

"You can't leave us hanging like that," Skye said.

"Yeah, tell us!" Graham insisted.

"There was… a mess. He said, are we sure that there's an anti-gravity chamber on this ship? Because… because…" It looked like Kyra was trying to contain herself, although her tongue was poking out of her mouth, but she delivered the last line with a howl of laughter. "There was shit all over the ceiling!"

The group broke out laughing, and got more foul looks from some of the other customers. Skye didn't even care, though, laughing so hard that it felt like tears were about to roll down her face. Truly, there was almost nothing as rewarding for Skye as a good company of friends, and they absolutely lifted her up in the wake of Elliott's demise.

"Well, it's a good thing there's only four of us," Skye offered once she was offered the bill. "Because a fifth person and we'd be in trouble."

"Why's that?" Graham asked.

"The total for the bill, is $402.38," Skye said, and the others gasped.

"That's like… A month of my part-time job in college as a tutor," Madison said.

"That's like a week for me when I worked as a waitress," Skye said. "Well, a slow week. AKA, it's a lot."

"Not that much," Kyra said, shrugging.

"Well, do you want to pay this then? No? Okay then," Skye replied.

"Privileged," Madison whispered to Skye, pointing at Kyra with her thumb, and Kyra shrugged. The group burst out laughing once again, and Skye felt a whole lot better than she had that morning.

***

The next week overall was a lot less eventful than the previous week.

There was the death log, which, even though Lex insisted that they personally could take care of it due to Skye's personal connections with the case, Skye insisted on working with. This was a part of a job, and it would continue to be a part of her job, no matter what. Even with this log, there was still a little bit of ambiguity as to the cause of death. Apparently, Representative Elliott's body was stored in the morgue and awaited transportation back to the ground, where an official autopsy would be conducted back on the surface in America.

"Grace Elliott. Date of Birth, July 17th, 1998. Time of death, June 3rd, 2048, 7:57 p.m. UST. Place of death, Meeting Room 01. Cause of Death, suspected poison ingestion."

The press was horrible for the ship, and Skye could tell that it seemed all of the guests wanted to get out of there as soon as possible. This was compounded by the fact that rumors quickly spread on board as to how the assassin himself had been an employee of the ship and had essentially vanished into thin air with an escape pod. The second part of that news rattled Skye: whoever it was that had killed a woman she'd looked up to, the commendable Grace Elliott, wasn't going to be held accountable at all.

The lines of people at the front desk purchasing to return to Earth seemed to grow quite long with every day. But the shuttles

101

only came around every couple of days, and all of the tickets available for purchase to leave the ISH were bought up within a day after the incident.

Skye was relieved that she technically wasn't interning within the marketing department, because dealing with the press was a complicated, horrific issue that she was grateful that she wasn't responsible for dealing with. She didn't have to imagine their meetings, however, because she shadowed some of them as the hostess over the course of the next couple of days. Alan Lusky presided over these meetings, and to say that he was a little bit worked up about it would be a grand understatement.

"We need to find a way to attract more customers!" Alan Lusky said at one point, slamming his fists down onto the table. The Chief Marketing Officer, a middle-aged Asian woman who kept her hair in a bun, shrunk into herself at the force of violence.

"It's in headlines all the way on Earth," she replied, surprisingly collected despite her obvious discomfort. "We are certain that this does not drastically change our forecast for earnings in the year 2048. This is just a temporary blip until something significant overshadows it and the public moves on."

"I don't care, Ai! Find a way to boost customer attendance, and I mean it, now," Alan Lusky said, before standing up. "I need to clear my head. You're the marketing team. I know 'dealing with the assassination of high-profile politician' wasn't on all of your mood board for 2048, but it's our reality now, and I expect results in the upcoming weeks, or I'm going to have to hold some of you accountable."

With that, Alan Lusky stormed out of the meeting. Judging by the demeanor of the man, it seemed that he was growing more and more unhinged. Skye didn't even try watching television from the room until a couple of days after the assassination had happened, but when it did, the headlines were mainly talking about the assassination, how the alleged killer had poisoned her and escaped into hiding before the Space Force mobilized, how this was the biggest high-profile assassination in U.S. politics since the assassination of Robert Kennedy back in 1968. Despite the tragedy of the whole situation, it felt oddly cathartic to watch the news. A crazy fact finally began to sink in as she watched T.V. alone at bed at midnight three nights after Elliott was killed.

While she watched the next politician sworn as the House Speaker, Bruno Melero, take the gavel, Skye knew she was one of only a handful of witnesses to see the most notorious assassination of the 21st century. Skye watched as the gavel that symbolized power of the house was turned over, and watched a segment as he delivered a short speech on their responsibility of guiding the country back to its former glory. He mentioned how only years ago, his family had been taken from him in a tragic accident: but that as dark of a moment as that was for him, acknowledged that millions were mourning the death of one of the most paramount political figures in the world. When the speech was over, and the members of congress clapped eagerly, Skye realized that witnessing Grace Elliott's death was something she would always have a hand in, and could never change, no matter how much she wanted to. When the news switched to China's military build-up and its aggressive drone flyovers over Taiwan, also covering how Turkey looked on the verge of war with Israel, Skye flicked off the television, Skye's mind still adrift over how eventful her experience had been so far, and it hadn't even been two weeks.

***

While the hotel looked a lot emptier for the next couple of days, the meetings certainly weren't.

"I just want an idea," Alan Lusky raged on at one point. The man had so much pent-up energy, Skye didn't know how the guy could continue living with his undoubtedly elevated blood pressure.

"What about a discount?" Skye blurted out.

Everyone in the meeting froze. Every single eye turned to look at her, and she could see the pure shock and caution that flashed in their glances, that she felt she had made a mistake.

"What? What did you say?" Alan inquired.

"Uh…"

"A discount… A discount… So obvious, and so simple and abrupt. Yes, that might work," Alan said, standing up, grinning. "I could see it already. Launch an agenda as a plan to commemorate our upcoming decade anniversary. Promising that we've bolstered security for the promotion."

"Okay, that's great, but isn't this going to be bring on some bad press?" An executive, who Skye knew only as Mr. Bertrand, commented.

"We'll think it through," Lusky promised. "I think if we navigate it well, we'll be able to drum up some significant publicity. Although, if we wanted to, we could maybe set up a sort of macabre museum exhibit in Meeting Room 01. After all, the room's been rather untouched. The only thing we've cleaned up is the minor blood stains. That set-up might also boost sales."

"That's… a bit too far," someone else piped in, and Lusky nodded understandingly.

"Yes, perhaps it is a tad tone-deaf," he admitted, before turning to Skye. "What's your name again? You're the intern from, well, you know. That tragedy."

"Skye. Skye Calvert."

"Good job, Skye. You may be young, but you have half the brainpower of everyone else in the room combined. Keep it up."

***

It was the same afternoon that Skye pitched the idea to Alan Lusky that she was confronted by two mysterious men. She had been working at her desk in the comms room when Franco entered the room, trailed by two men. Skye turned around from her spot, and was presented with two men in suits. Both of them were sturdy, and wore black tinted sunglasses, of which why they were wearing them on board the hotel in space, Skye had no idea.

"Is your name Skye Calvert?"

"Yes," she said, nodding. "Who may I have the pleasure of speaking with?"

"Agent Roa," one agent said, pulling out his FBI badge, startling her.

"And I'm Agent Barrett," the other man said, doing the same.

"Oh, oh my God…" Skye started, covering her mouth. "Am I in trouble?"

"You have nothing to worry about," Roa stated. "So long as you tell us the truth. We're just investigating the death of Grace Elliott. We only have a few questions to ask, and then we'll be out of your hair."

"Can I have a lawyer?" she asked hurriedly.

Roa turned to Barrett, who frowned, before Barrett sighed.

"Yes, but I think that process will be more painful and tedious for all of us," Barrett claimed. "We're not detaining you, or arresting you. All we're doing is asking you some questions. It shouldn't take more than a couple of minutes. We've already taken statements from Mr. Lusky, Mr. McFarland, as well as some staff in the kitchen. This should be brief."

"Okay…"

Roa pulled up a couple of chairs to the table to sit by Skye, and then Barrett started asking questions.

"I'd like to start with some basic information. How old are you?"

Barrett and Roa asked questions for a good ten minutes, walking through her background, college education, and experience on board the ship, and most of it was surprisingly straightforward and basic, apart from a couple of questions which made no sense to her.

"What do you make of the Black Tooth?" Barrett asked.

Skye frowned. "Huh? What's that?"

"Okay," Barrett said, scrawling in his notes before moving on to the next question.

"Does the date March 2nd mean anything to you?"

"No," Skye answered unflinchingly. "Should it?

"What do you make of the current diplomatic sanctions from China and Russia?"

"It's… very conflicting," Skye managed. "I don't know a lot of politics, sorry. I hope everyone just gets along."

Roa scrawled some notes at the response, appearing to assess her demeanor, and then they moved back onto the more regular questions about the course of events the day Grace Elliott had died.

When the questions were done after a few minutes more, Roa turned to Barrett.

"I think we have enough to go on," Roa said, and he and Barrett thanked her before departing the room. Interestingly, neither of them asked for her to turn over her phone as evidence, even though Skye had heard that the person she'd called had been the assassin. That presented two possibilities to Skye: either the U.S. government's investigation of the assassination was so lazy that they didn't even follow leads, or that they already had the information. Both scenarios were creepy to consider.

Franco crossed his arms after they had left, turning to Skye, who was exhaling in relief now that they were finished.

"Don't worry about it, kid," he said. "The feds are the feds."

"I still don't know what they want from me," Skye sighed. "I don't understand. They were talking about Black Tooth, whatever that is."

"The Black Tooth, it's a poison they suspect was used," Franco explained. "You ever read that one novel by Evan Gray?"

"Ummm… No," Skye replied. "I don't think so."

"Well, never mind. You aced the questions, I'd say."

Skye frowned. "Umm… Thanks."

***

A couple of nights later, and Skye was in deep reflection.

"You okay?" The question came from beside Skye, and she turned to see Graham sitting next to her.

Both of them sat staring over the planet Earth. Right now, it was nighttime, and she sat alone in the gazing lobby apart from a few other guests. It was a little bit past midnight in space-time, and down on Earth it looked like the time wasn't too far off, either. The International Space Hotel was orbiting over Central Europe currently, and both Graham and Skye stared down at the glowing lights which covered over the landscape, beautiful glowing polka dots on a tapestry of water and earth. There were so many of these lights, and Skye felt she really took for granted just how many people live in France and Germany. It was more beautiful than she ever could've imagined.

"Yeah," Skye answered. "Just reflecting on things. You know, everything's been a little bit crazy since Grace Elliott kicked the can. I got interviewed by some feds."

"By the feds, huh?" Graham asked. "How was it?"

"Not too bad. They asked me a couple weird questions about the assassination, what happened, and my background. It was awful, though, at the time. Felt like they were eyeing me down and looking into my soul. At least I think I'm in the clear now."

"Of course you are," Graham said. "I'm sorry to hear that. I had no idea… That sounds bad."

"Yes," Skye replied, "It was. Although things haven't been so bad overall the past few days. I even pitched an idea that got Lusky excited."

"That's… completely understandable," Graham said, sighing. "You've taken it in stride though. And the fact you get to talk to the CEO yourself? I mean, that's just awesome, and you're doing awesome."

"Yeah… I guess so. Gave him some discount idea, whatever."

"No, I don't guess it, I know it. You're doing incredible. You seem to really be on top of things."

Skye looked up at Graham, frowning. "Really? Because I definitely don't feel that way at *all*. I feel like I've lost my marbles."

"Well, you definitely seem very composed. I mean, I'm not saying you're good at hiding your emotions. You're strong. That's what I mean to say."

"Mhm." That was all she could manage, but then she spoke up again. "Well, I have managed to get by without getting any antidepressants or binge drinking, so I consider that an absolute win. I have used my fair share of sleeping pills, though."

Graham sighed, silent for a few moments.

"That's really beautiful. That cluster, there? Paris, which I'm sure you know. The Netherlands are what really surprise me. More lights than you'd think. The Netherlands are really underrated. I highly recommend it."

"Really underrated, huh?" Skye questioned, smiling. "I didn't know we were rating all these different countries. You been there?"

"Well, no. I know people… Er, a person who has, though, and I hope to visit it someday."

Skye nodded again, before changing the topic. "You know, you don't have to sit here and wait for me to be done. I know I've been here a while."

"I know. But I'm just looking out for you."

"Because you're concerned."

"No. Because I'm your friend. And friends look out for each other, no matter what."

Skye peered up at Graham, checked out his face and concerned expression, and, although she would've denied it, felt a little spark of something inside.

"You're very sweet. But I'm not a headcase. I'm just a girl working through a difficult time."

"I don't doubt that you're doing just fine by yourself. But it's getting late, and we have work tomorrow. So how about we head back to our rooms and catch some rest? Come on, Skye."

"Okay."

"Okay? Good."

"We should do something fun this next weekend. Anything to distract my mind."

"Yeah. We've got a few months on board the fanciest hotel in the world, so we better have some more fun."

Graham walked Skye back before returning to her dorm, and when Skye went to bed that night, she fell asleep, fast. The day was a Thursday that would lie in infamy. As it turns out, there wouldn't be any fun plans soon at all. The world as Skye knew it was about to be set on fire.

Chapter 13

The day started out like any other. Skye sat by Lex as they made the typical morning announcements. The first sign that something was wrong, however, occurred a little bit after lunch when Skye saw Lex's concerned face peering over what looked to be an email on their phone. Soon, Lex leaned over the microphone to make an announcement for everyone on board.

"Attention, all International Space Hotel guests and staff. The space shuttle for departure today at 3 p.m. has been suspended. All guests will be refunded and will be reserved tickets for a later date. All said guests will also receive their previous rooms to stay at in the meantime, free of charge."

Skye, who had been sitting at her desk peering through a couple of spreadsheets and surfing the ISH-approved side of the internet, closed her browsers and walked over to Lex, confused.

"What's going on, Lex? Why would we cancel the space shuttle?"

Lex looked up. There was a glint in their eyes, and it took Skye a couple of seconds to realize that it was the glint of tears welling.

"Can you keep a secret, Skye? I mean, I have a feeling this is going to be leaked soon, and when it does, shit's going to hit the fan, and rumors are going to spread around like wildfire."

Skye nodded before replying to the affirmative, although she knew she may as well be crossing her fingers, because there's no way she would be concealing any important news from Madison or Graham.

"We got a Code Black from Alan Lusky, the CEO."

"A Code Black? Seriously? Not a Code Red?" Skye swore she could feel goosebumps run down the entire length of her body.

"Yes, a Code Black."

A Code Black was one level above Code Red. The Code Red represented an emergency of the worst kind on board (apparently, Grace Elliott's murder should've incited a Code Red, but Lusky had been so determined to apprehend the culprit and keep everyone calm that he hadn't initiated one). Code Black, on the other hand, represented one level above Code Red, and indicated there was a global catastrophe of imminent or ongoing proportions. According to the videos played during orientation, there had never been a Code Black in the history of the ISH.

"That has to be a mistake," Skye said, but Lex showed her their phone, and Skye read the email, which was short and to the point.

Subject: CODE BLACK

To: Announcement-full-time-staff-list

From: Alan Lusky (ALusky@ISH.com):

To Whom It May Concern:

In all of my years of working at the ISH, I never thought that I would have to say this. Unfortunately, we have received credible intel from the United States government that we have a Code Black on our hands. We're talking about potential mass destruction on Earth, and my source says that if this happens, then it will happen in the next 24 hours.

Right now, our top priority is cancelling any outgoing shuttles, and bringing in our last oncoming shuttle safely. Please keep this information under the wraps until you hear an update from me. We don't need widespread panic on board. As we speak, the security team is preparing for major disruption on board this ship if it happens. I hope that in the end they end up being wrong about all this, but if they aren't, I feel safe knowing we have the expertise of all of you on board to keep things running smoothly. I understand these are trying times for all of us, but we need to set a positive example for everyone on board.

Bless you all,

Alan Lusky

Skye felt butterflies in her stomach. This was a Grace Elliott situation all over. She remembered back to what Alan Lusky said, and felt like throwing up.

If what you're saying is true, then we could have a World War 3 situation on our hands. And we might not even be able to stop them until it's too late.

It couldn't be true. It wouldn't be true… And yet…

"I don't know what this means," Lex said, shaking their head. "I mean, I've been here for three years, and I've never seen anything like this. I mean, I thought this was just kind of there, just for the hypothetical, impossible situation. Maybe it's a drill, I was thinking. Skye, are you okay? You seem to be zoning out."

Skye nodded, gulping. Alan Lusky had written the e-mail without any sign of emotion. As if he seriously expected everyone to remain calm in a Code Black.

"Yeah. This is some kind of secret you're entrusting to me."

"Well, if this Code Black thing happens, there's no way we're keeping this secret," Lex stated. "And there's hundreds of us on board. I have no idea what'll happen but my guess is that there'll be total pandemonium."

"What do we do?"

"What can we do? This is out of our hands, Skye. You know what. Take the day off. Although keep your eye on your phone. It's possible you'll be needed in one of our meetings. In which case we'll be relying on you. If we do need you, I doubt it'll matter if you're dressed up fancy or not."

Skye nodded, and then she stepped out. She didn't know what motivated her to go to the call center, but she felt herself going there before she could stop herself. She had to talk to her parents. Especially if, somehow, the disaster that Lusky's Code Black warned of was actually about to happen.

***

The call center had only one area open to use, specifically designed for employees, and in most cases, you had to book a time slot days ahead of time. But Marcell had once told Skye that if you weren't on shift, and you checked in the early afternoon not on a weekend, that often people didn't show up to their slots. And if that was the case, then she might have an outside chance. Knowing what was going to happen, she certainly felt the need to at least try.

It was a miracle that she arrived when she did. The place looked completely empty, she stood up at the front black desk, behind which another one of those human-like robots was posted, and waited for a few moments. When she didn't see anything, she cleared her throat and spoke up.

"Hello?"

"Hello, how may I help you?" The robot droned.

"I'd like to take a phone call with the surface, if I may."

"Right now, there is a vacant time slot from 2:00-2:30 p.m. Would you like to reserve this slot?"

Skye looked down at the time on her phone. 2:11 p.m. space-time. Her family lived in CST, which was 5 hours ahead. 7:11 p.m. *That's perfect.*

"Yes, please," Skye said. "I'd like that."

"Name, keycard, and ID," The robot commanded.

Skye scrambled to offer her keycard and ID as quickly as possible. The robot's eyes scanned red lasers over both of them before ushering her into the adjacent room, which locked shut after she closed the door behind her.

The next room was remarkably plain. It was a circular room with nothing but a single seat next to a giant phone attached to the table. It looked like a landline from the last century, and it was wired down to the ground, which no doubt concealed a great deal of technology in order to be able to connect to Earth. Skye set her phone down onto the table, leaving the screen on so that she could tell the time. It was 2:13:33 space-time, and she only had less than 17 minutes until the phone would stop working and the next person would be able to kick her out to make a call.

She dialed her father's number. It got to one dial tone, and then another.

"Come on, come on!" She said, frustrated. Straight to voicemail.

Hey, this is Terry Calvert, please leave a message at the beep.

Her father's nasal but kind voice unexpectedly caught her off guard, and she realized that this might be the last time that she would ever hear her father's voice.

No. It can't be.

Skye hurriedly called her mother next. This time, she picked up after only ten or fifteen seconds.

"Hello? Who is this?"

"Hi mom! It's me!"

"Skye… Oh my God! Hi, sweetie? How are you? Are you calling me from space?"

"Yes! I'm okay, I'm okay… Look, I only have almost exactly 15 minutes to talk, but I wanted to say hi to you, and hi to everyone."

"Oh, of course! Your sister's upstairs doing homework, or probably messing around if we're being honest, but your dad is watching your brother at a basketball game right now, so I think you're out of luck with them."

"What?"

"Oh, you didn't hear me? The reception must be spotty, so-"

"No, no, it's okay, I got it," Skye said. "They're gone."

"Okay, well, I don't want to talk about the elephant in the room, but how's everything gone with, you know, the whole controversy? I can't believe that Representative Elliott died. I was so worried for you when I heard about the news. Are you feeling okay?"

Skye could feel beads of sweat forming on her forehead. 14 minutes.

"Yes, I'm fine. That was a tragedy but I was unaffected by it."

"Well, how's space? Is it as beautiful as they say it is?"

"Yeah, it is. It's very beautiful. I know it's only been a week, but almost every day at some point I just sit down and look at Earth from one of the watching room things. It's very beautiful, and I think of you all."

"Friends? You've made friends already?"

"Why, yes. I already told you about Graham, he's the guy from Michigan, but there's this girl, Madison. Super funny student from Bates. There's also another intern named Kyra. And we've even made friends with a guy who's a couple years older than us. Okay, that sounds weird, but he's super nice and he's been very helpful, and he's only 24, for the record."

"That's fantastic, honey," Skye's mother said. "I'm very glad, but I'm pretty sure you said you thought you could only speak to us once for the internship. What's up?"

"Umm, not much," Skye stumbled. She always knew her mother could tell when she was lying, and she found herself on the verge of tears. "I just found an opportunity to say hi to you, and I wanted to."

Skye checked on the time remaining. 12:25.

"Well okay, it's been nice talking to you. You should sit down and talk to me when you have more time, if you can," Skye's mother said. "I love you, baby."

"I love you too," Skye replied, and she meant it with every ounce of her body. *The Code Black has to be fake. It has to be.*

"Could I talk to my sister?" She asked.

"Yes, let me go get her."

Skye tapped her foot on the ground impatiently over the next twenty, almost thirty seconds, until her sister was on the line. At this point, a single tear spilled from her eye onto her cheek, and Skye had to stop herself from breaking down.

Keep it together, Skye. Keep it together. If this is true, then they can't know. They can't know what's going to happen.

"Hey Skye," Her sister greeted her.

"Hey Emily, how are you?"

"Good, good. I've just been chilling this summer. You know how it is."

"How are things with Neil?"

"Neil? Oh, good, very good, you know. He took me on a date to a mall the other day."

"Oh, a mall. I didn't know those still existed outside of the MOA."

"Yeah, it was a little bit of a novelty, but I liked it."

"That's awesome."

"Are things good in space?"

"Yup. You should see the views of Earth from here. It's the most beautiful thing I've ever seen in my life," Skye said.

There were a few seconds of silence on the other side of the line, and then came the question that Skye had been dreading.

"What happened, and why did you call us? It's not like you ever asked to specifically talk to me when you were in college, and now you're asking to talk to me after a week of being up there? What's wrong?"

Skye bit her tongue. She was tempted. So tempted to tell her the truth. But if there was going to be a Code Black, she didn't know how much any warning would help.

"I love you, Em," Skye managed. "There's so much I want to say, but so little time."

"Skye?" Emily asked, her voice escalating in volume. "What's going on?"

"Listen to me closely," Skye said. "After I hang up on you, I want you to take mom and hunker down in the basement. You should stay on the lower level for the next day, just to be safe. Block the windows. Hell, if you want to go shopping and stock up, fine, but do it *immediately* after I get the call, or don't do it at all. You hear me?"

"Why? Skye, what the hell is going on?"

"Fine! One of my coworkers got information about a Code Black. That's layman terms for something very, very bad. As in, nuclear war or meteor crashing into Earth bad. I don't know what's going to happen, or if it will actually happen, it could all be some kind of mistake, but I heard it's going to happen in the next 24 hours."

"Skye! Slow down!"

"Please tell mom. Go help her. I am going to try to get a hold of dad. You should call him and bring him and Braydon home as soon as you can. Goodbye. I love you!"

"Skye!"

"Tell me you love me. Please?"

"I love you! I love you! But are you sure about this not being just rumors? A false alert? How do you know this!?"

"I'm pretty sure about this. The memo came from Alan Lusky, the guy who built the whole ship, and he has deep connections to the U.S. government. If I'm wrong, then it's better to be on the safe side. I love you, sis," Skye said, and then she hung up.

Skye didn't even check her phone for time, because she knew she was running out of it quickly, but instead hurriedly dialed her father. This time, he picked up after ten seconds.

"Hello? Who is this?"

"It's Skye!"

Skye could hear background roaring and clapping, as well as some sort of grunt of disbelief.

"Skye? You're calling me? That's great! How are you doing? You're really calling me from space, huh? That's nuts!"

"I'm doing well," Skye lied. Much like with the other calls, she was close to crying. "I found an opportunity to place a call down to Earth, and I took it."

"How great!" He said. "I'm in the gym right now watching Braydon's game, so how about you call me back in a half-hour?

Your little brother has been playing great today! He's got twelve points so far."

"I can't," Skye said, checking her phone. Two minutes, nine seconds remaining. "Dad, I can't, I have two minutes left on our call. I already called mom and Em. Please hear me out."

"Okay," Skye's father responded.

"I love you," Skye said.

"I love you very much, honey," Skye's father said. "It's only been a week but the house feels emptier this summer without you. Believe me."

"Dad," Skye said. "Listen to me carefully. Take Braydon, go home. There's something bad that's going to happen, and you need to be sure that you're all bunkered in at the basement and safe."

"Skye? What are you talking about? Is this related to that Grace Elliott business? Speaking of which, I hope you weren't affected by that."

"What? Dad, no," Skye lied. "I wasn't at all involved. But please, listen to me, you need to get Braydon, right now, and go home. I've already talked to Emily. I need you to back her up. God, I should've told mom, she probably doesn't believe her."

"Honey? Why? What's going on up there?"

"I got a memo from Alan Lusky. He's the CEO. He said there's a Code Black, meaning there's likely going to be something horrible hitting Earth in the next day. Just listen to me, please, dad. Go home now, and-"

The phone line disconnected, and a robotic voice played in her ears, as her phone alarm simultaneously turned on. She hit the stop button.

Your call time has expired. Please return back to the call center lobby.

Skye let out a cry, slamming her fists on the table repeatedly. "No. No! No!"

She tried desperately re-dialing the phone, but of course, he couldn't. It was done. She'd hit her limit. That was it. There was nothing she could do but return back to the lobby as the voice had instructed her.

Five seconds. Five seconds to let it out.

Skye let out a heaving sob for the next few seconds before wiping her face. It was time to keep it together again, and she hurried out of the call center, not wanting to draw the ire of anyone waiting, as her door had popped open. And sure enough, when Skye stepped back out into the call center lobby, she found that it was absolutely packed with employees, and a line several people long waiting in front of the robot. There was a low murmur of people speaking to each other, and Skye could tell by their expressions that they were extremely stressed. A woman who appeared to be next in line barged into her before clamoring to the call room.

"Excuse you," Skye mumbled at the woman, but when she saw the commotion that was behind her, she didn't blame her.

Some people in the line were getting agitated, trying to force their way into the room before their scheduled time. However, others in the queue managed to maintain order and civility, stopping the impatient ones from causing chaos by pushing their way into the call room.

But even though Skye left the room feeling devastated, she realized that she'd been so incredibly lucky for arriving when she had. She'd gotten to say goodbye.

Chapter 14

The next few hours were hectic, as employees and guests alike scrambled around the International Space Hotel as if they were chickens with their heads cut off.

Although nothing had happened from Earth from what Skye could see, it appeared that rumors about what was happening now had spread to the guests, and on board, there was a mass panic. It felt like every ten minutes Skye walked into the nearest gazing lobby (of which all of them seemed packed full of various employees and guests doing the same thing) just to observe a normal Earth. It didn't help that the first couple of times she checked they looked to be over the middle of an ocean, and Skye couldn't tell quite which from the angle she was looking at.

During the craze, Skye ran into Madison in the hallways. Much like many of the other guests, she was heading in the same direction that all of the call centers were located.

"Oh my God," Madison said, in tears, when she ran into Skye. "Is it true? The Earth's going to get destroyed?"

"I don't know, Maddie. It could be a false alarm, you know? Even the U.S. government intel is wrong sometimes."

"Right, right," Madison said. "Everyone thought we were going to die with the Bay of Pigs mess in the '60s. This has to be a false alarm just like that. I've heard things were getting bad, but it can't be *this* bad."

Madison nodded before running past towards the front of the ship.

"Where are you going?" Skye asked, jogging alongside her.

"I'm going to see if there's any chance that I can call my family. You know, say goodbye?"

"Maddie," Skye said, but Madison didn't even bat an eye at her. Skye grabbed Madison's arm, and Madison stopped in her tracks, as a couple of guests ran past them.

"What? What're you holding my arm for?" Madison asked. "Look at everyone passing us- now I'll never get in!"

"Maddie, there's no spots," Skye said. "I know because I got the news a while ago, before *this* was happening. I saw the place. There's no way."

Madison's face fell.

"I understand," she said. "But I have to try."

Madison continued running past her, down towards the call center. Skye sighed but didn't chase after her. She understood why she acted the way she did. She probably would've done the same thing, all things considered.

But there was nothing Skye could do, and whatever would happen to the world was well beyond her control, and the idea of sitting around until something catastrophic happened didn't sound too appealing for her. So she'd go back to the room, see if the news on Earth were publicizing the impending tragedy or whether perhaps Lusky had been completely mistaken, and then she'd watch something light on television. She didn't care if it was cartoons, or a romcom, but she needed something to distract herself from everything that was going on.

On the way, however, someone stopped her, stepping in front of her door. Skye assumed when the hand touched her shoulder that it was Graham, but when she saw it wasn't, she pulled away in shock and disgust.

"Hey, Skye." She remembered the voice, from the boy who seemed like he could never stop staring at her. Drake.

"Hi," Skye managed. "What's up?"

Drake's hands were balled into fists, and he looked nervous. Skye felt a lump in her throat. She didn't know what he was about to do, but she definitely didn't feel like it was going to go well, whatever it was.

"This sucks, right?"

"Yeah."

"Can I be honest with you, now that it sounds like everything's about to get messed up?"

"Sure."

"I like you. From the moment I first set my eyes on you, I thought you were the most beautiful woman I've ever seen."

"Okay…"

"I was wondering, would you perhaps consider going on a date with me? Grab a drink once things calm down? Maybe when things blow over a little bit… or we can compromise and make something else work if things are… bad here. I think it would help us both a lot. Especially if things do go bad, then, well, we'd have each other."

"That's very nice of you," Skye responded, at a loss for words. "I… I don't think this is a good idea, Drake. To be honest, I have so many things to worry about, and I think something like a relationship is the last thing on my mind."

Skye walked over to her door and entered with her keycard.

"That's a no, then?" He asked. As Skye stepped back into her room, he laughed in disbelief. "That's a no."

***

Skye locked the door behind herself. She wasn't taking any chances. Then she moved over to the remote and turned on the television. There was nothing but regular news headlines for a while; President Chu signed some sort of big legislation, The Netherlands voted to establish a carbon tax, and some sort of mysterious infection rumored to be a new strain of Ebola was spreading in Western Africa.

Skye was relieved and was able to catch her breath. But she knew she had thought too soon. A minute or two after the network cut to commercials, suddenly a breaking news headline appeared on the screen and there was a jump cut to the news anchor. The same news anchor with the black hair who'd looked collected and professional minutes before looked frazzled now, his face contorted in fear.

"Right now, we have some urgent breaking news," The news anchor said, his voice breaking at the end. "We've received reports of several unidentified military installations across the world in the atmosphere seem to have been activated and are supercharged. The United States government has accused New Russia and China of collaborating in an effort to destroy the West and has stated that if they do not disarm the installations in the next twenty-four hours, or if they use any of them, then they will face... harsh nuclear retaliation. Oh my God."

He covered his mouth for a few moments before setting the papers down. It looked like he was receiving some sort of news through an earpiece.

"Breaking news... It appears that there are currently four known installations in orbit. They are approximately located at the following positions. St. Louis, Missouri; Hamburg, Germany. And one seems to be drifting over the province of Shandong China, and the final one, somewhere over Russia. Hold on…"

There was commotion in the news room for the next few seconds, as the news anchor jumped up. Skye sat up on her bed, trembling in fear as the news anchor let out a yell.

"You're kidding me, right? There's no way-"

Then the television cut off, and was replaced with static.

Chapter 15

The International Space Hotel was orbiting over India. Or what was left of India, anyway. Skye knew because when she sprinted into the gazing lobby after the TV went out, she could make out the general shape of the subcontinent. The gazing lobby, which earlier had been full of nervous chatter, was now completely silent, save for a few people who were crying or sobbing.

The land was covered with multiple red and brownish splotches that blemished the surface like some bad acne over a teenager with raging hormones: but unlike acne, this damage looked irreversible, and certainly lethal to those involved with it. Skye could see mushroom clouds rising from the surface, and she knew what that meant: nukes had struck the surface.

"This can't be real," Skye overheard one of the other interns say. *Step 1 of grief: denial.*

That wasn't all that was strange. There was a powerful blueish beam that seemed to move slowly across the planet, leaving a trail of devastation, of red and brown, in its wake. It looked like it was frying the Earth itself, and the ray emanated from some sort of speck far away in the distance.

"Look at that thing," someone said, pointing at the beam. "What the hell is that thing? It's like it's another spaceship, but it's not. And what's that beam?"

"It's the installation," Skye said, and a couple of people turned to her, looking at her like she had gone insane. Not that she faulted them for that. "Just like the news had said… A weapon. Scorching the surface."

One of the guests, who was standing there with his younger son and wife, leaned over into a fake potted plant, and threw up inside. The situation appeared to be hitting some of them now for real, and many finally broke down into tears or yelling. Some people were so distraught that they collapsed into seats, or even lay prostrate on the ground. Skye, meanwhile, was still watching blankly, transfixed at the sight of the world's destruction.

"It's fake," one skeptical intern from earlier reiterated. "It's a conspiracy, a test!"

"It's done," Minnie replied, shaking her head. Minnie, like Skye, appeared to still be processing her emotions, because she hadn't shed a tear, either. "Accept it, Lucas. The world is *over*, and pretending that it isn't is not helping anyone."

But Lucas stormed out of the room, seemingly convinced that this was all a conspiracy. Skye wished she could believe it was fake, but she couldn't. Alan Lusky had been right about the Code Black after all. Much of the world had been set ablaze, and she guessed it would be left black, burnt charcoal and rubble. The name "Code Black" was oddly fitting.

***

Skye couldn't hang around there. The panic, the fear and depression were so thick in the air that it was as if you could cut it with a knife or even taste it. It threatened her sanity just being there and watching the world unravel. She had to go, and she had to go, now.

Skye's first priority was to find her friends, to find Maddie, and Graham, and make sure that they were okay. As it turns out, she found Maddie walking slowly towards her own room, a shocked expression on her face.

"Maddie?" Skye asked, rushing over there. "Are you okay? Maddie?"

She ran up to Maddie, who barely even blinked when she stepped in her path, but just stood there, blankly.

"You were right," Madison murmured. "There was a line… A big line… And now the call center doesn't even work. It doesn't work at all."

She looked down at her phone, checking it.

"Would you look at that? Our Wi-Fi network is down too. No signal. We're really *fucked*, aren't we?"

Madison broke out into a grin and Skye felt a deep concern for her friend.

"Come on, let's go back to your room," Skye said.

Madison giggled. "Okay."

By the time Skye led Madison back into her room and sat her down, Madison was cackling with laughter, loud and bellowing laughter that transformed into sobs as Skye gently set her down onto her bed.

"Oh, Skye! What are we going to do? What are we going to do? We have to do something. Now!"

"I don't know, Maddie," Skye said, about to pull off of her and go check on Graham. "I… There's nothing."

"Don't leave me! Please don't leave me!"

An announcement came over the PA system, and Skye recognized the voice. It wasn't Franco, or even Lex, but it was Alan Lusky.

Hello everybody. I know you are all grieving. But I wanted you to know that we're going to be okay up here. We have enough food, oxygen, and water to survive for the foreseeable future as we assess the damage to Earth and await further updates from the United

States government. Please stay safe. Don't do anything you will regret. We might be on the ground tomorrow, or it might take a little bit longer. But we're all safe. We will keep you updated.

That was it. They were just waiting to hear how destroyed planet Earth was, but there was nothing.

"I never got to say goodbye," Madison cried. "To my family."

"I know, I know," Skye replied. "I'm so sorry, Maddie." And she stepped back, looking at the door of the room.

"Don't leave me! Please!" She wailed.

"I need to check on Graham. To see if he's safe."

"I'll go with you," Madison insisted, and Skye nodded.

***

They knocked on his door. Nothing. Pounded on his door harder. Again, nothing. Madison repeatedly pounded on the door while Skye looked at the itinerary to see a map layout of the ship again. Where would he be working though? Potentially near the energy reactors or the engine room, but she just wasn't certain.

It turned out that Madison's knocking on the door did their job.

"Leave me alone!"

"Oh! He's in there! He's in there!" Madison said eagerly.

There was something else, some quiet murmur, but Madison's insistent cries blocked Skye from hearing what he'd said. Regardless, her knocking must've worked to convince him to open up, or otherwise annoyed him so much, because Graham narrowly opened the door. Through the crack, Skye could see a tearstained face.

"I don't…" he said, but Madison put her hand in and pushed the door open before he could close it.

"Come on, let's talk," Madison said. She was still crying, but she looked oddly relieved at the sight of Graham, as if her shared struggle validated her emotions. "H-how are you? I know I'm feeling like shit right now, and you look like it."

"Please don't make fun of me," Graham said, reaching to close the door, but it was too late already, as Madison pushed herself inside. "Leave me be, please."

"We wanted to make sure you were okay," Skye said, stepping in.

"I'm fine," Graham said through gritted teeth. "Just dandy."

"Look at you," Madison murmured, wiping her face. "You're clearly *not* fine."

"You're right," Graham said, nodding. He turned around and covered his face. Skye went to put her hand on his shoulder, but he pulled away. "The entire world just got *fucking* destroyed, and we're all going to die. So no, I'm not fine."

"We're not going to die," Skye said coolly. Even though she could feel the tears building up once again, she was determined to not show any weakness, not here, as the pillar of strength in the friend group. She wouldn't let anything out until she was alone. "We're here, together."

"Are we though?" Madison rasped. "I-I never thought about that, but it's only a matter of time. They'll run out oxygen, water, and we'll all die. Oh my God. This is it. We're living through the actual end of the world. *Fuck* my life."

Madison's breath quickened. It looked like she was descending into a full-blown panic attack. She sat down on the foot of the bed, and Skye sat next to her, hugging her as Graham paced around the room.

"We have oxygen," Graham said, wiping the tears from his face, which quickly replaced itself. He kept wiping, averting his eyes from Skye and Madison in humiliation as he thought out loud. "And water, they reuse it. At least we're okay for some months. I'm an engineer, I've thought about this shit, you know, like a daydream. Like what would happen, if we were stuck up here. But now my daydream is a living *nightmare*. We don't have the food to sustain ourselves. I reckon we're all going to die."

"No, no, we're not going to die," Skye said. "There's probably more food than either of you could imagine. We don't know what's in the storeroom, none of us work there."

"K-K-Kyra," Madison sputtered. "She would know!"

"Yes, she might know," Skye said, as Madison leaned her head on Skye's shoulder. "How smart of you."

Graham went over to his windows, ripped open the curtains. Only there was nothing on the other side but the endless expanse of space due to the hotel's rotation. Some mixture of a loud snort and sob escaped from his mouth, and Skye looked over to him as he stared at his reflection.

"You don't need to hide," Skye said.

"I wish I'd gotten to say goodbye," Graham blurted out, whipping around to face Skye. "You know, my brother and I had a bet. We had a bet, you know, on how fast I'd want to give up. He said I'd get sick of space, fast. Call home within three weeks. That was our bet. I'll never get to know if I'd win. I was almost about to win, but I'll never be sure. I mean, I missed Earth but I felt lucky because I got to make friends, y'all. I mean I just stumbled here, and I finally felt like I belonged. And I made more friends in one week than I ever made in three years of college, even though I felt unworthy, even though there were no textbooks or study guides on how to make real friends. I mean, what the *hell*? It made me realize there was more to life than just being this try-hard with a stick up my a-, my rear, maybe I could finally live my life like a normal person, and enjoy it for once, and then this had to happen, right away."

Skye looked up at Graham. She wanted to say something, but it looked like he was going on and on, delivering a full monologue for apparently no one but himself. Even if this oversharing was uncalled for, it looked like this was needed, and Skye hoped it would make him feel better.

"It's like some kind of sick joke. The ultimate middle finger from the universe and God, if there is one, which I doubt there is because what kind of sick *twisted* God would let this happen to the world. Now nothing matters anyway. My brother's likely dead anyway, and if he isn't, the radiation or starvation will probably do him in."

"Graham, I really think you do need a hug," Skye said. She gently eased away from Madison before walking over to Graham and hugging him. This time, he accepted the gesture.

"Skye," Graham said, choking on his tears. He pulled away and wiped his face. "Thank you. For being here."

"Yes," Madison concurred from over on bed. "Thank you. I… I can't help but think we're together for a reason, you know? I have a boyfriend, Fuego, you know, he was a firecracker… I used to do his biology homework, almost every day, all the time. Now I can't stop thinking about him. Burned. To a crisp. What a waste. And my dad!"

She wailed for a few moments, as Skye hugged her again.

"It's okay. It's going to be okay," Skye said, although she didn't know if she believed it. "Your family's fine. Your dad's fine, your mother's fine. They're all fine. We have to believe."

But even though Skye said this, her shaky voice betrayed her calm demeanor, and she felt like her she was going to break down any second.

"My mom's dead," Madison snorted, wiping her face, "and my stepmother can burn in the fifth circle of hell for all I care. But I hope everyone else is okay."

Skye raised her eyebrows, but didn't prod. Instead, she turned to Graham, who looked like he was the slightly more collected of the two at the moment. "Can you look after Madison for me if I step out for a bit?"

"What? Why?" He looked back at Madison and nodded. "Yeah, I feel like I want to just disappear, but I'll make sure… you know. We'll be fine, is all I'm saying. I got s-space to look at."

"I'm going to go check on Kyra," Skye said.

"You'll come back?" Madison asked.

"I'll be back as soon as I know she's okay, all right? I just feel a responsibility for everyone."

"You're a good friend," Graham said. "I wish I'd made more of an effort to meet with you you earlier at school, I really did."

"Maybe check on Marcell too," Madison suggested. "He's got to be… very, very sad."

"I bet he's got his hands full with his job right now," Skye said. "But if I run into him, I will definitely check on him."

"Good call," Graham agreed.

Chapter 16

Skye remembered Kyra's room number based on the conversation within the bowling alley the other day.

Room 166, Kyra had told her, *I got Satan's number.*

Room 166 was just a couple of minutes away from Skye's room via the escalator track, but those minutes felt like hours. Only a minute or so after stepping into the hallway, emergency alarms started blaring and some red lights in the hallways began flashing. Skye had no idea what was happening, whether there was a fire, or some other emergency, but the alarm played over and over as she approached Kyra's room.

A few people ran through the hallways, including a couple of security guards. Some were also clearly disturbed by the blaring alarms and opened their doors. Some of them went out into the hallway to investigate, while others shut their doors momentarily in an attempt to muffle out the noise. However, Marcell was nowhere to be found, and he was the only one she knew she could get to help her enter Kyra's room.

She tried to get the attention of one of the security guards to come with her, but he ignored her, flashing a look of fury when she grabbed his arm.

"Just help me!" Skye said. "I need to check on someone, but I can't access their room!"

"I have my hands full right now!"

"This is important! She could've *done* something!"

"Well, we're all worried about here! Someone's trying to open the emergency exits right now and I'm trying to get things under control!"

"Just let me swipe one of your master cards, please!"

But the man broke free from her grip, and with that he was gone, disappearing down the hallway. Skye moved over to Room 166. She tried the handle. It was, of course, locked, as it always would be without having the proper keycard. She looked under the door, and found that there was light glowing out from underneath, indicating that someone was in the room.

For a couple of minutes, she pounded on the door, calling for Kyra, only for there to be silence on the other side.

"Kyra? You in there?"

"Are you okay? I just want to talk to you."

"I want to make sure you're okay, can you please let me in?"

"Kyra? Kyra! Please."

She knew there was a good chance that she was somewhere else, panicking, and yet she didn't know why, there was a knot forming in her stomach. The fact that there was a light there meant that she probably was inside, and yet there was no response from the other side, not even movement. She remembered back to when she'd gotten the audio tour of her lodging. It had been a moot point, something she'd never thought about since then, but that was now on her mind, more salient than it had ever been.

Lights will automatically turn off within five minutes if no individual is detected inside.

Any second she expected Kyra to be there. But there was nothing.

Skye didn't know how long she stood out there knocking and calling her name, but she was confident that it was more than five minutes. Soon, she knew there was nothing she could do, and she hoped she was just sitting in the bathroom. She wouldn't have blamed her at all. If Skye wasn't too concerned about her friends, she probably would've been doing that herself.

But there was no response, none at all, and Skye was growing impatient. She checked her phone again before resolving to do something drastic.

Lex. She didn't know what drew her to running back to comms, but she knew that if anyone would know anything, and perhaps be willing to explain the situation and help her, then it would be them. Skye ran back to comms and flung open the door. After the door slammed shut, she subtly slipped the lock on behind herself.

She was lucky, as Lex, and not Franco, was there manning the comms and looking on a screen, their face showing signs of anxiety, of exhaustion.

"You're back," Lex commented.

"Hi Lex," Skye said. "I need your help. I need you to help explain what's really gone on."

"Why? Can't you tell I'm a bit busy right now? And what makes you think I know any more than the next person?"

"Nonsense," Skye said, pulling up a chair from over where she typically sat during her shifts next to her. "If anyone would know anything, it would be you or the CEO."

"I… I don't know what you want me to tell you, Skye," Lex said.

"I want you to tell me what you've heard."

"I don't think that's a good idea."

"Try me. Just tell me," Skye said, leaning in next to Lex. "I know I've only known you a couple of weeks. But I thought we'd have developed a little bit of a rapport at this point that we'd be honest with each other. That you would trust me."

"It's not that I don't trust you," Lex replied, squirming in their seat. "It's that I don't trust everyone on board to maintain their sanity in the event that I let the truth out. And if you go out and go blabbering to everyone, that'd be violating my orders and what Lusky told me himself. I need to do my job."

"Job? You're worried about your job?"

"Let's just say I'm not concerned about my paycheck. But I would be worried about getting in trouble at a time like this, yes."

"Things are bad, then?"

"Skye."

"Come on. People deserve to know the truth! Or if they don't, at least tell me, so I can report what's going on. People are on edge. They deserve answers. And you aren't giving them, or me, any answers right now."

"I could call security right now, but they seem to have their hands full already. You really want to know, that bad, what's going on? The stuff I've heard, it'll change you. Makes me wish I'd never heard what I did."

"Yes, Lex, I do."

"Fine. I'll play the previous conversation I had with Earth earlier. Don't tell me I didn't warn you."

Then Lex hit play, as Skye stepped forward, leaning a hand on the comms and pressing a button to broadcast the recording over all the rooms on the ISH. The whole time, she simply pretended to simply casually brace herself against the equipment. Lex was too absorbed to even notice.

***

"This is Bunker 11 reporting out of Louisville, Kentucky. Can anyone hear me?"

Graham perked up, looking up into the air. He wiped his face. Madison, who had been sobbing, abruptly stopped crying. A recording was playing into their room.

"What's going on?" Madison sniffled. "Where's that coming from?"

"Sounds like it's coming over the PA system," Graham said. "But it's coming in the room."

"Must be the emergency system," Madison speculated. "I guess important announcements can play into any room."

"Is anyone there? I repeat, is anyone out there?" The voice sounded desperate. "I repeat, this is Bunker 11. Is anyone out there at all?"

"Yes, yes, we're here," A voice said. Although neither Graham nor Madison could identify the voice, it sounded like one of the PA announcers. That was because the voice belonged to Lex.

"Who is this?"

"This is the International Space Hotel speaking," Lex answered.

"Ah, the space hotel! I'm glad to hear that you are all safe."

"What… Who… are you?"

"This is Bunker 11, sanctioned by the United States; we're a group of soldiers, civilians, and government staff living underground in a military base. I am the commanding officer."

"What's the condition down on Earth? Is it safe to return?"

"Is it safe to return?" The man was in disbelief, and he chuckled a little bit. "The entire surface of the planet has just been struck with nuclear missiles, no, it isn't safe to return."

"Our communication lines with Earth have been unable to make any sort of connection at all. You're the first person we've talked to."

Graham gasped. "This doesn't sound good."

"No kidding," Madison replied. "What the hell is this?"

Graham stood up and looked over to the door. "I don't know. I kind of want to see what's going on. Is this conversation being broadcast live, or is this some kind of recording?"

"Me too," Madison agreed. But both of them were too engrossed listening to move.

"It's no wonder why. You've received no updates from Earth, at all?" Lex was asking the radio controller from Bunker 11.

"No."

"Okay. Listen closely. At around 7 p.m. eastern standard time, foreign military installations were activated on Earth. The damage was catastrophic, and it triggered a global nuclear war. We thought it was the Chinese, and the Chinese thought it was us. But before we knew it, nukes were deployed. We don't know if it was India, or Pakistan, or Iran, that fired next, but it was too late to go back after that. Our defense systems failed to stop most strikes from connecting."

"What military installations are you talking about?"

"I don't know. I don't know! But these installations—giant military installations, mind you—shot lasers from above the clouds, from what I heard. We thought it was the Chinese that started it, but they accused us of doing the same thing. What I do know is that we've been in contact with several other bunkers across the United States and across the world. We haven't gotten much luck anywhere else trying to contact survivors."

"How bad is it down there? Do you think we can get into contact with the Federal Aviation Administration to greenlight when we could attempt a landing back down on Earth?"

"The FAA? I doubt they even exist... I don't think you understand, so let me spell it out for you. D.C. is gone. So are most of the other cities of the Western world."

"But how can you be certain about that? Maybe the EMT blasts have simply cut off most sources of communication."

"I wish we could believe that. But no, trust me on this. The damage is irreparable, and almost every major American city has been struck at least once," the commanding officer explained. He sounded exhausted as if he'd not slept in days, and his words also sounded a bit detached, as if he had prepared these lines and rehearsed them in front of the mirror. "We deployed some drones, drones that remained intact through the EMT blasts by being stowed in secure locations. As of right now, they're searching the landscape, evaluating the condition of everywhere in the contiguous United States, combing the rubble for survivors. And it's looking rather awful... and like it's a lost cause."

"My God," Madison exclaimed, covering her mouth. "So, it's true, then."

"Hey! Hey! It's okay," Graham said. He patted her shoulder but felt awkward about it and pulled away.

"I'm all right," Madison said, although she was dabbing her face with tissues.

"What are the estimates for the damages?" Lex inquired. "Surely there's someplace that's intact."

"The financial cost... incalculable," the commanding officer responded. "The human toll... They say there are over a billion dead, and tens of millions Americans, increasing by the minute. That's some scientists' estimates. If there's any place intact, in my opinion, it's going to be in the middle of nowhere. But then there's also nothing to go back to, either."

"What are we supposed to do up here? We have limited supplies, and our systems can only operate for so long without any shipments."

"I wish I could help you. But there's nothing we can do. If I were you, I would hold out from returning to Earth as long as possible before you even consider coming back down. Certainly not for months, since the radiation is at lethal levels. It's not safe."

"I need to talk to your commanding officer. See if I can get in touch with anyone higher up, any politicians."

"Are you dense? I told you. I am the commanding officer of this bunker. Washington D.C. was destroyed. As far as I've heard, the President, every member of her cabinet, every senator: they're all gone!"

"What are you saying?"

"What am I saying? I'm saying that the United States is gone. The world is gone. You guys should stay where you are because you are far safer up there than you would be on the surface."

"I… That can't be true. You have to be mistaken."

"I'm glad to hear all of you are okay. You should consider yourself lucky to be safe, to be alive. I almost think I'd rather be up there, in the sky, than rotting down below in these bunkers. But we're done. All we have to do is live with the consequences, live realizing everything we've ever known, everyone we've ever known personally in our lives, they're all dead. If not already, then they will be soon. The second they step outside, the second they will be exposed to extreme levels of radiation. We're talking about hundreds of rads of radiation in much of the country. You should tell everyone on board the ISH sooner rather than later. Rip off the band-aid."

The voice on the P.A. announcement ended abruptly, leaving Graham and Madison there, standing in silence. They waited a few seconds, unsure if announcement would resume. After Graham and Madison were certain the broadcast was over, they opened the doors and stepped outside into chaos. The once peaceful hallway was now filled with pandemonium, with people crying and talking loudly. In the distance, they saw a couple of security guards sprinting towards the front of the ship, clearly in a hurry.

"Are you alright?" Graham asked Madison loudly, as she started walking down the hallway fast. "Where are you going?"

"I need something to calm me down," Madison answered. That explanation was enough, and Graham nodded. "Can you keep a secret? No matter what?"

"Of course," Graham said, but as he watched her smirk, he doubted himself.

Chapter 17

The door to the comms room that Skye had, in essence, hijacked, flew open quickly. A couple of guards, flanking Alan Lusky, barged into the room, aiming their guns at Lex and Skye. Skye and Lex instinctively jumped back, raising their hands in the air in submission.

"What is the meaning of this?" Alan barked, as he directed one of the guards, not Marcell, to slam the button to stop the recording that had played over the intercom.

"They deserved to know the truth," Skye started, "but-"

"It was a mistake," Lex interrupted. "An accident, I swear. We had no idea that it was playing over the intercom."

"A mistake! Look at what you've done! Listen!" Spittle flew from Alan's face as he slammed his fist down on the metal dashboard, and Skye could see red marks left on his knuckles when he pulled away. He pointed back to the door as one of the guards propped open the door to reveal the distant sound of shouting and rapid footsteps.

"You've set the entire ship into a panic! You fool! Do you know how much damage control this is going to take?"

"Sir?" Lex asked, trying to get in a word as Lusky continued ranting, fuming.

"This never would be a problem if we had more security guards! But *nobody* wants to work anymore! Everyone crying about their mental health, about how they want to be leave back for their family and their new jobs, so I had to bring in a new batch. Do you know how hard I work my *ass* off to make things work? And now we got only a dozen guards to handle this shitstorm! And it's all your fault!"

"I-" Skye attempted to speak up, defend the cause, but Lex clamped their hand down on their shoulder hard and interrupted them.

"Well, it's done now, isn't it?" Lex asked. "I'm sorry, Mr. Lusky. This wasn't supposed to happen like this. But it's over! The cat's out of the bag. Maybe this could be an advantage for us."

Alan Lusky was so furious that he was shaking. He raised his fist into the air, as if he was going to bring it down again, perhaps back down on the dashboard, or, worse yet, down on Lex. But he didn't. All at once, he let out a giant sigh, and his skin lost much of its red hue. He looked like a defeated man now.

"You're right," Alan replied. "I didn't think it was time. Not yet… But maybe it's best like this. No more lies. No more secrets."

Alan Lusky turned to the two guards, one of whom was a woman with a ponytail who Skye had seen around a couple of times, and the other whom she hadn't seen before. Skye looked at their nametags on their body armor and saw that their names were Audrey and Joshua.

"I need you both on patrol. Make sure no one robs anything. Lock up everything that isn't locked up already, although I know we've taken care of the storage and the armory. I want every knife accounted for. Then I'm going to need you to run some wellness checks in as many rooms as possible. I don't want anyone doing anything they'd regret."

"Got it!" Joshua exclaimed.

"What about you?" Audrey asked. "We need to ensure your protection. Someone could try to hurt you."

"I'll be fine," Alan insisted, waving his hands. "I'm going to make an announcement right now. Before I think any better of it."

Alan stepped over to the microphone. Lex nodded approvingly as Skye moved to walk out of the room. Lex followed her out into the hallway, closing the door behind themselves and stepping well out of earshot of the room.

"Skye."

"Thank you, Lex."

"You put us on a very slippery slope, you know. Alan usually can be reasoned with, but I was worried for a hot second…"

"But you covered for me."

"It's only been a few weeks, but I liked you as an employee, for what it's worth. You got grit. Talent. I guess you could say you're a go-getter, although between you and me, I hate that word. Just stay safe."

"Okay."

"You're lucky. You just don't know how lucky you are yet."

"Thank you."

Skye turned to open up the door, and there was a buzz and a static edge as Alan Lusky appeared to have pressed the on-button for the announcement system. Lex looked at Skye questioningly, as if they wanted to say something else, but thought better of it.

"Be safe," Lex said, stepping back into the room. Skye could hear Alan's voice as she turned around, deciding to stop back and check on Kyra again. He was improvising over the intercom, and he sounded a whole lot less professional than he had in his email.

"Ahem. This is Alan Lusky speaking. I understand that you just overheard a transmission that played out between our announcement coordinator and someone down on Earth. Yes, that conversation is authentic and real. But… in these trying times, we need to remember… we need… We have each other, and we have the safety of the International Space Hotel."

There were the sounds of something thumping and the noise of a clang as if Alan Lusky had knocked something over, and Skye could hear him quietly curse under his breath. It would've been funny if her worry for Kyra hadn't been growing at an exponential rate.

Her worry was so strong that now she was running on the flat escalator, almost tripping in the process. It seemed like many people retreat into their rooms, and she saw what looked like an Indian or otherwise South Asian family running into their own hotel room, holding their hands together, and she couldn't help but feel a pang of jealousy at the sight. At least they had each other, their family. They were maybe the luckiest people on board.

"I ask that everyone remain calm at this time. Don't do anything you would regret. Our guards are patrolling to make sure each and every one of you is safe. And at this time, I need to tell you. We will make it together. We have the resources, the manpower, the brainpower, uh, the… willpower. All the power. Please don't loot. Don't harm anyone, be it yourself or anyone else. Please just make your way back to your rooms in the next couple of hours. We have put a mandatory curfew in place for 11:00 UTC, or space-time. That's, uh… In an hour. Please return to your rooms in the next hour. This situation will be sorted out tomorrow and we will update all of you with our plans moving forward. Thank you for your time. God bless."

With that, Alan clicked off the announcement. And there was a giant sound of metal whirring. Skye stopped in her tracks for a couple of minutes to see metal gates locking down in the front of a store. It looked like all the shops were closing for the business, their gates closing in front of them.

By now, Skye was almost at Kyra's door. Right as she reached the door to knock again, however, she had a stroke of luck. A little bit further downward, Marcell was standing next to a water fountain and leaning against the wall of the hallway, a look of concern on his face. Given the way he lounged, his face creased in apparent exasperation, it looked like he was taking a breather, and Skye bounded over in his direction. He quickly noticed Skye approaching, and raised his eyebrows.

"Skye."

"Marcell. I need a favor from you."

"Okay," Marcell managed.

"Okay?"

"Okay. I'm tired. A lot of stuff's been happening. People are flipping out, trying to loot things, or are otherwise going wild." He paused for a second, putting his finger on his ear as if he was listening on his earpiece. "Shit. It looks like they need me. Again."

"Let me into that room," Skye said, pointing to Room 166. "You can do that much. You have a master key, right?"

"Do I?" Marcell asked out loud. "Yes, I do, and I'll do that. Then I need to hurry or my ass is toast."

Marcell jogged over to the room, unlocking the door with his keycard before turning around.

"See ya," Marcell said, not sticking around long enough for Skye to communicate her worries about her friend's well-being. Skye grabbed the handle, turning around and calling for Marcell to wait, but the words caught in her throat, and he was gone within seconds.

"Marcell!" Skye shouted, but she turned back to the room, figuring her endeavor was fruitless.

Skye instead pushed the door forward, propping it forward. From the angle of the doorway, she couldn't see her friend Kyra.

But she could see the T.V., which had nothing more than the black and white static flashing on its screen. There was the desk lying underneath, from which the chair was missing.

Oh no.

Skye instinctively tried the handle to the bathroom, but it pushed open to reveal that it was empty and dark.

"Kyra?" Skye called out. "Kyra, are you there?"

Skye's head was spinning. Her heart was racing. She felt the dread wash over like the waves of a typhoon crashing to the shore, but she stepped forward and looked to the left. Her eyes flicked between the bed and the couch.

First, she saw the chair. Then the legs, dangling. And then she could see the glowing light, from which the rope hung, a rope which pulled tightly around Kyra's throat. Her skin pallor had taken on a horrifying blue tint, and she foamed at her mouth. Her eyes bulged out of her head, and her face was distorted in an expression of pure shock, and of pain, of regret. It was as if, in her final moments, as she neared asphyxiation, she'd seen ghosts: although Skye didn't need to check her pulse to know she was one now.

And then Skye screamed. She could feel the world coming on top of her. She shook, fell onto the ground in front of Kyra, and grabbed at her legs to try to pull her down, smelling the distinct pang of urine that had soaked her pants. But she was tied up tightly, and the rope wasn't budging. She needed a blade to cut her down.

"Kyra!" Skye sobbed, screaming at the top of her lungs. "Kyra! Oh my God! Help! Help! She's dead! *Dead*! Dead!"

Skye collapsed onto the ground, body racked with sobs, as footsteps pounded into the room. One thought, worse than anything else she'd ever thought, flashed across her mind. *It's my fault. I killed her. I killed Kyra.*

Chapter 18

"I don't approve of this, seriously," Graham told Madison, who had snuck into the pharmacy using her keycard. "This is not okay."

Without flicking on the light switch, Madison moved over to the giant desk in the back room. She ran her finger along the surface, until she found what she was looking for, and pulled open the lower drawer.

"So, you draw the line at prescription pills and opioids, but getting absolutely wasted, that's okay?" Madison asked, crouching down and rummaging through the bottom drawer.

"Well, yes," Graham replied. "There's a substantial difference."

"Is there, though? Because last time I checked alcohol has probably killed more people and ruined more people's lives than opioids and prescription pills. As a matter of fact, the only reason we think it's okay or not okay is due to these other drugs being stigmatized by our culture."

"I said I'd keep a secret," Graham said. "I just was hoping at first that your secret wasn't going to be raiding the pharmacy's cabinets to get high."

"Well, what can I say? Did I disappoint your high expectations that I wasn't a damsel?"

"A *damsel*? What, huh? No. Not a damsel, just… just…"

Madison's face lit up as she pulled up a metal object with a jingle, holding it up in the air to let Graham know she was holding keys.

"Just what?"

"Normal," Graham muttered, almost under his breath.

"If you want someone normal, I would recommend you look no further than a self-portrait. Or Skye. Sweet girl, though."

"That's not nice of you to say."

"Oh no, you're lucky," Madison said, standing up. "Neither of you are as fucked up as me. You're lucky. It's a compliment. And Skye's a good friend of mine."

"Madison," Graham said, in a pleading tone.

"Now it's time for the cabinet," Madison said, ignoring Graham's comment and moving over to it. She was about to insert the keys inside, but then Graham was standing there, as firm and upright as a chiseled marble statue, blocking her path.

"Get out of the way," Madison said.

"You could get into serious trouble," Graham reasoned. "I mean, think about it. What if this thing is rigged with an alarm at night? And it activates? If that happens, I can't cover for you."

"Move it, buckeroo," Madison said, but she sighed before shaking her head. "There's no alarm, Graham. Just look at the thing. Everyone's distracted as hell and I don't think we'll be taking inventory ever because we're never going to get a shipment again."

"You're not only asking me to be a bystander," Graham replied, crossing his arms. "You're asking me to be an accomplice. That's *really* not cool, Maddie. I mean, come on, now."

"I told you because I trusted you, okay? I have a problem. I've had a problem... I..." Madison sighed once again, loudly, sniffling a little bit. "Look, Graham. I'm not going to bitch and moan about what a hard life I've lived. I'm not a victim. Sure, half my family got deported, and I almost died from an overdose the past couple of years. But the world just ended, and I wanted to be around someone, someone who I could trust, and be forthright, forthright about my, uh, problems… And at least have this before I inevitably die up here with the rest whenever we run out of food, oxygen, or water."

"People could need these medications," Graham countered. "You may be forthright with me, Maddie, but you're not with everyone else on the ship who you are depriving of whatever you steal. What if someone died, but they wouldn't have if you hadn't swiped this medicine?"

"Well, let's pretend I'm not in the mood for a philosophical discussion. Would you snitch on me, Graham? Get me in extreme, potentially capital, punishment?"

Graham hesitated for a few moments, and his face fell. "No, Maddie. You're my friend. I don't like this. I'm… I'm just going to go back to my room, okay? Just knock on the door and I'll let you in."

Madison nodded, and Graham stepped out of the way, hurrying back, back down the hallway and to her rooms. Madison stood there for a few moments, doubting herself. Graham had brought up some good points, and she couldn't help but feel a pang of guilt for the way she had treated him, and for the compelling reasons he had argued.

But the temptation was too strong. Soon enough, she had clicked the cabinet open and swiped several containers of pills and various other vials. The only issue was that she couldn't fit it all in her pockets, so she managed to take one of the brown bags that you could almost mistake for a lunch bag from the pharmacy and packed the medicine into the bag. Now she simply had to return to her room, acting as nonchalantly as possible.

She was almost about to leave the room when her phone vibrated. She pulled it out of her pocket, expecting some kind of message from Alan Lusky. But it wasn't. It was actually a phone call from none other than Sarah. Madison picked it up, speaking quietly, as she opened up the door, checking both directions to make sure there was no one she recognized. There wasn't, the hallways, still lit, empty in this sector as they could be, and she felt like a cartoon character when she tiptoed her way down the corridor.

"Uh… Hello?"

"Hi Maddie, it's Sarah. I need you to get to Room 166 as soon as possible."

"Uh… So, I'm assuming this job is still on?"

"What do you mean, your job is still on? I'm counting on you still."

"Okay. Well, sure, but I'm not dressed up in uniform right now."

"I don't care. Right now, the EMTs have their hands full and there is a body to pick up. I need you to take it to the morgue."

Madison froze for a few moments. The room number was oddly familiar, although she couldn't quite remember why. "What's going on? What happened?"

"Some people, Maddie, they simply have lost the will to live."

***

Madison managed to sneak back to her room and stow what medicine she had underneath the desk before she headed to Room 166. It wasn't an ideal location, but it would have to do for now. Then, she hurried over to the room. She saw a small crowd had formed on the outside of a door, and she pushed through the crowd, which was speaking in a low murmur. Dwarfing the murmur, however, there was a noise. It was an unpleasant sound. It almost resembled like the cries of some wounded wild animal, until Madison stepped into the room, and recognized it as human wailing. But it wasn't just the wailing of any random human. She knew who the cries belonged to, now that she had come closer.

"Skye…" She said. Her jaw dropped and she rushed inside before stopping in her tracks.

There was a body in a bag now, and a female EMT whom she hadn't seen before.

"Thank God you're here!" The EMT said. "It's total chaos right now."

"What the hell is going on?"

"Kyra," Skye sputtered out, collapsing down onto the ground again. "It's Kyra."

Madison felt her heart race. She knew it was true, and yet, somehow, some part of her couldn't buy it.

She slowly reached her hand down to the bag, which rested on top of a dolly (one that wasn't supposed to be for bodies, Madison guessed), and unzipped it. When the flap opened and she saw the pale top of her forehead and her tangled hair, Madison felt her head spin, and she stumbled backward, gasping for air.

"Are you okay?" The EMT asked.

"I know her," Madison said. Her eyes were close to clouding with tears.

"You need to take the body to the morgue, right now. I have to deal with some other things."

"What about her?" Madison asked, pointing at Skye. "She's a wreck. What am I supposed to do with her?"

"You take her to her room," The EMT replied. "I'm sure you can handle that."

"Okay," Madison responded. "Okay, okay, I'll do it."

***

The morgue. Madison had only been there once so far, and that had been way back when Sarah had given her a tour of the pharmacy and the nearby facilities. It was not a huge room, with only about ten slots to place dead bodies into the mortuary fridges and only a single metal table in the center of the room for the mortician to work on. But despite its small size, it seemed a whole lot larger than it was due to how empty it was. Then there was the strong smell of disinfectant, which entangled itself in Madison's throat and make her choke.

Madison moved over to the lowermost, leftmost fridge and pulled it open. There was nothing inside, and she pulled out the drawer all the way so that she could lift Kyra onto the table. She looked around once again, felt like there were eyes bearing down on her. But there was no one nearby, and Madison had to reassure herself that she wasn't being watched by ghosts. Death, Madison imagined, wasn't too common on the ISH, although she had an uneasy feeling that there would be a whole lot more frequent if the Earth really had been as devastated as they had said.

Madison dreaded touching the body. But she had to. There was no other way that this body would be placed in the fridge otherwise. If she had gotten Skye back to her room, surely she could do this much.

"No, no, no," she mumbled under her breath. "Why did this have to happen? Kyra…"

She reached towards the body, touched the bag, and stopped in place. She felt butterflies forming in her stomach. Then, Madison reached down and grabbed her shoulders. Stiff. Stuck. Still. She had only felt Kyra's shoulders a couple of days ago, when she had hugged her goodbye, and they had felt warm, soft, and pulsing with life. Now she was as lifeless as any tiny meteor that hurtled itself through the empty void of space outside the space hotel.

"You could have talked to me," Madison mumbled under her breath. "You could have talked to me… But it's time to move you now."

Madison took a deep breath before lifting her up. She gasped for air, exasperated. The body slouched forwards for a few moments, and Madison had to recover herself.

"Oomph!"

Madison almost dropped her to the ground like a sack of potatoes. Only after several seconds of exertion did she manage to get the upper part of her torso onto the table, and then, the legs followed shortly after. For a few minutes, she stood there, hesitating. Part of her wanted to look at her face for real one last time; the other part of her knew that there was no good that could come of that, especially if she'd just taken her own life, and this rational part won herself over quickly. Madison hurriedly shut the fridge, leaning up against the back wall and breathing deep breaths for a few moments. Her phone vibrated again, and she wiped the sweat off her face before accepting the call, supposing there was already another emergency medical situation on board.

Chapter 19

While Madison, Graham, and Skye had experienced devastating emotions over the course of the night, that was not necessarily the case for everyone else.

Marcell was so busy with the various emergency calls that same night, that he hardly even processed what was going on. Some people were taking measures into their own hands, and partying like it was their last day alive.

"Yes, sir," Marcell said over his earpiece. "I understand. Room 339, disturbance and curfew violation. I'm heading there straightaway."

On the way, Marcell caught up with Noah, another fellow security guard, who was taking his sweet time slowly strolling through the hallways. When Marcell passed him up, judgmentally staring at him, he hurried his pace to match his speed.

"So, what's our gameplan here?" Noah asked. His face was pale, and he looked emotionally and physically drained. Even though it was two a.m., all hands were on deck when it came to the security crew on board the ISH, and Marcell hoped he had some caffeine on hand, because he knew they were in for a long night.

"I don't know," Marcell said. "Let's just find whoever runs the party, tell them all to disperse and be quiet. If anyone resists, then we detain them."

"I wish we had more reinforcements," Noah replied. "Two of us might not be enough."

"Oh, me too," Marcell agreed. "That's what happens when we're understaffed."

Noah and Marcell could hear the commotion from a good hundred paces away from their destination. Even though a strict curfew had been instituted, it was apparent that many people were not respecting it. The door was propped wide open, and a small crowd of men and women, most of them, but not all of them, younger than fifty or so, were funneling around the entrance. It looked like some people were entering or leaving, as if this was a night out on the block and people were bar hopping.

A few of the onlookers hanging around the exit noticed Noah and Marcell approaching, and dispersed fast. Others, however, were more stubborn, and tried to ignore their presence.

When Marcell entered into the hotel room, he caught a glimpse of what he wouldn't have expected on a night like this. A disco ball, which Marcell had absolutely no idea as to how it had been acquired, let alone brought into the ISH, was set up in the center of the room, spinning and sending its flashing lights around the room. The room was full of a dozen more chairs than normal, and around twenty to twenty-five people were crammed in this relatively small space. Empty cups were piling on the ground, as were empty cans and bottles, food wrappers, and crumbs. Wet stains of countless alcohol beverages splattered across the room; and in the center of the room, a small throng of people, including a few men and women who had stripped completely naked, were dancing in the center of the room to the blasting pop music that played from a speaker against the wall. One man was on his knees, throwing up into a garbage can, which was practically filled up to the brim with at least a gallon's worth of vomit inside, and probably other various bodily fluids that Marcell didn't want to think about. There was also loud moaning, seemingly from multiple people, coming from behind the bathroom door. It reminded Marcell of the wildest college party he'd never been to, which made him oddly nostalgic. Even though this debauchery was directly counter to the rules Lusky and management enforced, it gave Marcell hope that some people's impulses and reaction to the end of the world wasn't to harm themselves, or to lose all hope, but to party. Marcell liked to think that if he didn't have a job, he probably would've done the same.

Noah looked at Marcell, at a smile that had inadvertently slipped onto his face, and laughed.

"Well, this looks harmless!" Noah said beside him.

"I know," Marcell admitted. "But there's a curfew, and our orders are clear. We got to stop this."

"Boo!" The crowd roared when they saw Noah and Marcell enter into the room, waving for them all to leave.

"All right, everyone!" Marcell tried to say, but the loud blasting music drowned him out almost completely. The man responsible on aux had used his phone to crank up the speaker while he spoke (even though their network was off, phones still had their uses, it seemed). Marcell wrestled the phone away, and Noah shoved the rowdy man away when he stood up to try to take control of his phone again. Marcell muted the speaker, and all of a sudden, everyone in the room had turned against them, their presence extremely unwelcome.

"Boo!"

"Fuck you!"

"We don't want you here!"

"Come on, man!"

"Baby, don't do this!" A woman next to him cried out in a voice that Marcell couldn't decide was pleading, or seductive. The woman had a half-empty bottle of wine in her hand, and grabbed Marcell's crotch, but Marcell shook off her hand of in disgust, stepping back.

"This party… is over!" Marcell yelled. "Everyone disperse in the next five minutes, unless you live here! If you don't, then you will be booked for violating curfew and imprisoned in a holding cell. And believe me, you do *not* want to experience our prison cells."

A good deal heeded his warning quickly, and most of the nude individuals began dressing up again. But not everyone listened.

A few people stayed around, crossing their arms and drinking in their seats, and the man who'd turned up the speakers (who Marcell quickly learned rented the room) cursed them out. Marcell did his best to ignore him, but the same drunk woman who'd touched Marcell earlier ripped off her top.

"What's the crime here?" The drunk woman asked, flashing her breasts within a foot from Marcell's face. "Baby, you can't do this!"

"Leave him be," Noah said, standing in his path. Noah was well aware of Marcell's previous altercation with some other security members (who'd ultimately been reassigned back on Earth) a few years ago, and seemed to know how much this woman bothered him, because he stepped in. Marcell was grateful in that moment for his intervention. He didn't know what he'd do, otherwise.

"It's the end of the world," the woman said, hiccupping. "Why can't we have some fun?"

"You're violating curfew," Noah replied.

"I'll give you a little something if you let me stay here and party," she responded, grinning. "You want it? I'll blow you if you let me stay here for the night."

Marcell looked at his colleague, saw the weakness in his face, and then almost decked him.

"Noah," he said, and his stern tone was enough to get his younger colleague to react.

"Out," Noah growled, and he grabbed the woman by the arm and escorted her out, but not before she re-dressed. In the process, those participating in the presumed orgy in the bathroom had either finished or caught wind of what had happened, as the half-naked two men and two women emerged from the bathroom to be promptly kicked out of the room. All that remained was the drunk host with this phone.

"You all leave," Marcell commanded, but he didn't, instead sipping on their drinks in protest. In the meantime, the host stood up, his fists clenching by his side. The man was heavyset, with a wide hairy chin. He looked like he'd usually be a pleasant guy to drink with at the bar, but now his face was scrunched with rage.

"You all make me sick," he said. "My family's dead, and I can't even drink to them? A party to commemorate our families, and you break it up? You pig. You authoritarian pig."

"Sir," Noah said. "Back away."

"Listen to the man," Marcell said, raising his hands in the air. "You can drink all you want, but disturbing everyone else, that's where I cross the line."

The man snapped, throwing his fist to slug Marcell, but his hand-eye coordination was likely impaired, because he missed. Noah and Marcell looked at each other, in shock, and then they tackled the man to the ground, Marcell slapping his handcuffs over his wrists. The sight of the arrest was the final motivation it took for the remaining stragglers to ditch the party, but not without them bringing their drinks with them, and a few choice words from the last man, who turned back to look around the corner and accost them while they finished detaining the man.

"Fuck you all! No fun police! Screw you and this hotel! I want a damn refund, you hear me!? I'll sue your ass so hard you'll wish you were dead!"

***

Graham didn't find out about what had happened to Skye that night until the next morning when he was awoken by a loud knocking on his room's front door.

"Go away," he said, rolling in his bed. But the pounding persisted, and Graham walked out of bed, grumbling.

"Goddammit."

Since Graham was wearing only pajama pants, he threw on a white t-shirt before finally throwing open the door. He was expecting it to be Skye and was shocked to see that instead, it was a bedraggled Madison. She appeared to have black bags underneath her eyes, and she was wearing a ruffled pair of pants and a t-shirt that made him question whether she'd even changed her clothes the last day or not.

"Hey," Madison greeted him. "Can I come in?"

"You look terrible," Graham sputtered. "Are you okay?"

"I'm tired," Madison replied, shaking her head before opening her mouth wide in a yawn so large that it looked like her jaw would unhinge like a venomous snake.

"Come in," Graham said, ushering for her to come on inside with a giant wave. Madison stumbled over to her bed, sitting upon it before yawning deeply once again.

"What time is it?" Graham asked. Somehow, in his malaise he forgot he could've just glanced over at the clock.

"It's about 8 o'clock in the morning," Madison replied. "8:02, it says."

"Geez, 8 o'clock," Graham said. "Maddie, you look super tired. You should probably go back to your place and get some sleep. You look like you haven't slept at all."

"Yeah, yeah, I know," Madison said. "I will. Probably. And I did sleep. Just for only an hour or so. Not healthy, I know, but I was too busy last night. It was call, after call… God, I'm exhausted. I just wanted to talk to someone."

"Busy?" Graham asked, raising his eyebrows. "What do you mean? Why?"

Attention, all employees and residents at the International Space Hotel. Today at 10:00 a.m., or in approximately 2 hours from now, we will have a hotel-wide meeting in the Entertainment Hall. This meeting is mandatory, and all guests are expected to show up. Our CEO, Alan Lusky, will provide key information as to our living conditions as well as the current situation on Earth.

The voice was familiar once again, spoken by Lex.

"Wow," Graham said. "We should definitely go to that, then."

"Yes," Madison agreed. "It was only a matter of time before they tried damage control, but it's good that they do that."

"Yeah. Oh, and back to my question. Why?"

"Uh…." Madison said. "What was your question?"

"Why were you busy?"

"I was on call all night. Medical emergency after medical emergency… Four people killed themselves last night, Graham. But there were a lot more failed attempts. Over a dozen. I was working until 5 a.m. helping pump out the stomach of one of the hotel's clients because he tried overdosing with all of his medication. Then I had to go give some woman stitches who'd slashed her arms a bunch, blood was all over, it was like a crime scene from a murder mystery."

"Oh geez. That's horrible."

"The ER's booked to hell. They only had four EMTs on staff, a few doctors, and a couple of nurses, and they're all working right now. They sent me back only because I'm an intern and Sarah, she's the pharmacist who's working with them right now too, said she doesn't want me to collapse. I don't know."

"That's horrible. I had no idea. I just headed straight here after, well, you know…"

"About that…" Madison laid back on the bed. Her eyes felt heavier than ever before, and she felt like sleeping, but then the face of Kyra flashed in her head. "You remember Kyra, right?"

"Yes, I do. Why?" He asked, concerned.

"She's dead, Graham."

Graham fell silent. He paced around for a couple of seconds, his face falling. When he spoke up again, he sounded like he was on the verge of choking up. "We really can't have nice things, can we?"

"No," Madison replied. "We can't."

Madison yawned. She might've cried at an earlier time, as she had earlier in the operating room or after she'd found out the world had simply unraveled, but now she was too tired, and too drained of tears, to even be able to.

"How is Skye handling it?" Graham asked.

"Not great," Madison said. "Not that you can blame her…"

She sounded like she was going to perk up for a second, say something else, but her eyes closed.

"Yes," Graham drawled. "Poor Skye."

"Let's go to the meeting at 10," Madison said, and without another word, she started snoring in the next minute.

***

Graham had thought many times about the first time he would ever sleep in the same bed with a woman who was not a relative. Never before would he have guessed it would've been Madison, and never before would he have thought it would've been under these circumstances.

There was nothing weird about it, either. She was simply so tired that she fell asleep next to him. When his alarm that he'd set for 9:45 rang, he woke up with a start to see Madison's arm entangled over his face.

"Huh… Huh…"

Graham carefully took her arm off of his face before sitting up. Maddie lay on the opposite side of the bed but was splayed out like a dog stretching out on the couch.

"Maddie. Get up, Maddie," Graham said, rolling off the bed and walking across to the other side. This time he shook her, and she stirred, her eyes opening wide for a few moments.

"Where am I?"

"You're in my room, remember?"

"Oh, yeah. I'm tired. Let me sleep."

"I know, I know. But there's some kind of important speech going on. I think we should go. Some important announcements from Alan Lusky."

"I don't care," Madison said, and then she yawned. "I'm too tired. Tell me what happens. Good night." And with that, she fell back down onto the bed, loudly snoring.

Graham sighed but didn't press the issue further. She had one heck of a night, after all.

And Kyra's dead. Graham could hardly process that fact. Kyra, who he'd had lunch with a few times. Gone. Too soon. He didn't know how she could do something like that. Only when he thought about his family, there was a deep pain in his chest again, threatening to push him over the edge, and, in some way or another, he understood. He would never have the courage to do something like that, but he did understand how it could motivate someone to act in such a way.

Graham grabbed some of his clothes from his closet before walking into the bathroom. He locked the door shut, just to be safe so that somehow Madison wouldn't stumble in on him in the nude. Then, after changing, he grabbed his phone and keycard and headed out towards the Entertainment Hall.

The halls were packed full of guests and staff heading towards the Entertainment Hall. Even though he hadn't memorized the locations of where everything was, Graham simply followed the crowd and it took him straight to the Entertainment Hall.

When he arrived, there were a whole lot of unfamiliar faces, guests he'd never seen before in his life. He thought about Skye, and wandered around looking for her. But be it as he would, he could not find her, and after a couple of minutes of fruitlessly searching he was certain she must've been much like Madison, sleeping due to the exhaustion of the previous night. She deserved it, especially if she wasn't taking it well like Madison had said.

Although there were many in the crowd that Graham didn't recognize, it wasn't all unfamiliar faces. At one point he bumped into a couple making out, and he had to do a double take when they pulled away and he saw who it was.

"Graham. Good to see you," Drake told him.

"Drake, right?" Graham asked. "And you are…?"

"Minnie," the woman answered, offering him his hand, which he shook.

"I had no idea you were dating," Graham said. "Assuming that's what this."

"Oh, of course," Drake said. "Well, it's a little bit of a recent thing."

"The world has come to an end," Minnie explained. "He asked me, why not live on the edge?"

"Uhhh… I guess that makes sense," Graham replied, frowning.

Drake looked around. "Where's Maddie and Skye? I always see you talking with them at all the intern functions."

"Maddie's sleeping, she had to work a lot as an EMT with, you know… And Skye, I think she's probably tired too."

"Emergency meeting… Yeah, I heard about what happened," Drake said. "Kyra took her own life last night."

"Such a tragedy," Minnie said, shaking her head. "I can't believe it."

"Coward's way out," Drake said, and Minnie looked up into Drake's eyes. Graham looked at her and felt himself shaking in disgust. There was some sort of odd glint in her eye—it was almost *hunger*—and it turned him off and made his mood fouler than it would've even been otherwise.

"Shut. Up," Graham hissed through gritted teeth. "You don't get to talk about her like that."

"Oh, well, I'm just telling it like it is," Drake said, leaning over and pecking Minnie on the cheek before facing him again. "Anyway, Maddie and Skye. You dating one of them or something?"

"What? Umm, no," Graham answered. "It's not like that. We're friends."

"So then, you're not even a boy toy," Drake replied. Minnie giggled.

"He's their white knight," Minnie offered. "Their white knight in dull armor."

Graham stood there, seething for a few moments until he muttered something that resembled a farewell and stormed off. Drake, dating Minnie. Something about the whole thing felt off, and it certainly perturbed him more than anything, although part of Graham wondered if he was just jealous of Drake for being in a relationship. Graham looked around and saw a few familiar faces. He even saw a woman he swore was Eva, with a few individuals clustering around her, only she was not wearing a drop of makeup or a fancy outfit, only sweatpants and a loose-fitting shirt livened with a colorful floral print. Graham hadn't even realized she was still on the ship. Now she was in the same condition as almost all of them, with little to no family or friends alive anymore, and with potentially no more worldly possessions left intact on Earth. No one seemed to bother doting over her, either. It was as if she was as forgotten and screwed over as everyone else on the ship, the destruction from yesterday a great equalizer.

A couple of minutes later Alan Lusky moved onto the stage. When he did, the crowd, which had been talking quietly amongst themselves, fell silent. He stepped towards the center of the stage. Graham remembered how only a few weeks ago a spotlight had flashed on his spot and they had cheered upon seeing him. Now there was nothing but the din of dread-filled murmurs, echoing together like some sort of low predatory growl, as people anxiously waited for news.

"Good morning," Alan Lusky started, before pausing. Graham disagreed greatly. It wasn't a good morning, there wouldn't probably ever be a good morning again until the radiation decayed to a survivable point and whatever crumbling remnants of society managed to rebuild themselves. But Graham also knew he was looking into his words a lot more than he had to.

"Yesterday, as you know, tragedy struck the Earth. There was widespread devastation experienced across the world. This day will lay on in infamy for the rest of our lives, and the rest of the generations succeeding us. We've deemed that day of destruction, the Red Day, for much of the Earth… was on fire."

Graham looked back at the door and saw Marcell and several other guards flanked around the perimeter of the room. They were armed to the teeth with guns, and Graham wondered if they were here to control the crowd in the event of a riot. Graham backed away a little bit, ready to leave the room if anything looked like it was taking a turn for the worst.

"I think, first things first, I need to reassure all of you that we are safe here in the hotel. That this isn't the end. I know it seems like the end because it sounds like everything on Earth is destroyed beyond repair: but it's not. Not as long as we survive up here. Even if. Even if… God forbid, the world is as bad as they said it was, which, to be clear, they cannot be certain about, then think what our family members down there would want for us. Because I know everyone down there would've wanted us to keep living. Not just for its own sake, or for our own sake… But for theirs as well."

The room was silent. Everyone was silent, mesmerized by his words as if they had been hypnotized by a pocket watch.

"Things are going to change. I can't deny that. Our resources will stretch thin, and our food reserves will be depleted. But we have a contingency plan, and we have the technology, the crew, and the supplies to be able to make everyone together. I know our Wi-Fi networks will no longer function, and it's inconvenient, just like our assistant androids and the virtual assistant ROB have been permanently turned off to conserve energy, not to mention some of our extra room functionalities and our gaming room have been disabled. We should be grateful, however, that our oxygen center, as well as all of our engines and generators, remain intact. That's what matters. This new life is going to require an unprecedented amount of cooperation. It's going to also involve adherence to the rules and codes that we lay out today and in the upcoming days. I know all of you clients came here for a great vacation, but right now, it looks like for the time being, you are all going to be here to stay. Certainly, for the next few weeks, or maybe months."

"Send us back down to Earth!" A lone voice cried out from behind Graham, hurriedly shushed by someone else in the crowd.

"I can't, in good conscience, allow any of you to leave. I want to emphasize this point: all escape pods right now are restricted. You cannot access them right now. They are turned off. In the event of an emergency, that policy might change. But I cannot, in good conscience, allow any of you to leave this ship. Not only would no one save for some of the staff know how to pilot the ship, but leaving would deplete the ISH of its required manpower to remain functional."

A few boos broke out from the crowd. Graham peered back at Drake to see his reaction, and it looked like he was squeezing Minnie's hand. Graham felt like gagging.

"You can't stop us!" Someone else yelled. And then there were a couple of other loud yells, except the words weren't in English so Graham couldn't understand what was being said. If he had to guess, it was a couple of the guests cursing Lusky in their native tongue.

"I know, I know, many of you are unhappy. But this is the best thing for everybody, I truly mean it when I am saying that I am looking after all of your best interests. In addition to these escape pods being strictly prohibited, so too are any access to firearms except for authorized personnel. As you know, many of the staff went around collecting knives. This is a temporary arrangement and was a preventive measure to make sure that there were no incidents of self-harm or assault yesterday. Just as we had to arrest several different guests who were disrupting the peace and attempting to loot yesterday. It is only temporary. However, what isn't going to have to be temporary, what is going to have to happen, is that all of you guests are going to have to step up. I understand that you came here looking to relax. But you are all going to have to work. Work with us to ensure that we all survive. Our employees will train you, when needed. And you will be crucial in ensuring the safety and well-being of everyone on board the International Space Hotel."

There were more murmurs, a few boos, and a few yells. But it didn't deter Alan Lusky at all, who continued talking unfazed.

"Rules are changing, just like times are changing, and we will be sure to update you as we come up with our decisions, and we will act swiftly to enforce them. For example, we are instituting a permanent curfew at 10 p.m. from here on out. That means that all the doors to each and every individual's rooms will be locking up for the night, except for approved staff, at 10 p.m., and will not unlock until 6 in the morning. Please note that your emergency buttons will still be active during the night in the event of an emergency. Along these lines, we are going to have to start conserving our energy. That means that we will be more stringent in enforcing the lights-out policy than before, and we will do everything we can to conserve energy where we can, such as disabling voice activated controls. We apologize for this inconvenience. Do keep in mind, we are able to track the energy consumption of each individual room. We will warn those who are consuming excessive amounts of electricity to cut back, or we will discontinue power to their room completely, and that would mean living in pure darkness."

That's crazy, Graham thought. *It looks like I'm living in a real-life dystopia. This is too much.*

"Our rules will be subject to change. Even as of this second, I have a team working around the clock for the next few days to help lay out the ground rules as well as. These will, as I mentioned before, be updated as they come in, and we will notify you with important news through the public announcement systems. That's all I have today, folks. Thank you for your patience. For now, please return to your rooms."

And with that Alan Lusky whipped around, disappearing behind the curtains. Graham decided to step away and return to his room, lest any altercations break out, as the crowd started to disperse, most everyone else doing the same. Although Graham had countless questions floating around in the recesses of his brain, one thing had been made abundantly clear: they were going to be there for the long-run, and it sounded like Alan Lusky would do whatever was necessary to benefit the greater good and keep them all safe.

Chapter 20

It's not my orders. It came from management."

Marcell looked up at his boss, Fritz, who had just spoken those cutting words. Fritz was a couple of decades Marcell's senior, but his head looked even older than his age, with a gray goatee and receding hairline. Some people could claim that their youthful appearances aged like fine wine. Fritz, unfortunately, appeared to have aged like milk left out in the simmering heat. Despite that, he was in insane physical shape, with the muscle mass of a Greek God, and that made his face a stark juxtaposition to the rest of his body.

"Look at them," Marcell said, gesturing through the pale windows to the holding cell beside them. Inside, six men, as well as a single woman, sat, spaced apart, sitting on benches in a room completely bare outside of the benches and a single toilet. This was the largest cell of them at all, but what it had in size it lacked in amenities. At least the five regular prison cells had toilets, beds, and sinks.

"They are a harm to no one," Marcell insisted. "I mean, take that guy, Patrick, over there for example. He hosted a party. And he looks miserable, probably because he's nursing the hangover of a lifetime."

Marcell excluded the part where he'd thrown a punch at his face the previous night.

"Okay…" Fritz said, his voice trailing off. "Your point is?"

"I can't let him go free for something so petty? Or even head in there to give him a glass of water?"

"I get you," Fritz replied, sighing. "But orders are orders, Marcell, and that's that. How about you stroll the perimeter, and make sure no one's forced their way into one of the locked-up shops? Take Route 3."

"I… Yes sir," Marcell replied.

"Marcell. You should know. Someone lodged a complaint against you, day before yesterday."

"Really. Who?"

"I can't say, confidentiality and all that. But this seems to be a pattern with you."

Marcell laughed. "Right. Blame the gay guy dealing with homophobia in the 21st century. I swear to God, security is a century behind in terms of these things. I might've gotten the last boss taken off from the job, but I'm pretty sure you're safe now."

"It's not about that, Marcell," Fritz responded. "I don't give a shit about whether you like women, men, hell, if you're into the weirdest kinks known to man. What I don't like is the attitude. So, go and stretch out those legs in a long walk, won't you?"

"Yes, sir," Marcell said, strolling off away from the prison cell, grumbling. It wasn't fair at all. Alan Lusky was a loose cannon. However, loose cannon as he may have been, Marcell knew where his loyalties lay, and that was still with the people of the International Space Hotel. Falling in line would best support his philosophy, so he did as he was told.

Although he started his way on the patrol, it was not going to be a normal shift. He soon found himself called over towards the main lobby.

"We got a disturbance in the main lobby," Fritz told him over the line. "Get your taser ready, if need be. It looks like some of the residents aren't taking the orders to return to their rooms very kindly, and have been trashing the lobby. Idiots."

As Marcell approached his destination, he heard shouting and picked up the pace, breaking into a jog. When he finally entered the main lobby, he came to an abrupt halt. He reported back to Fritz, informing him that he had reached the scene of the disturbance. A crowd of about twenty-five people had gathered in the lobby.

On the small stage where the incoming interns had checked in a few weeks earlier, stood an intern named Lucas. Guests, employees, and interns were all watching on the floor below. Chairs were overturned, giving the room the appearance of a tornado having swept through. Marcell walked over to the scene. Another couple of guards were there to break up the scene, and the closest one nodded when he saw Marcell.

"This guy's a whacko," he whispered, and he looked to say something else, but whatever else he wanted to say was completely blotted out by Lucas.

"I mean, think about it!" Lucas hollered at the top of his lungs. "Think back to what the conversation said: how the world had totally unraveled, been destroyed!"

"What are you getting at?" someone from the crowd asked. "And you don't need to yell so loudly: you're going to disturb the whole hotel."

"Well, good! They need to hear this! They need to hear the truth!" Lucas replied, although judging by the way that he spoke on a much lower level now, it was as if he had heeded his words to some extent. "What I'm getting at is that this is all fake! It's not possible. Believe me, I've done the research: not only is this war impossible, and I'm not just talking about the global armistice, but also what the Earth looked like. Most importantly, that "conversation" played over the P.A. system was anything but real. It was scripted beyond belief!"

"Hey!" Marcell called, stepping towards the stage. "I understand that you are in the first of the five stages of denial, but what you're saying isn't true."

"See! The guards! Even they're in it too: part of a grand scheme."

A few more individuals had funneled into the lobby at the commotion, while a few more also evidently had failed to suspend their disbelief, because they now walked away from the crowd and the lobby and back towards their rooms.

"So kid, if what you're saying is right, then, somehow, this is what, fake? You're in space. That much is apparent. How in the hell could we fake what the Earth looks like?" Marcell asked. "You really think this is all special effects? That it is all just a lie?"

"I don't know why! That's what I'm trying to figure out. My running theory is this is a grand social experiment. And right now, we're all failing. We're all falling in line like lemmings about to jump off a cliff."

"He's right," an older man, with a wide forehead and thick gray beard said. He wore a blue suit, and he clambered onto the stage. Judging by the way that he swayed, he appeared to have been at least somewhat intoxicated. "This is all a ploy. A ploy by the Jews! I always knew that they would take over the world. We must unite to defeat the lizards!"

A collective groan escaped from some of the spectators, and the reality check of a slightly deluded old man ranting about the Jews appeared to have ignited in a spark in the crowd to the implausibility of what they were all saying. The crowd began to part and then dissipate, much to the chagrin of Lucas, who lightly shoved the old man, who took the hint and didn't try lecturing the audience again.

"Come on! Don't leave! We need to escape the International Space Hotel! We need to go back down to Earth!" Lucas begged the crowd.

"What would we possibly gain from this?" Marcell called back. "Wasting all of this money? Ruining everyone's emotions, and mental well-being? Nothing! You all need to be safe. Don't be so stupid. Go back to your rooms!"

"Damn you!" Lucas shouted back. "Don't you all leave! Come on, don't you see?"

"Should we take him in?" Marcell asked Fritz over his earpiece, much quieter now. "The leader of this unrest: should I take him into custody?"

"Leave it for now," Fritz replied. "We just got an order from Alan Lusky to release the captives with a warning."

***

"Skye."

Madison stood at the foot of Skye's bed. She yanked the sheets down that she had been cowering under, and despite Skye's flailing arms, the outer blankets were off the bed.

"Skye, come on," she said. Skye looked to be wearing the exact same clothes as yesterday; she hadn't even bothered to remove any of them, except for the socks which lay at the foot of the bed.

"No," Skye firmly responded. She grabbed the sheets and pulled them back. Madison was surprised with the strength of Skye's grip, which almost threw her back down onto her bed with the blankets, making it readily apparent that, if Madison ever had to play a game of tug-of-war with her, that she would lose.

"Don't be like this," Madison begged. She thought for a few moments, trying to think of something to say. This emotional support thing, it was difficult, and where Skye had adeptly comforted her the day before, right now, with their positions reversed, Madison was having a much harder time.

"I mean, what I want to remind you. Is that I'm here for you," Madison managed.

"Doesn't sound like you're there for me," Skye replied. "You're trying to pull my blankets off me. When I just want to sleep. And lay here."

"I'm your friend," Madison said. "I mean, you're *my* friend. Uhhh…"

"Just stop pretending you care," Skye replied apathetically. "You don't need to do this game, Maddie. It's obvious you're way over your head. Just let me be."

"You've been here all day long," Madison said. "The most you've gotten out of bed is for water and the bathroom. The cafeteria is opening up again. We need to get you food."

"Why?"

"Why? Food's important, Skye."

"But why? Why is it important?"

"To get strong again… To feel better, mentally and physically."

"What if I don't want strength? What if I want to sit here, and drain, and lose my physical and mental faculties? Maybe that should be my punishment. I mean, I've already pretty much lost the will to live, so."

"It's not your fault," Madison spilled out.

"Yes. Yes, it is," Skye replied quietly.

"She took her own life. In no way did you have anything to do with that. That was her decision. Doesn't mean it was the right one, or even was an okay one. It wasn't. But she's dead, and nothing's changing that."

"I killed her," Skye murmured. "Even though she was the one who technically did it, I may as well have been the one to tie the rope. It's completely my fault."

"You never did anything wrong. You fought, tooth and nail. You're still here."

"Maybe I shouldn't be."

"You don't mean that. You wanted the truth to get out. That's why you did what you did. I talked to someone at the scene. Announcement coordinator, their name was Lex. They're your boss, right? They told me about what had happened. How you knew people deserved to know the truth. You told them."

"And she died as a result."

"She died as a result of her own actions. She didn't die as a result of what you did. As a matter of fact, even if you hadn't done what you did, played it out, the truth would've come out, sooner rather than later. You may have been the bearer of bad news, but that bad news is what made her act, not you. Besides, you don't even know if she did it before you played that recording."

Skye finally perked up from behind the covers. Her face was scrunched into a frown, but it was a thoughtful one.

"How do I forgive myself?"

"You don't," Madison responded. "Not for a long time. But you keep on living."

"Keep on living, huh?" Skye asked. "Are you telling me that I have to drag my ass out of bed, and actually keep doing work? Doing whatever… *this* is going to be now, just to survive, and probably die in the end?"

"Sounds like shit, huh?" Madison said. "Yet, I know you have it in you. I also know from Graham that apparently, we're all going to have to keep working. I know you have a job to do."

Skye sat up. She managed a very slight smile, the sight of which caused Madison to break into a grin.

"You're not so bad at this, after all," Skye said.

"Thank you," Madison answered. "I learned from the best."

***

One by one, Skye read off the names into the registry. Even though Lex said they could do it, Skye had insisted.

"It's my job," Skye had told them. "I gotta do my job, you know?"

"Of course," Lex said. "You do that."

There were five names total. Five people had killed themselves since Skye had played the announcement over the speaker, and since Lex had saved her from facing any sort of punishment from Lusky. And that was only counting the successes; the failed attempts were likely much higher. Three of the dead were men, presumably separated from their families forever. Two of them had been business executives on the same trip. And then there was a middle-aged woman. Her family had left on the last flight back down to Earth, and, due to the seats being booked out, she'd had to reschedule. Of course, Alan Lusky had canceled the last flight when the whole Code Black had been initiated. There'd, surprisingly, only been one person under the age of thirty to die, and that was Kyra. In this case, she had no clear-cut time of death, as with a couple of the other suicides; the coroner was too busy as is, and McFarland with the forensics lab wasn't interested.

"I have no interest in estimating a time of death for an open-and-shut case of suicide," McFarland had once said, cold as ice.

Thus, Skye logged all of their deaths, capping it off with Kyra, which was far more difficult than the others.

"Kyra Powell. D-date of Birth, September 22nd, 2029. Time of death, June 15th, 2048. Place of death, Room 166. Cause of death, asphyxiation."

After Skye was done, she headed to Lex, who was working at their desk with Franco by their side.

"What else can I do?" Skye asked. "Surely I can be of use."

"There's nothing we have for you to do, right now," Lex admitted. "There are no announcements to make. As you can imagine, any sort of business meetings or other previously scheduled meetings have been canceled. Right now, there's nothing we can do but wait."

"Okay, well," Skye said, "There's got to be something I can do. *Please.*"

Lex looked up at Skye. They seemed to have detected the desperation in her eyes, but evidently couldn't do anything about it.

"There isn't, I'm sorry," Lex apologized. "But I promise the second I can think of something, I'll put you on it."

"Thank you," Skye mumbled.

With no work to distract herself, Skye returned to her room, fuming. Her anger at herself soon shifted onto Kyra, and she found herself punching pillows, which was, somehow, very cathartic.

How could she do this to me? How could she give up so easily? And leave all of us, to clean up her mess? These questions whirled around in her head like a hurricane over the next few hours, and they still clung to her as she went to the cafeteria with Madison and Graham.

It was readily apparent that things had changed when they entered the cafeteria. Usually there were several restaurants open, but today, half of them were closed already. The lines usually were also manageable, but now, there was a giant backlog of guests and employees alike waiting for their share of food. Every couple of minutes, an announcement played.

For the time being, guests and employees are allowed meal swipes free of charge. Simply present your room's keycard at the station and you will be offered a portion of food.

"It's free for the guests," Graham commented. "How strange."

"Good deal," Madison said. "It's about time the hotel cut patrons a break."

"Or maybe fiat currency has been rendered worthless," a voice answered. "Therefore, there's no point charging us money when money has no value."

The three friends whipped around to see Drake standing straight behind them in line. He held hands with Minnie next to him.

"How are you feeling, Skye?" Drake asked. When he didn't get a response, he continued speaking as normal. "It's like I said. There isn't much left on Earth, so right now they're rationing food."

Madison's eyes narrowed.

"What do you know about this, you finance smart-aleck? Stop pulling this out of your ass."

"I don't think you should talk to my boyfriend like that," Minnie snarled.

"Boyfriend? This thick-skulled dimwit is your boyfriend?" Madison asked, laughing. "A match made in heaven. Or, more like hell."

Graham stared off into the distance, awkwardly, while Skye raised her hands pleadingly.

"Please don't fight," Skye begged. "I've been through enough the past couple of days."

"I'm sorry for your loss," Drake offered. "I heard about what happened."

"Thank you."

"I don't want to be a pessimist," Drake continued, "But I have a bad feeling that this is going to only get worse, and the pressure is just going to keep on mounting."

"Yeah, sounds like we got a psychologist here now," Madison replied sarcastically. "What do you know about what's happening? Or about what will happen?"

"You seem to just feed off of negative energy," Graham added. "Seriously, I'd tell you to touch grass if we're out on Earth."

"Yes! Good point," Drake said. "Who knows about the adverse effects of living in space full-time, without access to normal levels of sunlight and nature?"

"I don't know," Minnie admitted. "But I know I have you."

"Ooh, yes. In times like these, the best thing we have is each other. I love you."

Drake leaned forward to Minnie, passionately kissing her.

The line couldn't move forward fast enough. Skye wanted to scream. This man was insufferable.

"I hope you're using protection," Madison commented, before whispering in Graham's ear. "God help us all if Drake reproduces. There're enough idiots in this spaceship already."

Chapter 21

Marcell, meanwhile, was left reeling by a plan that had just been proposed by the ship's leadership.

"We can't seriously consider this plan," Marcell exclaimed. Fritz, standing next to Marcell, slapped him on the side. He didn't take the hint.

"I know," Alan Lusky said. "I've considered everything, thought about this. But there are no other options. And no offense, I appreciate the input, but who even are you?"

Alan Lusky sat at the head of the table in the meeting room, flanked by his upper management team - or at least what remained of it after the Code Black and the loss of all communication with Earth. The Chief Marketing Officer, Chief Information Officer, and several Vice Presidents of different ranks were gathered around the table. But there were a few unexpected faces too. Alan's wife sat right beside him, drawing occasional glances from the other executives. Dr. Chetana, the Head Doctor of the International Space Hotel, was also present. Finally, there was Mr. Xiong, one of his Engineering Department contacts who had irked Marcell by arriving seven minutes late to the meeting.

"My name's Marcell, Marcell Hopkins," Marcell introduced himself. "I'm a senior security guard. Been working here for the last five years."

"A senior security guard, huh?" Alan Lusky laughed.

"Very funny," The CIO said. "What's your salary? 40 an hour?"

"Well, no, actually I make a bit over-"

"I'm being facetious," The CIO interrupted. "What I mean to say is, you're stepping out of line here."

"Indeed," Alan Lusky replied. "However, I believe there's some quote there. From Teddy Roosevelt… Or no, I think it was Winston Churchill. Some men change their party for the sake of their principles; others change their principles. I hope you're not all becoming my yes men. Otherwise, I'd feel a bit unhappy."

"We…" The Chief Marketing Officer hesitated.

"What is it, Ai?"

"I just… This is a bit extreme, right?" She asked, sweeping her black curls out of her face. "I have to think about their perspective. If we just kick people off the ship, think about the message we're sending to everyone else. And if it is as bad as they say… Then we have no right to take their life. We're company executives, not dictators."

"It's a shame Andy isn't here to debate that," Alan Lusky replied. "But perhaps she has a point. I still think getting rid of the interns and most of the guests will increase all of our chances of survival, and allow us to actually consume a set number of resources that we can sustain in the long-run."

"There's a different route," Dr. Chetana replied. "A middle way."

"I'm assuming you would be familiar with the Middle Way, being Indian," Alan Lusky remarked. A couple of Vice Presidents shuffled uncomfortably in their seats at the racist remark.

"No, that's Buddhism, and I'm Hindu," Dr. Chetana said, sighing. "We let them go. Whoever wants to go, we let them travel down back to Earth. Everyone else stays."

Marcell's mouth opened, but again, Fritz poked him in the side and shook his head. This time, he fell in line. He had to.

Alan Lusky thought deeply for a few moments. "You know, I think she may have a point. They will decide their own choice, in two days' time. Until then, everything can continue as usual. I know we're understaffed because of all those quitters, but I want everyone working double time. We can't let this get out, and we need to at least pretend like we're perfectly in control."

The group assented before the conversation died out. After a minute of silence, Mrs. Lusky was the one to speak.

"Honey, what did you tell me about looking at the Earth? Just to see how the situation was?"

"Yes," Alan Lusky replied. "The impact analysis. Ron, have you any complete projection as to what the situation looks like? Because that certainly might help sway my feelings one way or another."

"No," replied Ron, the CIO. "What we have done so far is charted every clear impact point that we can see on Earth. There's still a lot of progress to be made, but we are in much better shape than yesterday, that's for sure."

"And? What big findings have you realized?"

"Well, we would strongly advise against letting any escape pod return down to the United States. There's a whole lot of impact points there, relative to just about every country."

"We have to let them," Alan Lusky countered. "If we want them to willingly go, then the only way anyone will even want to return back to the Earth is if they can go back home. Over half of our clients and staff are based out of the United States."

"That's not right," a different Vice President jumped in. "That's not who we are."

"Yes," Dr. Chetana agreed. "If we simply let them blindly return to only the United States, we'll be enabling their death. That isn't right. If we're going to let them go freely, then they deserve to have an honest disclosure about the state of the world. To improve their chances of survival."

"I think we let our boss decide what's right," Mr. Xiong said.

"Okay," Alan Lusky responded. "I need to think about this. We'll figure out that part, tomorrow. This meeting is adjourned. Oh, and one other thing."

Alan Lusky looked at Fritz for a couple of moments. "With the chaos of this whole situation, I think it's a good idea to have a full-time personal security guard. And by that, I don't just mean having guards posted outside my room at night. Someone to watch my back."

Marcell thought that was funny, considering how understaffed they were after the last batch of guards had recently left.

Fritz nodded. "Well, sir, I'd be honored-"

"Could I take that Marcell of yours off your hands?" Lusky interrupted.

"Marcell?" Fritz asked. "You want Marcell?"

"Yes."

Marcell frowned, perplexed.

"Sure," Fritz replied. "He's all yours."

***

"Now… it's the welder's turn," Mr. Xiong told Yusef and Graham.

Two welders, positioned in front of them, were now welding a spider-like contraption to one of the generators in the electrical room.

"The prototype of this GCM, Generator Conservation Machine was developed in the labs," Mr. Xiong practically had to yell over the noise of the sparking of the welding. "This has the potential to make things a lot better for all of us. It will help double our output."

"I thought each generator was capable of producing up to 10,000 kilowatts," Yusef said. "So, Mr. X, why is this such an issue?"

"I wouldn't worry about it," Mr. Xiong said. "It's just, I don't think we're going to be getting any shipments from Earth soon, whether that's more parts for repair or manufacturing, or more crew members. What that means is that every single generator is all the more valuable, as is each single amp that is drawn from all these generators."

"You're making it more cost-efficient," Graham reasoned. "You can maybe even power one off. Save it just in case."

"Hypothetically, hypothetically," Mr. Xiong answered. "In general, saving electricity is key. One of our top priorities. It's why when the curfew time hits, the majority of uninhabited rooms will lose access to our electricity. Only the hallways and other critical rooms will retain their access to electricity. Of course, our heating and oxygen systems will remain untouched."

Graham didn't like the sound of that. Not one bit.

***

Graham was trying his best to look cool, but failing miserably.

His face, usually rather expressionless most of the time, showed a look of exasperation, and was so sweaty that it looked like a waterfall of sweat was draining from his face: Skye noted this, and appreciated his hustle, but was also slightly concerned. There were a few dozen people throughout the giant gym right now, but it looked like Graham was applying himself as wholly as anyone.

"Where's anti-grav when you need it?" Graham rasped.

Madison walked over, having run on the treadmill for some good time, and chatted with Skye for a minute before Skye commented on Graham's performance.

"Don't overdo yourself," Skye said, setting down the five-pound weights she'd been lifting back down on the rack of weights. "Maybe you should start with something lighter."

Graham finished the last few reps before slamming them down onto the ground. He wiped the sweat from his forehead before shaking his head.

"Heck no," Graham replied, standing closer to the two women. "How am I ever supposed to get buff lifting twigs? No offense, Skye."

"None taken," Skye responded.

"My god, you're sweaty, though," Madison said. "I don't want you tearing your muscles. I don't need another patient in the ER."

"Stop it," Graham responded. "That isn't going to happen."

"He's really pushing himself," Skye said. "I'm impressed."

"What can I say?" Graham said, exhaling. "If we're going to be stuck up here for a while, then I may as well be productive."

"Look at him, though," Madison said, pointing her thumb in the direction of Drake.

The three turned to look at Drake. Right now, a couple of older men who were presumably clients just working out at the gym were spotting him as he benched a bar with a couple of extremely heavy looking weights attached to the end. He was effortlessly lifting the bar up and down for a few moments, Graham frowned, his face curled in displeasure.

I need that muscle tone, He thought. *I'm not even close. And lifting twenty-pound weights isn't going to cut it.*

"I've been so bored, with next to nothing to do the past couple of days, except feeling bad for myself," Skye said. "We should do this more often."

"I haven't been doing much, either," Graham admitted. "Our production line is pretty much halted. Saving energy and all of that. I've just been walking around with my manager to make sure all of our systems are operating effectively. Doesn't exactly make for a full day of work, considering how many other people are doing that."

"Heh, I've still been busy," Madison said. "Well, like I said, there were a few people who killed themselves, but there were more yet who tried and failed."

"What do they do with them, anyway?" Skye asked as the three friends slowly walked out of the gym.

"A couple are on active watch, and are being treated," Madison responded. "We can't let them go because we think they're active threats to themselves."

"Can't do anything about that," Skye replied. "Why not let them go? It's their own choice."

"Geez," Graham managed, shocked by the bluntness of Skye's remark. It was like she was a completely different woman than a few days ago when she'd come across Kyra's body. Far more blunt and far less emotional than before.

Right before the three friends exited the gym, Graham spotted Yusef walking inside, and he gave him a nod of acknowledgement on the way. Madison and Skye noticed this act.

"Oh, you know that guy?" Madison asked as they all stopped in front of a drinking fountain, before plopping themselves down on some nice cushioned chairs in front of the gym.

"His name's Yusef," Graham replied. "I know people."

"*Ooh*, he knows people!" Madison exclaimed, prodding Skye. "Our boy is all grown up!"

"Stop it," Graham responded, blushing.

"I know," Skye said, squeezing his bicep. "His bicep's grown up too. Well, not all the way. Maybe it's still in puberty."

"That's embarrassing," Graham replied, turning an even deeper shade of red and whipping his head back and forth so much it looked like it might rotate fully around like an owl. "Would you lay off? How would you feel if I squeezed your body without your consent?"

"He's got a point," Madison replied, and Skye patted his arm before pulling away.

"Anyway, I bet I could bulk up more if I had more food to eat," Graham continued. "But apparently that's not possible, the way that the cafeteria has been skimping us on portion size."

"I know, right? Isn't it weird?" Skye asked.

It was weird. Ever since the news, their food options had been limited: before, you would have to pay, but you could acquire as much, or as little, food as you wanted. Now, you could only pick a single entrée from a single menu. And these entrées, while sufficient, were nothing to write home about: Graham could swear that the portion size had been slightly reduced over the past few days as well.

"I don't like it," Madison replied. "And I don't think any of you happen to have any inside information about what our food situation is going to look like, do you?"

"No," Skye replied. "Maybe Marcell knows."

"Good point," Graham replied. "I bet he knows a lot more than any of us. We should try to talk to him more."

"Yeah," Skye agreed. "Can't talk to Kyra. I bet she would've had a lot to say about our food."

The comment was enough to kill the mood, and almost the conversation.

"It's not like Marcell telegraphs his schedule," Madison replied, deciding to ignore Skye's comment. "I've knocked a couple times, and got no answer. And besides, what are we supposed to ask him? Hey, can you find a way to sneak us some extra garlic bread?"

"Why not?" Graham asked. "What's the worst that could happen?"

"He could report us, and we get ejected from the ship," Skye speculated. "I'd say that would be pretty damn bad."

"Oh, come on," Graham replied. "He got us booze on our first day here. I think we should ask. We know his room number, right?"

"Yes," Madison replied. "Room 248."

"Let's go there tonight."

Skye was going to open her mouth and probably make some snarky comment, but just then, another announcement came from over the line. Even though Lex had said that they hadn't needed Skye's help, they seemed to have their hands busy.

Attention all clients and non-essential staff of the International Space Hotel: today only, we are providing you all with an opportunity to return to Earth. In one hour flat, we will be meeting in front of the Entertainment Hall. Anyone who wishes to return to Earth may have the chance to do so. You may bring one suitcase or bag. It will be on a first-come, first-serve basis. It is ultimately up to the staff of the ISH to determine how many of you are allowed to leave, but we can promise at least 20 spots right now. The escape pods will be deployed to land back down where the space shuttles launch from in Florida. There are no exceptions.

"Wow," Skye said, sitting up. "Holy shit."

Chapter 22

A line of guests had formed in front of the Entertainment Hall. Many of them carried suitcases and lined up with desperate expressions on their faces. By the time Graham, Skye, and Madison arrived, there might've been a couple dozen people queued up, the numbers quickly growing.

"I should go back and pack," Madison said. "It looks like everyone's bringing some stuff with them."

"You can't seriously be thinking of going?" Graham asked.

Skye thought of her family. Of Emily, and of Braydon. She thought about that last phone call she'd desperately placed. It had been less than a week ago, but now it already felt like a month or a year ago. It had been a completely different time. She'd thought of them so deeply, of how they had probably died, and felt oddly disconnected. It was as if she had almost forgotten them. She'd gone through such a rollercoaster of emotions since the Red Day, especially with what had happened to Kyra, that she felt emotionally broken. But she did know one thing. She loved them. Now she could see them again.

Skye had seemed to take every chance she got to catch a glimpse out the window and look at the massive oceans, which she imagined were tainted with fallout, the desolate deserts, and the scorched patches that likely marked former cities out the windows of the ISH. She had spent so much time wondering what it was like on Earth. Now it was finally time to reunite with her family. No more daydreaming.

"I am," Skye answered. "We should go back, right now. If we hurry, we should be able to pack some essentials and have a couple of minutes to spare before the flights leave."

"Now hold on a second," Graham replied. "Something feels off."

Skye paused and looked at the line as her eyebrows formed into a crease.

"Wait," Skye said nervously. "Do you recognize anyone here? Like, staff?"

Most of the people were completely unfamiliar to Skye. There were a couple of people she recognized from the first intern meeting, but most of them she didn't know at all.

"Not really," Madison replied. "I think I saw that guy at the intern meeting. Tony's his name, I think."

"Isn't it strange," Skye commented, "That they said, all clients and non-essential staff…"

"Yeah, that's to be expected," Madison responded. "I mean, the place can't run without essential staff."

"I don't know," Skye hesitated, the rational part of her brain starting to take over. "It sounds fishy."

"It does," Graham asserted. "It sounds textbook sketchy to me. Like, maybe this and the food situation are related. They're trying to willingly offload the ship when they can."

"Pull your sticks out of your asses," Madison said. "We have a chance to finally go home, and see our family, and now you're saying we shouldn't do it?"

"Think about it, Maddie: if we go back down to Florida," Graham replied. "Think how irradiated it could all be. There was a nuclear war, and a bunch of the U.S. got hit. Y'all could die. Plus, your family is in California. You really think you can safely get across the U.S. to your family? Or Skye back to Minnesota, me to South Carolina? No can do."

"We'll make do," Madison responded. "I need to see my family again, and I'm going down. Period."

"Don't do it!" A quiet voice hissed from behind.

The three turned around to see Marcell. He motioned for them to come closer and whispered with them.

"I don't have much time," he whispered. "Just don't take it. Go back to your rooms, now."

"Why?" Madison asked. "Tell us why."

"The world's fucked," Marcell replied. "If you go on, you'll die. Take my word for it. Just stick it out here for at least a month or two."

Marcell looked around frantically, as if he was being followed. Then he hurried away, down the hallway. The three friends stopped for a few seconds in shock.

"Marcell! Wait, Marcell!" Skye called, but he was gone.

With that, Marcell disappeared away from the crowd. Madison, Graham, and Skye hurried away. They could hear the sounds of commotions, of a voice shouting to not trust them.

"Lucas," Graham speculated. "I heard the kid is off his rocker about some conspiracy theories."

But they didn't look back or go to see what was going on. They couldn't. Skye knew if she looked back again, she might second guess her decision, even with what Marcell had told her.

Chapter 23

Madison knocked Marcell's door so hard that her knuckles felt like they were about to bleed. The door swung open, and Marcell, wearing a white t-shirt and gym shorts, answered.

"You look hungover," Madison commented.

"I'm not. I'm just about to catch some shut-eye," Marcell fired back defensively. "It's late. Curfew's about to start in fifteen minutes. You should return to your room."

"I know. I just needed to thank you for saving our lives," Madison replied. "It means a lot."

"No problem," Marcell responded. He stuck his head out the door and looked down both sides of the hallway. There was no one in the immediate vicinity.

Madison peered into the room, and saw a couple suitcases, as well as a few boxes scattered throughout.

"You moving rooms?" Madison asked.

"Yeah," Marcell replied. "Tonight."

"Where?"

"Alan Lusky's condo," he explained. "I'm moving in, full-time."

"The hell," Madison replied. "Why?"

"Uhhh… I'm his full-time bodyguard now, apparently."

"That's… crazy," Madison responded. "I mean, that's great, right?"

"Yeah, I don't know if I'm so excited, but he chose me for some reason, so I guess I have to deal with that."

"You should give us the inside information," Madison suggested. "My friends are wondering about food, whether you can maybe hook us up with some more. It's not that it's horrible, but it's just not quite good enough. I always feel like I'm slightly hungry."

"That's not up to me," Marcell replied. "That's the kitchen."

"I know," Madison replied. "But I find it difficult to believe you can't help us here."

"Look, let's not talk about this now," Marcell said. "I'll catch you later at your room, okay?"

"Are you sure? Promise to visit us tomorrow evening, before curfew? Because this is important for us."

"I promise I'll try," Marcell offered. "Even us security guards get some free time."

***

The temptation was simply too much for Madison to bear. Knowing that she'd missed out on what was maybe her final opportunity of ever seeing her family again placed a heavy burden upon her shoulders. An announcement a couple of hours earlier had said that forty individuals had safely departed the International Space Hotel, and that they bid them a kind farewell. Madison trusted Marcell's words, but that made her all the more confused and emotionally conflicted. How could they do something like this? How could they send them down to their death? Maybe it was a sign that everyone she knew was dead forever after all.

Madison's family was different from many of the Mexican friends and family members she knew. Sure, they valued family, and their cultural heritage, so much, as was relevant in their home in Southern California. But they wanted to be American, so badly.

Madison's father and his first wife had immigrated to the United States when they got the chance of a lifetime with a visa. Both of them had been professors in Mexico and found an excellent research employment opportunity. They immigrated with Madison's older brother Juan. But then, tragedy struck when her father's wife died in an accident. Madison's father was quick to move on. So much so that her father married a white American woman, which, ultimately, had spawned her into existence. Her mother had been close to Maddie, until she wasn't. She divorced her father and moved across the country, cutting off ties. But Madison's father was not yet done: he divorced his new wife and re-married another miserable American woman, while helping bring many relatives over to the United States, illegally. But he couldn't do anything as Madison's *tío*, *tía* and *primos* were all deported with the conservative crackdown of the previous presidency, trying to control the immigration inflow into the country. At least Chu had kicked President Parrish's butt in the election.

"I'm such a fuck-up," Madison said aloud to no one but herself as she reflected upon these things. Her mother had abandoned her, and her stepmother never loved her. She unscrewed the lid of the opiates, took out a few pills and dropped them into the palm of her hands. She raised her palm up to her hand again before letting it fall onto the ground, the pills spilling out onto the carpet.

I can't do this, Maddie thought. *Not again.*

She had been clean for over a year before after being on the hotel. And for good reason. These things were like an indestructible reel of a fishing line, and she, like some idiot fish about to be snagged up and served fried and battered. When the urges pulled her in, it pulled her in almost for good. She'd almost died; it was only through detox and rehab during her second semester freshman year that she'd gotten everything together. Somehow, she'd gotten clean just in time for her first internship interview last summer. Now explaining that gap of a semester of schooling had led her to a deceptive stretch of truth to the ISH interviewers, that she'd gotten into a major accident and stepped away from school for health reasons. If they'd known she was a junkie, they wouldn't have even hired her in the first place.

"Stupid, stupid," Madison told herself. Then she took a pill and swallowed it. Madison stuffed the remaining pills back into the vial, hiding it back underneath the desk. Then she slunk back to her bed in shame, waiting for the effects to kick in.

***

Alan Lusky, meanwhile, was sharing his thoughts with Marcell.

"You look like you want to tell me something. Don't hold back."

Marcell's face wrinkled into a frown. Alan Lusky had confronted him in his living room while Marcell stood watch.

"I don't know what you're talking about, sir," Marcell said. "I'm here to protect you and your family."

"Do you like the place?"

Marcell looked around at the luxurious condo. It was huge, probably a few thousand square feet, with a second level accessible via a fancy private stairway. The living room he stayed in right now was lavishly decorated, with a statue, postmodernist artwork, fancy furniture, and even a fish tank that took up half of one of the walls. But when Marcell looked inside at the shimmering of some of the fish, it became clear that the fish were actually holograms.

"It's nice," Marcell answered. "Very nice, actually. And very big."

"Indeed," Alan Lusky said. "As I've said, all the security systems are active. Make yourself at home in the guest room down here. You just need to watch the front entrance and make sure no one goes up these stairs."

"Can I ask you something?"

"What is it?"

"Why did you choose me?"

"What?"

"You chose me as your personal bodyguard because of everything that's happened, right? So why would you possibly choose me? It doesn't make any sense."

"I appreciated the way you stood up to me at the meeting. Got the ball rolling. You can't teach that trait. You stood up for what you believe in. And I like that."

"You want a free thinker as your security guard? That seems pretty counterintuitive, no?"

"I want someone competent," Alan Lusky replied, before yawning. "Most of the guards here can't think in emergency situations to save their life. You seem to be smart. Certainly, physically agile. And what about you? Are you okay with this arrangement?"

"I don't think you want to know that."

"Really?" Lusky asked, his interest piqued. "Please tell me. In fact, I order you as your superior to tell me."

"Truthfully?"

"Yes. Truthfully."

"I think you're a chickenshit coward who sent dozens of people to their death today. I think you've done something so unethical and cruel, that I don't know how you can live with yourself. As for this 'arrangement', I would tell you to shove it, but I don't want to be disobedient, and I want to do whatever's best for the ship, anyhow. So, if that means falling in line and protecting you, then I will do that."

Lusky turned around, walking up the stairs. He raised his eyebrows, chuckling for a moment.

"I'm so sorry you feel that way," Lusky called back down. "But I'm glad to know that you're loyal."

Chapter 24

W ithin the next two weeks, the International Space Hotel felt a whole lot less like a hotel and a whole lot more like a prison.

It wasn't all bad. Marcell managed to work something out with Madison the day after he told them to not take the optional flight back down to Earth. He stopped by Skye's room to catch her and Madison. They both were playing chess with a set that they had borrowed from the rec room, but paused to talk with Marcell.

"The appetizers are kept for us," Marcell explained at one point. "They give some of us staff a lot more food than any of the clients or the interns. It's a strategy to conserve our food supply."

"Wow," Madison replied. "That's not fair."

"Okay, to be fair, they have some tough work to do," Skye replied. She moved her queen forward. "Check."

"Rookie move," Madison jeered, moving her knight forward to block the check and attack the queen. "You've only accelerated my development."

"I can get the food to you," Marcell said. "I can drop it off to you in a plastic bag every couple of days."

"Okay," Skye replied. "We'll keep it and share it with only a couple of people."

"That sound fair?" Marcell asked.

"Fair and square," Madison replied, as Skye dropped her queen back a few squares, only to find it captured by Madison's dark-squared bishop.

"Crap!" Skye exclaimed. "I didn't see that."

Skye tipped over her king.

"Good game," she managed, shaking hands with Madison as Marcell chuckled.

"Bye guys," Marcell said, waving goodbye.

"See ya," Madison said, as the door shut close behind him.

"I used to play chess in high school," Madison admitted. "I was the top player at my high school and ran the chess club. Don't feel bad."

"Really?"

"Well, yeah. Let me guess, I'm a nerd, right?"

"No," Skye replied. "That's not weird at all. That's super cool."

"I just quit," Skye said. "Got wrapped up with my ex and made bad decisions. He got me into drugs, too."

Skye didn't know what to say. The friends had opened up to each other within the past week, but this seemed uncalled for.

All the time, Graham, Skye, and Madison found themselves a lot more bored, although now they at least felt adequately fed with the extra food drop-offs made by Marcell. The three kept the food to themselves. Perhaps it was selfish, but they didn't want to tell anyone lest they somehow accidentally spill the beans and get Marcell in trouble.

***

There were some interesting developments with the International Space Hotel over the span of this time. One of the gazing lobbies developed into a place for prayer.

There were no priests on board. The International Space Hotel was a location that was as secular as any other places in America in the year 2048, which was to say that it was pretty secular. And yet, despite that, a place for prayer for different faiths had been set up on board. There were multiple tables pushed against the side walls. Some of them contained offerings such as water, flowers, incense (although not food, since that was too valuable to not eat), while others contained various icons of their faiths. On the ground, there were a few bibles, as well as some other holy texts, available for anyone who wanted to pick it up and read it, as well as some crucifixes and prayer beads. There were also even a few prayer rugs set up aimed at the Earth, indicating that there were a few Muslims still completing their faithful rituals on board. Even now, there were a few guests who sat on their seats, hands clasped in some manner of prayer, or who stood in front of their religious tables or the window to the Earth, in deep contemplation.

One day, Madison invited Graham and Skye to accompany her to the prayer room. She knelt on the ground in front of the window, looking down on Earth, holding the crucifix necklace around her neck in her right hand.

It was night on Earth, and it looked like they were over the Mediterranean region now. Looking down at Earth was a glum sight: sure, pretty much all of the fires by now had burned out, so that the Earth no longer looked like it did on the Red Day, but the Earth had been scorched, much of the green rendered a depressing brown. And now, that they orbited over what remained at night, there were next to no visible lights shining from the ground anymore. It was an indicator that either the electricity was cut off almost everywhere due to a widespread collapse of the electrical grid, or that, worse yet, almost everyone was dead.

Madison absorbed the sight for a few moments, before she closed her eyes, and Skye could see her lips moving up and down silently. Skye and Graham watched without saying a word for a couple of minutes, and then Madison stood back up onto her feet, and joined them towards the back of the room.

"You don't want to join me?" Madison asked.

"I'm okay," Graham replied.

"Yeah, me too," Skye added.

Madison paced around, showing off the various tables to Graham and Skye. Ironically, having the various faiths collaborate in one room had fostered an environment that she felt was far more cooperative, far more supportive, than any divisive religious institution from back down in Earth, back when people often took everything that they had for granted and used their faiths as a weapon to alienate others, to propagate their own world views.

"Not the religious type, huh?" Madison asked quietly.

"Nope," Skye responded. "I'm atheist."

Madison nodded. "How about you, Graham?"

"Grew up in a Methodist household," Graham answered. "They raised me to never swear, and that's why I say darn and heck quite a bit."

"Do you still believe?" Madison asked, as Graham looked at an icon of Mary on one of the nearest tables, realizing that this particular table was for the Catholics.

"I'm not sure," Graham said. "I don't really think about it too much. I'm too busy thinking about the world, and about our survival. My job."

"You don't have to," Madison said. "But it's good for introspection."

"I don't need that," Skye responded. "It'd take a fucked-up kind of God to let this Red Day happen. Besides, the way I see it, if you need the threat of hell to prevent you from acting sinfully, then you're probably not a good person."

"Touché," Madison replied, chuckling. "That's not what it's about, though. It's empowering, it's freeing. It's a feeling of there being something more important, and it gives you something else to live for, and live by. Take this room, for example. A bunch of differing religious people here, and we all get along together. Isn't it great?"

"It is… something," Graham admitted. "I'm glad people have this space. I never thought I'd see Muslims and Christians praying together in the same space in such perfect harmony."

"Me neither," Skye agreed, "I'm impressed."

The three of them exited that room shortly after. Skye and Graham never returned; but Madison made the trip almost every single day, praying for Jesus to lend her the strength to kick the drugs: it didn't happen.

***

Even though the boredom was real, it wasn't the boredom that affected the friends so much. It was the thoughts of home, and the longing experienced for them. In Skye's case, she was haunted, still, weeks after the fact, by Kyra. It seemed like every night that horrifying discovery flashed in her head, Kyra's face contorted in regret, and Skye would wake up, drenched in sweat, gasping for air.

But life continued. In Madison's case, she still worked in the medical wing.

One day, Madison was shadowing in the doctor's room, working with Dr. Wells when a patient was ushered into the room. Madison raised her eyebrows.

"Minnie?" Madison asked.

"Hi," she said. "W-what are you doing here?"

"I'm a medical intern," she explained.

"What may I do for you today?" Dr. Wells, one of the three medical doctors on board alongside Dr. Silva and Dr. Chetana, asked.

"I don't know if I can say it with her in the room," Minnie admitted, looking up at Madison.

"I can leave," Madison offered, standing up, but Dr. Wells told her to stop and motioned for her to stay.

"You can trust us," Dr. Wells promised. "Anything you tell us is protected by doctor-patient confidentiality, and all of us, including interns, abide by these rules. Isn't that right, Maddie?"

"Yes," Madison replied.

"Okay," Minnie replied. "I've been throwing up. I'm tired and my emotions have been out of whack."

"When did these symptoms start?" Dr. Wells asked.

"A week ago," Minnie replied.

"Okay," Dr. Wells replied. "Now I hate to ask but-"

"I think I'm pregnant," Minnie blurted out.

Madison's eyes widened.

"Okay," the doctor said, turning to Madison. "Now I think you *can* leave."

Madison stepped out of the room, shaking her head after she stepped out. Even though she was under the influence of addiction, she was glad she at least wasn't *that* kind of fucked.

***

Even though the secure Wi-Fi networks had been completely down since the first day of the nuclear devastation, the radio systems weren't. That much was made apparent to the public when Franco announced over the line that they had made contact with another base on the surface. Skye didn't know why the ISH hadn't maintained regular contact with the other bunker, but what she did know was that this time they were talking to a different bunker. Bunker 4.

Unlike last time, the conversation wasn't played over the PA System, but Skye did have the luxury of listening in to the conversation herself to confirm what had been said.

"You're not trying anything funny this time," Franco mouthed, more of a statement than a question, and Skye nodded.

The conversation in question involved a brief introduction before they dived into talking about the current situation. At some point, Marcell, Alan Lusky, as well as a couple who Skye assumed were business executives in charge of the hotel, burst inside. A couple of security guards, including Marcell, followed them in, and Skye stood back to give them space. Lex also entered the room shortly after. Skye made eye contact with Marcell, managing a shy wave in his direction. Marcell mouthed a "hey" and that was that.

"How long do you think we ought to stay up here?" Franco questioned at some point.

"To be perfectly safe," the radio controller answered, "three months. Reasonably, two months. At a bare minimum, a month and a half."

Franco whistled. "That's a long time."

"Our models think it should be mainly clear by then. The fallout was much heavier than we anticipated. Not to mention the wildfires that scorched God knows how many miles of land across the world."

"And what about the losses? Any news about what cities were hit?"

"Almost every major city suffered a direct strike, from Los Angeles to New York. It's had a crippling effect on infrastructure as well as governmental organization. Initial reports say that our defense systems only managed to stop the first nine of fifty-three strikes. The situation is FUBAR. That means-"

Alan Lusky stepped forward, leaning into the microphone.

"We know what that means. I can imagine President Chu declared martial law immediately, then," Alan Lusky reasoned.

"President Chu? She's missing, presumed dead. Washington D.C. was devastated more than almost anywhere else on Planet Earth."

"She's dead?" Alan Lusky asked. One of the executives leaned over and whispered into Alan Lusky's ear, and then he spoke up. "That's confirmed now? Okay then, what about the Vice President?"

"Same news. He's gone."

Skye's heart sank. President Violet Chu, and Vice President Hugh Boone were both gone for good. She'd voted for them for the 2048 election cycle, and now they were both dead.

If the President of the United States, and the Vice President, with the best intel of the entire planet, didn't manage to survive the destruction of the United States, then how could I even believe that it is possible my family is alive?

Skye felt sick to the stomach. Surely there had to be some kind of positive message. Some sort of sliver of hope to latch onto.

"Who's the President, then?" Lusky asked.

"Bruno Melero," The radio controller responded. "He was sworn in as Speaker of the House after Grace Elliott got killed up on your station, and survived the destruction unscathed."

"Is there any way I can get into contact with the president?" Alan Lusky asked. Skye raised her eyebrows at this question. Just who did Alan Lusky think he was, in the position to just hop on a call with the president of the United States?

"He's occupied with business, presently. He's on board the S.S. Washington, if I'm not mistaken."

"The S.S. Washington? You're telling me that their spaceship made it into orbit?"

"Yes."

Alan Lusky mumbled under his breath. "Why in the hell haven't we heard anything from them, then?"

"Are there any functional airports we can make a landing in?" Alan Lusky inquired, this time speaking much louder.

"No," the radio controller replied. "We're not on the surface. I've heard Hawaii only got struck once, so that might be the safest bet in terms of not being dangerously irradiated. But even then, why go back down when you can stay in orbit in the ISH?"

The conversation stalled after that. Alan Lusky asked for some details for the bunker situation, to which it was explained that there were seven functional bunkers maintaining radio contact through the United States; and then it was only a couple of minutes more until the ISH lost contact with Earth and nothing but the sound of static came through. At that point, Alan Lusky ushered the executives out of the room into the hallway, but not before asking some questions first.

"How is it that we've only gotten into contact with them twice?" Lusky asked. "Shouldn't we contact more of them?"

"The radio receivers only work when they're aimed and calibrated properly," Franco replied. "And given we're still in active orbit, the prospect of maintaining contact for long is impossible. Especially since I'd guess some of the bunkers don't even have long distance radio."

Lusky nodded. "What a piece of work."

***

Alan Lusky looked oddly pale that same night when he asked Marcell to accompany him.

"Are you okay?" Marcell asked. "You look ill."

"I'm okay," Lusky told Marcell. "I think I must have eaten something bad. You don't need to worry about me."

"Of course," Marcell replied. "Are you sure you don't want me to stay and watch the door? Protect your family? Maybe you should stay in, too."

"What?" Alan Lusky asked. "Oh. Well, let me ask you something. Have you ever felt pinned between a rock and a hard place?"

"Of course," Marcell replied. "Who among us hasn't faced adversity?"

"I mean, now," Alan Lusky said. "Now that I'm in charge, I'm directly responsible for 246 people's lives. I say that after 41 people left with the escape pods a short while back. Which I know you weren't a fan of."

"Yes," Marcell replied. "That must be tough, having that responsibility."

Marcell had to hold his tongue. He let them go. He simply let them go despite the fact that Lusky, and the other executives, had admitted that they had no idea whether they would be safe in any way going back down.

"Did I make the right call appointing you as my bodyguard?" Lusky asked.

"I don't follow," Marcell remarked, confused. "What's going on?"

"Come with me," he said, taking him through the hallways of the ISH. Most of the hallways were rather dimly lit, and they were next to empty apart from a couple of other guards who Marcell acknowledged as they snaked their way past. Since the flat escalators had been powered off, the walk across the hotel took much longer than it would during the daytime.

Eventually, Alan Lusky stopped in front of Room 306, moving up to the door. Marcell dug deep into his memory to remember if anyone he knew lived in this room, but couldn't think of anyone.

"You wait here," Lusky said. "I need to have a conversation with someone. Make sure no one tries entering the room."

Marcell didn't even have a chance to respond until he was knocking on the door.

"Who is it?" A voice called.

"It's Alan Lusky, the CEO," Alan said. "Let me in."

The door flew open, and Marcell caught a glimpse of the man's face—he recognized the man as someone he'd seen in the comms room with Skye earlier in the day—before he beckoned Alan Lusky inside.

Lusky stepped over into the threshold, sneaking one glance back towards Marcell before the door slammed shut. Marcell wanted to step closer, press his ear onto the door. But orders were orders, and he stayed back, unable to hear what was being discussed at all.

Not much happened for a few minutes. Marcell grew restless for a couple of minutes. But then he heard the sound of a crash, and heard loud cries for help.

Marcell rushed over to the door, grabbing the door and yanking the handle and finding that it was locked tight. Of course it was—the doors always remained locked unless the settings for the doors were changed, which they hadn't been yet. Fortunately for Marcell, he carried around a master key and he was able to swipe it hurriedly over the card reader, throwing the door open.

Caught in a tangle on the ground, kicking and punching each other, was Alan Lusky and another middle-aged man. The other man appeared to have the upper hand in the tussle, and was on top of him, pressing his forearm down on his neck hard and delivering a smackdown.

"Hey!" Marcell asked, rushing over the scene. He could hear the door slam shut behind him.

"Get the fuck off me, Franco!" Alan roared, managing to buck him off and roll away, exasperated. It looked like there already was a large bruise on his cheek, and he was breathing heavily.

Franco wasn't letting up, though; he rushed forward, wrapping his arms around Lusky. It could've been a bear hug if it wasn't from behind, and if he wasn't lifting him off the ground. Marcell was there though, like a streak of lightning, prying him off like he was trying to rip a leech off human skin. Marcell was in top shape and his work-out regimen must've worked because he pulled him off of Alan, Franco screaming all the while.

Once Marcell pried Franco off, he threw him against the lamp, sending the lamp toppling over onto the carpet. Franco managed to stay on his feet. Marcell fought off Franco's punches and landed a punch to his jaw which snapped his head back and stunned him. He toppled over to the ground, and Marcell kicked him hard in the chest, once, twice, enraged at the show of defiance.

"You murderer!" Franco yelled, gasping for breath. "You really expect me to go along with your plan!? Monster!"

"Taze him!" Alan yelled. Marcell looked back at Alan, and in the window of time that it took, Franco had retaken his feet, smacking Marcell across the face and delivering a blow below the belt that led to him falling down onto his knees.

"Fuck," Marcell winced.

"I'm calling for back-up!" Alan was yelling, as Franco bolted for the exit.

Despite the agonizing pain, Marcell turned around and whipped out his taser from his belt, pulling it out and launching it towards Franco as he neared the door. The line launched over straight onto his back, sending him to the ground, his head slamming the door and his body falling to the carpet, twitching, as Alan Lusky pleaded for reinforcements over the radio.

Chapter 25

"You won't believe it," Skye told Madison the following morning. It was a Saturday morning, and they were eating their small rations of uniform pancakes with freeze-dried eggs. The eggs were runny and rather unsalted, the pancakes so chewy that they may as well have been a piece of taffy. The syrup was pretty much the only thing that made the meal palatable, so much so that Skye had almost drowned her plate in it. Graham set his tray down next to her with a forlorn look, not impressed with the food at all.

"You won't believe it, either!" Madison exclaimed.

"You first," Skye said.

"I think Minnie's pregnant."

"Pregnant?" Skye asked, her jaw dropping. "You don't mean to say… she got pregnant? How?"

"I mean, how do you think?" Madison asked, bringing her left hand into a circle and thrusting her right pointer finger in and out.

"Real mature," Graham commented, rolling his eyes. "Are you serious, though?"

"Yes," Madison replied. "The doctor kicked me out after she brought it up."

"So, what is she going to do then?" Graham asked.

"I don't know," Madison answered. "Like I said, I wasn't there. But assuming it's true, probably abort the thing."

"Idiots," Skye said. "Maddie, Graham. Can I be honest with you?"

"What's up?" Madison asked.

"Day that the shit hit the fan, The Red Day, Drake asked me out."

"No way," Madison replied. "How the hell have you kept that from us?"

"Yes way," Skye responded. "I don't know, I feel like that's something a little bit private."

"Good thing you said no," Graham said, frowning.

"Well, I wouldn't make a stupid decision like that," Skye replied. "I'm not about to stop using my head just because the world may be in trouble. I'm better than that."

Graham stared down at the table, not wanting to make eye contact with them. He was emotionally conflicted. Even though Madison's antics with the drugs a couple of weeks ago had agitated him, and certainly set him apart from Madison emotionally, he knew he was attracted to Skye.

"How was it?" Madison asked.

Skye looked up. "How was what?"

"His romantic gesture, him asking you out."

Skye blushed. "Extremely awkward."

Madison clucked her tongue. "You know, I'm not surprised. Still, part of me is surprised half the ship isn't banging all the time, with the world ending at all."

"That's because we're well behaved," Graham responded.

"You don't know what goes on behind closed doors," Madison countered.

"Oh yeah, speaking of closed doors, my news," Skye said. Her face fell a little bit as she recalled the conversation. "Chu and

Boone… They're presumed dead. Bruno Melero's the President. And a lot of the United States is wiped out, or next to wiped out, it sounds like."

"Are you sure about that?" Madison asked shakily. "Did they say anything about California?"

"No, they didn't say anything about California," Skye answered. "I'm sorry Maddie. But yes, I'm sure about it. It's official."

"Well, geez," Graham muttered. "Looks like things are really that bad, after all."

***

Skye was called to host a meeting the very next day between Alan Lusky and another executive, despite it being a Sunday. Skye had been in her room, alone. She'd borrowed a book from Graham, who had apparently brought up a few books, and was kicking her own legs back, finally starting to get into the science fiction novel she had recently acquired, when she'd received a knock at her door. Skye rolled off her bed, opening it up. She was surprised when she saw Lex.

"Hi," Lex said meekly. They looked pale, weak, and their hair was bedraggled.

"Is something wrong?" Skye asked.

"No," Lex replied glumly. "You have a meeting to go to, in forty minutes flat."

Then they gave them a room number, disappearing down the hallway.

Unlike last time's unexpected meeting, she wasn't asked to dress up; and, unlike this time, there wasn't an active kitchen to get drinks from, let alone place a phone call anymore. It reminded Skye of how much had changed in only the course of a month.

Inside the room, was Alan Lusky and another man she recognized from some of the meetings she'd attended.

She looked around for Marcell, knowing about his current role as the personal body guard for Alan Lusky through the window of the meeting room, but he was nowhere to be found. Alan Lusky raised his eyebrows.

"Looking for someone?"

"Oh, no," Skye lied. "I was just curious whether anyone else was coming in or not. It's just you two."

"Please, sit down," Alan Lusky replied. "It's just me and him."

"I really shouldn't," Skye hesitated.

"This is my friend, Ron," Alan Lusky said. "He's the CIO. Do you know what that means? Not that I would expect you to."

"I don't know," Skye said, hesitating. "Chief Intelligence Officer?"

"Close enough," Ron answered. "Chief Information Officer. I get all sorts of information. Obviously, I work with our computer systems. Our communications system. It's an important job. Without me, the International Space Hotel doesn't function."

"Okay," Skye said, not sure where this was going. "Is there anything you need me to do? Bring a drink? Perhaps I can grab you two some food?"

"I just… wanted to see you," Ron replied. "Mr. Lusky told me about you."

Skye gulped. She didn't like where this was going.

"Oh, don't be so stiff," Alan said, patting down on the seat of the chair. "Take a seat."

Skye pulled out the chair and sat next to Ron. The room was silent for a minute. Alan turned to Ron, as if he was waiting for him to speak.

"How has your stay been?" Ron asked.

"It's been an okay few weeks now," Skye said. "Just about as okay as the world ending can be. I've kinda lost track of time."

"As have I, as have I," Ron replied. "I can imagine, you've gotten quite lonely. You must miss your family."

"Yes."

"Me too. I miss them very much," Ron continued.

He leaned over and touched Skye in the leg, grabbing her around her thigh in a way that sent shivers down her spine. Skye pulled away, slapping at Ron's hand and jumping up from the seat. Ron sat up straight, stunned, as if the notion that she would reject his advances was completely unexpected.

"Stop it," Skye barked. "I was wondering what the hell this was all about, and this is it!? Trying to hook me up with one of your employees!?"

"I told you, she wouldn't like it," Alan Lusky chortled. "She is, unfortunately, one of the "good girl" types. Oh, well. It was worth shooting your shot."

"What is wrong with you!? What do you want with me?" Skye screeched, standing up.

"I want to help you," Ron said. "I really do. But in order to do that, you have to take my hand and accept your role as my wife."

"*Fuck* you!"

Skye turned to exit the room as fast as she could, but words from Ron stopped her in her tracks.

"You're going to regret it if you leave this room."

Skye turned around, bewildered by the threat. "*What*?"

"My wife isn't up here with me," Ron said. "She's down on Earth. Dead, I would wager. Just like everyone you know from home. But you and I, we're alive, and we're going to stay alive. If only you stay in this room, and hear me out like an adult. And do as I say, like an obedient housewife."

"You should listen to him," Alan Lusky warned. "For your own good."

"Or what?" Skye asked. "Just let him come onto me, the pervert? I have control over myself. I'm lonely, too. But you must be out of your *damn* mind if you think I'm going to my own bodily autonomy for you just because you say so. So, tell me: I should listen to you or what?"

Ron looked like he was going to say something, but Alan raised a finger to his mouth and shook his head. Skye didn't know what this apparent move of mediation meant, but she wasn't going to stick around to find out.

"Or you'll die alone," Ron threatened. "Longing."

"Better to die alone, than to die with shitty people," Skye retorted. She stormed out of the room, and this time, neither Alan Lusky nor Ron tried to stop her.

***

Alan Lusky pulled Marcell aside once he returned back to the hotel.

"I'm back from my meeting," he announced. "Come Marcell, sit with me." He gestured for him to take a seat next to him on the leopard print couch in the living room.

"Ah, sure, I mean, of course, sir," Marcell stumbled.

"Let me ask you something: if you had to get rid of any group on the International Space Hotel, then who would it be? I am, of course, saying if you absolutely had to due to dwindling resources."

"This is purely hypothetical?" Marcell asked.

"Of course," Alan Lusky answered.

"Okay," Marcell replied. "Because it doesn't sound very hypothetical to me."

"Work with me here."

"I guess I'd get rid of the most expendable group first, and then I'd work down from there."

"The interns?"

Marcell didn't like that question. Not at all.

"No," Marcell responded. "I wouldn't start with them. I'd start with the guests. The ones who can't give back. So, probably the old ones first."

"Fascinating," Alan Lusky replied. "Your logic is sound."

"The interns at least have a usage," Marcell answered. "They do provide labor for the ship, plus they are young and agile."

"Yes," Alan Lusky responded, but his face was wrinkled into a frown. "I don't imagine you have any personal stake in that answer, though."

"No," Marcell replied. "Why?"

"Forgive me for my prying eyes," Alan Lusky said. "But one time, after I let you go, I had another guard, I won't tell you who, shadow you. They told me that, at some point, an intern came up to your room, had a conversation with you. I had them track down who it was. Madison Flores, I believe her name is?"

"Don't confuse my kindness with friendship," Marcell lied through his teeth. His heart was racing, and he could feel beads of sweat forming on his forehead. "What you saw was an intern trying, unsuccessfully, to work out some kind of arrangement with me."

"Arrangement?"

Fuck. Fuck, Marcell thought, *I can't think of anything that would work in this situation, except for the truth.*

"Food," Marcell confessed. That part was true, and although he knew his deal with Madison and the others was through only shortly after even being made. "She wanted more food. Was asking about the situation. That's all."

"I'm going to be completely straight with you. We're down to 246 people on this ship," Alan Lusky replied. "That's simply too much."

"Why are you telling me this?" Marcell asked. "And what can I do about it?"

"Because good executives have to seek the advice from their underlings," Alan Lusky replied. "I decided to seek the advice of someone who wasn't directly in my line of management. I mean, all employees are technically under me, but I think you understand what I mean. I respect you. You saved my ass a few days ago, what with that one employee assaulting me. You may be my most trusted employee who isn't a chief officer or senior VP."

"I appreciate your words," Marcell replied. "I really do. But that's my job. And if I can ask, what *was* that about? He called you a murderer."

"We had a difference in philosophy," Alan Lusky responded vaguely, dodging the question. "Back to my point. There's 246, and I have to trim it down. What should I do?"

"How many of us can this ship sustain, long-term?"

"One-hundred," Alan Lusky said. "And that's off a subsistence diet, only around 1500 calories."

"Why do we have to decide now?"

"We have a week's food left," Alan Lusky said. "At that point, we'd have to start harvesting some food from the gardens. Obviously, our lab can continue churning out our genetically engineered meat, but that only produces so much. Maybe three days total factoring both in."

"Jesus."

"If only Jesus was with us, to feed all of us with however few loaves of bread and fishes," Alan Lusky said, sighing. "I'm not a bad guy, Marcell. I'm just struggling with my choice, how I want to do this."

"I had no idea the situation was this dire," Marcell said, and he hadn't. This was alarming.

"You see my problem? We usually have food shipments every single week here. We're already digging deep into our reserves of frozen food. Sure, we could cut the food size to stretch it out a few more days. People are already upset over how little they're being fed, though."

Lusky was right. The food portions for most of the guests, as well as low-level employees, was definitely more than enough to subsist on, but it was nothing to write home about. Madison made that clear when she had described to Marcell how the food was almost enough, but not satisfactory.

"You should have told me earlier. Honestly, you should've made the situation abundantly clear to all of the guests at the start of all this."

"And send everyone aboard into a panic?" Alan Lusky asked.

"Maybe they would, maybe they won't," Marcell replied. "Sooner or later, however, they're going to find out. You've had us lock up all the guns, confiscate pretty much all the knives on the ship. There's what, ten of us in security, including our manager, Fritz?"

"Yes. There's ten total."

"I think ten armed security guards, plus a few dozen other employees, can hold their own against a couple hundred rowdy, unarmed guests."

"That's your stance then? Tell them about how fucked we are?"

"Yes."

"What about the food? That doesn't solve the underlying problem of us starving to death."

"I don't know," Marcell said, hesitating. "Why can't we just all go back down when we run out of food, together?"

"You heard that conversation with the radio controller," Alan Lusky said. "We have to wait, at least two months, if we want to be safe. We'll probably run out within a couple of weeks if we keep everyone on board, and it'll only be a couple weeks after that we start dropping like flies."

"Maybe they're wrong."

"Sheesh," Lusky groaned, frustrated. "I'll shoot straight with you. I'm thinking of offloading some extra weight in a few days. Getting our count down to around a hundred. The remaining of us will stay the next two to three months, and then we will all return back to Earth once it's safe."

Marcell stared at Lusky.

"*What?*"

"You heard me right," Marcell said. "You promised me you were with me some time ago. Do you have any doubts about that?"

"What? No," Marcell replied. "Okay, so then, how do you suggest going about this? How do you choose who is worth keeping around, and who needs to go?"

"I've already ironed this out in our private meetings, which you were not in the room for," Alan Lusky said, handing Marcell a few pages stapled together. "Here's a hard copy of what we came up with."

Marcell flipped through some of the list. A list of names appeared in each section, arranged alphabetically by last name, also containing information about the person's own gender identity, age, and occupation. In the *clients* section, it seemed like one in three were marked 'Stay', the vast majority 'Exit'. In the *full-time employees*, a good deal was marked stay, apart from what looked like some lower-level staff like those who supervised the now-disabled robots or worked in the cleaning and hospitality crews. He also saw his own name among this list.

Marcell Hopkins | 24M | Senior Security Guard | Stay

Then he switched to the interns. A vast majority of them were marked for exit. He rolled his eyes down, quickly, so as to not draw attention from Lusky, but he managed to see the three interns who he'd stayed in contact with, interspersed between many of the other interns.

Skye Calvert | 20F | Communications Intern | Exit

Madison Flores | 21F | Medical Intern | Exit

Graham Scorsone | 20M | Electrical Engineering and Repair Intern | Stay

"What do you think about the list?" Alan Lusky inquired, as Marcell finished looking through the pages and looked back up to Lusky. "We have an even gender split, and most of the stay list is under fifty. I had to obviously keep the upper management and their family around, you know?"

Marcell felt a ball of panic in his stomach. What could he say?

"It's a good plan," Marcell said, nodding. He knew by Alan Lusky's fierce stare that he wasn't just looking for validation. That he was being tested.

"This will be done the most ethical way you can imagine," Lusky said. "They'll be given escape pods to go back down to Earth. If anything good ever came out of the Titanic, it was that all of our major boats and spaceships were over-endowed with emergency ships and pods."

Marcell nodded. "That's good, sir."

Alan Lusky stood up, patted him on the shoulder.

"I'm glad you're on board," Alan Lusky said. "Tomorrow, you're going to deliver the news to the security team while I work out some of the details with upper management and work out the semantics of this new Operation Exodus, as I call it."

"W-when? When is this going to happen?"

"When?" Lusky asked. He looked down at his watch. "Three days' time… So that's what… Wednesday?"

"I think so," Marcell answered.

Marcell gulped. He was scared: scared for the future of the ship, for his fellow guards and his own safety, and for everyone who would not be fortunate enough to stay and likely be given the equivalent of a death sentence by radiation poisoning. But oddly enough, that didn't hold a candle to what terrified him most of all from a personal standpoint.

What scared Marcell the most is that he knew he had to make a choice, to pick a side, and he didn't know what he would do.

Chapter 26

Only a few hours later, and Marcell found himself drinking alone at the bar.

Marcell remembered how back in his early 20s, he had always scoffed at those people who sat by themselves in bars at night, those who would sit alone in the interactive movie theaters and restaurants sipping their drinks and chowing down on their food with no possibility of human connection to anyone else except potentially via a phone. Only as he matured with age during his stay aboard the ship did he realize the importance of solitude and solace. Except now, he knew what he was experiencing wasn't solitude, but loneliness: deep, profound loneliness, the kind that would fester in his brain and cause him to sulk with each passing second that he dwelled on his realization.

Marcell was an outcast, no matter what way he cut it. No matter how many friends and family he surrounded himself with, in the very end, they would only go so far. Marcell's family was gone, dead. And despite being popular in college and high school, his stint on security with predominantly cis-men had gone surprisingly poorly. Marcell attributed this to the macho backwards culture and toxic work environment than anything else. Still, Marcell had dove headfirst into his work. And for what? Living, he guessed, a life that he was struggling through all alone.

But he wasn't entirely alone. The bar was packed with guests at this late hour, who were allowed a maximum of two drinks per adult using their card swipes. There wasn't much to do on board the ship anymore for the guests, and Alan Lusky's promise of training guests to help operate the ship had never been fulfilled. All the essential staff were too busy keeping the ship operating. This was not a surprise to Marcell. Time is money, and when it came to money, Alan Lusky was always cutting costs.

Cutting costs… Cutting lives. Marcell was now going to be an accomplice to that, and as much as he hated Lusky, he knew that loyalty was one of the most important virtues in the world. Marcell wasn't going to betray the ship. At least he would live. He just wished that there was as much food as alcohol on board so that no one would have to die.

Someone slid into the stool next to Marcell, clearing their throat, and Marcell turned, not sure what to expect.

He certainly didn't expect the frog-looking man. The man was familiar, only he looked even worse than last time: greasy hair, yellowed teeth, and a general B.O. stench that made him almost double take. It was the man from the party that Marcell had broken up, and now he was sitting beside him, a mixed drink in hand.

"It's you," the man said, clucking. "Well, isn't this quite a surprise?"

Marcell looked up at him, took a sip, and said nothing, looking ahead. There was nothing more to say.

"Did you feel good about that?" The other man pressed.

Marcell kept staring forward, where behind a glass panel a line of emptied alcohol bottles was exhibited. Standing in front of the transparent cabinet was a human-like android, only it contained several arms, splayed out like some kind of supervillain. The bartender had been disabled during the Red Day to conserve energy. It always did a good job at randomizing drink selections for Marcell. He wondered how much energy it would take for him to reboot it, just for one night. Just to get blackout drunk and pretend to be one with "the boys" at the night out.

"No," Marcell muttered, barely a whisper, and the man snorted.

"No, huh?" The man said, sipping. "That hits the spot. You know, I've thought about that night, and how I deserve an apology."

"Huh."

"You sack of shit. At least *look* at me." He slapped his hand down on the counter in tandem with the demand.

Marcell turned to him, saw his snarl, and sighed.

"Are you trying to start a fight again?" Marcell asked. "I'm not in the mood."

"No," The man replied. "I already told you."

"Patrick," Marcell said, "Please, leave me be."

"You remember my name," Patrick said matter-of-factly, and Marcell nodded. That warranted a slight smile, until his face hardened again.

"I came here for an apology, and I'm not leaving until I get one."

"I was following orders," Marcell hissed. "How difficult is that to understand?"

"You were rough, you attacked me. It was uncalled for. You could've let it slide."

"That's not what happened," Marcell replied. "You tried to punch us, and we arrested you. That's it."

"Trying to gaslight me into making this my fault, are you?" Patrick questioned. He tensed up, setting his drink down on the counter, and for a second, Marcell was certain there was going to be a fight again.

"I'm sorry," Marcell said, and Patrick looked shocked, easing back into his stool.

"I'm sorry for all of this shit," Marcell continued, "I'm sorry no one gives a shit about your opinion, and your freedom. I'm sorry for our negligent leader not training you all to be useful, as he promised, because he's too busy up his own ass. I'm sorry everyone's dead. I'm sorry that we can't get our own lives back."

Patrick was flabbergasted into silence for a few moments.

"Here, have the rest," Marcell said, sliding his half-empty glass of beer across the counter.

"Seriously?" Patrick asked, eyebrows raising.

"There's no backwash," Marcell promised. "Though I understand if you don't want to drink it. Germs and all."

"Fuck it," Patrick mumbled, accepting the glass and setting it in front of him, "I don't care. I'm at my limit for the night, and they weren't wrong when they said getting drunk is way easier in space."

"That it is."

The conversation died out, and Marcell was about ready to leave, now that he'd exhausted his allotted two swipes, only before he could swivel around, a comment to his side stopped him in his tracks.

"You look like you're fighting a battle inside, brother."

Brother. The word was so unexpected, that Marcell was almost shaken to the core.

"I… I don't know what to say," Marcell responded, turning back to face him.

"You don't have to say anything," Patrick answered, raising his own glass into the air and chugging the remainder of his own mixed drink down, a few driblets of his pink-looking beverage splashing onto his face and meandering down his scruffy chin like streams carving canyons in the mountains.

"No," Marcell agreed, "I don't. And I can't talk with the therapist, either."

"No," Patrick said. "Only therapy nowadays is booze… Only thing that's stopped me from trying to kill myself, between you and me."

Marcell nodded. "Question… Have you ever had to make a difficult decision, and there seems to be no correct answer?"

Patrick slammed his empty glass down onto the counter, and smiled. "Oh, for sure. All the time."

"Well, what's the right answer?"

"I dunno," Patrick said, reaching for the remaining beer. "Being a bit more specific would help."

"Let me put it like this. Do you go with your brain, or with your heart?"

Patrick thought deeply for a few moments. "Back in the day, your brain. Human rationality always would lead to the best outcome, least hurt emotions. But, nowadays, out in space…? With the whole world gone to hell? I say *fuck the brain*. The brain's done enough destruction to the planet already. I live with my heart, and I'll die with it too."

Marcell stood up, smiled. He knew what he had to do.

"Thank you, Patrick," Marcell said, as he turned around to go.

"Thank you… Hey? What's your name?" Patrick called.

Marcell turned around, waved before leaving.

"Marcell. My name is Marcell Hopkins, and I'm about to go live with my heart."

Chapter 27

It was a miracle that next day that, after unsuccessfully pounding on Skye and Graham's door, the third door opened. The only reason Marcell was even off the hook and able to try to make contact was that it was Alan Lusky's mid-day afternoon nap, which meant he had until precisely four to warn them about the impending plans. Following his night of reflection off at the bar, it was like he was almost busy with his assignment all day, every day.

When Lusky had gone to sleep and Marcell had wanted to leave, Lusky's wife and seven-year-old daughter had gone downstairs, making it impossible for Marcell to exit undetected. It wasn't until after three p.m. that he finally had a chance to leave, but time was ticking. He knew he had less than twenty minutes to return before the risk of getting caught and punished, potentially even executed, for leaking confidential plans became too great. Marcell had hardly slept the night before, burdened with the knowledge of the oncoming purge on board. For his conscience's sake, he knew he had to let someone know.

But Marcell had already tried knocking at Skye's door with no response. Now, he was hoping for a miracle, that Madison would happen to be home. "Open up! Fucking shit, open!"

The door opened, and Madison was on the other side.

"Thank God! You're not working!" Marcell said.

"Yeah," Madison said. "I've scaled back to three days a week, or when they need me. Nothing's as deflating as having to watch patients on suicide watch, let me tell you."

Madison looked up and saw Marcell's concerned expression, and was shocked. He pushed his way inside of the room, slamming the door shut behind him, but not before he'd checked to make sure there were no other security guards in the vicinity who could've possibly snitched on him.

"What's wrong?" Madison asked. "Marcell?"

"Listen to me," Marcell said, leaning over and grabbing her by the edge of the arms. He looked like a parent trying to make eye contact with their child, only his eyes weren't full of reproach or love, but of desperation, so pure and primal that it looked like he was being pursued by a deadly predator and wasn't standing in the International Space Hotel on a Monday afternoon.

"In two days, on Wednesday, shit's going to hit the fan," Marcell told Madison. "Operation Exodus."

"What? What are you talking about?" Madison asked. "Hold on. Slow down."

Marcell let go, pacing around the room anxiously. He impulsively pulled at what little hair was on his head, and then he scratched at his beard as if there were lice crawling on his face.

"They're going to kick you out," Marcell said, deciding to be as direct as possible. "You and Skye. Graham is on the list, so he's safe."

"The list?" Madison asked. "What list?"

"Gah," Marcell said, checking on his phone. "I don't have a lot of time until I have to go. But I'll try to explain."

"Okay," Madison replied.

"It's Monday now. On Wednesday night it's going to happen. They're going to remove you from the ship and send you back down to Earth."

"What?" Madison questioned. "How? Why?"

"They're running out of food next week," Marcell said. "They're taking matters into their own hands. If they keep everyone on board, then we'll starve out in the next few weeks."

"I'm confused," Madison responded. "They're sending us to Earth to kick us out. Isn't that a good thing?"

"No, it's not good," Marcell disputed. "The Earth isn't safe right now. Not yet. Not for weeks more. If you go down right now, your skin will probably melt off and you'll die an excruciating death."

Madison's face flashed a look of fear. "I don't like what you're saying."

"Yeah, well, me neither. I'm trying to think of ways of saving you, but I can't think of any."

"Okay," Madison replied. "Tell me more."

"It'll happen Wednesday night. They have a list of people who they're going to remove, and like I said, you and Skye are going to be on the list. They're trimming down to 100 people."

"That can't be feasible," Madison offered. "They can't just get rid of all of us. There's too many of us, and most of us won't agree. I definitely won't, the way you've described the situation."

"You don't have a choice," Marcell responded. "They'll lock all the doors at once at night, so you can't exit your rooms. Then we'll go and clear out all the rooms we need, one by one. There's ten of us armed security guards and we'll be able to help and tie up everyone as needed, and then we launch all of you all out through the escape pods. Just like that, it'll be too late."

"You can't seriously go along with this…" Madison said, shaking her head. "That sounds like murder."

"I didn't have a choice!" Marcell insisted. "Look, I'll help you if I can. I just knew I needed to tell you, to help you all have a chance. This isn't right. Alan Lusky isn't God, but he sure is acting like it. We don't have a right to decide who gets to live and who dies. That's wrong."

"So why are you telling me this?"

"I have a conscience," Marcell said. "I'm trying to save you."

"What do I do?" Madison asked, desperate. She felt shivers running down her spine, and the panic was growing with each passing second.

"I don't know!" Marcell barked, pacing around the room and looking back at the door.

"Maybe I can go and warn everyone," Madison said.

"No, Maddie," Marcell begged. "Please don't do that. If you do, then there'll be an investigation about who leaked it, and they'll find out about me going to your room. You'll screw all of us over, and it won't do anything except maybe delay it a few days."

"Okay," Madison said. "You have my word. I won't be a whistleblower."

Marcell checked his phone, shaking his head in disbelief.

"You can tell Graham, and Skye," Marcell said. He dug out a keycard from his pocket and handed it to Madison. "I don't know why I'm doing this, but I don't think I can do this alone. You might have a better shot of maybe somehow fixing this, of somehow stopping this, with you and the others. You seem like a bright bunch. Here's my master keycard. It works in every single room in the building, unless the keycard is remotely disabled. Which it shouldn't be, unless it is reported as missing. Which I won't do, obviously."

"Wouldn't this leave a… digital footprint?" Madison asked.

"The ship's security doesn't check when keycards are activated, so as long as you don't draw suspicion upon yourself, there'll be nothing to find. Essentially, they won't be checking on Wednesday, and, knowing how security has been the last couple of weeks since the Red Day, we won't even be looking at the logs at all."

"Thank you," Madison said. "What about you? How will you get around without this?"

"I have a couple other ones," Marcell said, pulling out two more keycards. "A personal keycard, and one for Lusky's room. I'll be fine."

"Okay," Madison said.

"I have to leave now. I'll try and catch you or Skye again if I can. If I can't, know I'm going to try to help you, in whatever way I can without endangering myself. They can't get away with this."

Madison didn't know what to say. So, she just stared as Marcell turned around and left the room without another word. Madison groaned when he had gone, collapsing onto the bed and curling up into a ball like some sort of armadillo.

A great blackness formed around her vision, around her heart, over the next few minutes.

I'm going to die, Madison realized. It felt like how she'd felt weeks ago, on the Red Day, but somehow worse, and more draining. Because even though then, she knew that there had been a switch that had been pulled, a point of no return, that had uprooted her life so much, at least then she had clung onto hope. Skye had comforted her; so too had Graham; and they were her friends. But now, there was no hope. They were going to send her back down to die, as Marcell had predicted would happen if they returned. That was it. Two days left to live, an impossibly difficult situation. It may as well have been like they were trying to solve two equations with three unknown variables, that was how hopeless they were. And Marcell had told her, of all people, thinking she had a solution to the situation. They were going to be abducted by ten people with guns.

What the hell does Marcell think I can do?

With this newfound realization clouding Madison's brain, there came an urge, an insatiable hunger that spread through Madison's body. The reaction wasn't just emotional; it was physical, too, bleeding over in the form of fatigue in her limbs. She prayed she wasn't getting hooked onto the opiates again. But she also knew that there was nothing left that she could do, so she may as well give in to the temptation. It sounded better than wallowing in her own misery like Kyra had before she'd killed herself, after all.

The urge was so strong that, before Madison knew it, she was digging underneath her table again for some of her stolen drugs as eagerly as a prospector in the Gold Rush would have sifted through their wide pans for nuggets of gold. This time, Madison needed something strong to numb the pain, and when her hands closed around a vial of morphine, she knew it would do the trick. She grabbed a needle she had stolen from work some days ago, grinned. She didn't know what was going to happen—she actually hadn't tried it before—but she couldn't care less, because she *needed* it.

Chapter 28

Graham noticed something was off when he was looking through circuitry. He and Yusef, along with Mr. Xiong, were working on a trivial repair in the front cabin of the ship, when, among the bunches of red and yellow cords that snaked around like dense vines through the rivets of a jungle, he noticed something had been disconnected.

"Look at that," he said, pointing further back to a couple of wires which had evidently been pulled from socket plugs.

"What?" Mr. Xiong asked.

"I see what he's talking about," Yusef said. "We should plug it back in."

"Oh, no," Mr. Xiong said, shaking his head. "You don't need to worry about that."

"But sir," Graham asked, confused. He stood up and saw what no longer was drawing electricity. There was a button on the dashboard that no longer glowed like most of the other ones. And etched on the top of it were the words *ALARM*. "It's the alarm system. And it's just unplugged. That's strange."

"Of course it is," Mr. Xiong said, sighing. "Look, with everyone on edge. There's no reason to activate an alarm anyway. If there's an alarm, it'll do nothing but spread a panic."

"It's intentional?" Graham asked, confused.

"And we should leave it?" Yusef chipped in.

"No," Mr. Xiong said, backtracking on what he'd said a second before. "Plug it in, obviously. Now that I think about it, I'm sure it was a mistake."

Graham frowned as he plugged it in. That didn't sit right at all. And now that he thought about it, he had seen a lot of other engineers and electricians early in the morning, both in the electrical room, engineering facility, as well as roaming the hallways. But that didn't make any sense or explanation to some alarm being unplugged.

Graham couldn't connect the dots. There was no apparent reasonable explanation to what was happening, so he just wrote it off as an accident and went about his business.

***

Skye tried knocking on Room 115 multiple times, with no luck.

"Maddie!" She called, again and again.

But there was no response at all. The lights were off, too, indicating to Skye that she was either fast asleep, or gone out of the room. But it was early in the evening, and she hadn't been to dinner at the cafeteria at all.

After trying for a couple of minutes, she left to her room, ready to maybe settle down for another chill evening of relaxation. But she was too full of curiosity and decided to knock on Graham's door.

"Hey," Graham answered.

"Hi," Skye said. "How are you?"

"Okay," Graham replied. "You?"

"Good. I read that book you recommended. The one about the dude with the predictive powers and the time traveling."

"Ah. Good choice. That's one of my favorites. Well, no, it isn't, I should clarify. It's one of my favorite light science fiction novels, which isn't what I read too much."

"I have a question," Skye said. "Have you seen Madison today?"

"Now that I think about it, no," Graham replied. "I didn't see her at breakfast, or dinner, either."

"I haven't seen her since dinner yesterday. I'm worried for her."

"Oh, Skye," Graham said. "You're kind. But you're a worrywart. I'm sure she's just been busy with the doctors."

"This is uncharacteristic of her," Skye replied. "She always eats lunch and dinner with me, and they scaled back her hours with the internships, so I don't know why she wouldn't at least say hi."

"I guess so," Graham said. "Do you want to go look around for her? Maybe we can try knocking on her door again."

"I tried," Skye said. "Maybe we can reach out to Marcell, and get his master card."

"Yes, but remember what Madison said? She said he got moved to protect Alan Lusky or something. I don't think we'll be able to find him if we even want to."

"Yeah," Skye said. She flipped her hair in a way that Graham didn't know she did because she was angry, or because somehow, she was attracted to him, exhibiting herself like a dancing male peacock would show off its colorful blue feathers to a mate.

Or maybe she's just getting the hair out of her eyes, Graham concluded. *Yeah, I'd say that's the most likely option.*

"Let's go look around for Marcell," Graham said, and the two friends set off to go look for him in the hallways of the ship.

***

It had started with a feeling that was good. So unbelievably good, Madison couldn't put it into words how good she had felt.

Pure happiness had never been obtainable in Madison's life. It was as evasive and mystical as the searches for the El Dorado and Fountain of Youth must've felt to the colonists a half millennia ago.

There had been waves of pleasure. Pure euphoria, better than full-body orgasms, better than anything she'd ever felt before. But it became apparent that she must've put in more into her syringe than she should've in her haphazard, careless state. Her breathing grew shallow, and she soon passed out completely. Although it was all buried under an angelic feeling, like she'd been floating in heaven, that feeling disappeared as quickly as it had arrived. Instead, it was replaced with nausea, with muscle pain and a sense of detachment and time displacement.

Madison woke up drenched in sweat, her sheets damp. It was readily apparent because of the smell that she'd wet her own bed, but it turned out that was pretty much the least of her concerns.

"Oh God," she said, gasping for air. "Oh God. What have I done?"

Something was missing, and she couldn't remember what. It was extremely strange. She knew she had to get up, get herself together, and yet she couldn't concentrate, couldn't focus or remember for the life of herself what she had forgotten. Within a minute, she was running over to the bathroom, throwing up into the porcelain for a good minute straight. When it was finished, it felt like the sickness had been purged from her stomach. She flushed the cloudy yet relatively clear fluid, and then she ran the sink for a good minute before drinking. She was parched, so much so that she felt like she'd just completed a strenuous desert expedition rather than taken a nap.

Because I didn't take a nap, Madison thought. *I was high.*

Madison's head was spinning, and she rushed back into the bed before anything. She saw the needle sitting on the nightstand, and there was a flicker of memory, of something so awful that was going to happen, and some attempt at escape, but then she felt herself pulled under the feeling of sickness and wrongness and she was back asleep before she knew it.

***

Meanwhile, in the corner of one of the hallways, Marcell had pulled aside another security guard to interrogate him. It was the Fourth of July 2048, marking the 272nd year of America. If you could say America even existed. Marcell was still in the gray when it came to exactly what the country's status was, and he didn't much enjoy thinking about it. In his head, everything was okay, and his brother Reese had led a prison breakout, and returned to the countryside with his family, living like the old Pioneers, except with much more advanced farming methods.

This supposition was, of course, preposterous. But if any intrusive thoughts suggested otherwise, Marcell always pushed them away.

Usually, the fourth of July celebration would entail an American-themed dinner in the Entertainment Hall for all guests willing to purchase the tickets, as well as all staff, who were given these same tickets free of charge. Marcell wanted his artificially grown ribs, baked potato, and craft beers: but there was no opportunity for that this year. All that existed was preparation for the oncoming Operation Exodus, the constant meetings with the other security guards and with Alan Lusky. Even though Marcell hadn't gotten the chance to talk to Skye and Graham since he'd contacted Maddie (he didn't have much free time at all), he demanded answers for himself. To know what had happened to the man who he'd seen fight with Alan Lusky.

"Come on, Joshua. I think I deserve to get some answers," Marcell said. "Everyone I've talked to said that you know."

Joshua cracked his knuckles, sighed. "Come on, Marcell. What good would come from me spilling the beans? Who are you, Sherlock?"

"I'm higher ranking than you," Marcell said. "I can discipline if you don't tell me."

"Which is bullshit," Joshua mumbled. "I'm older than you, and have worked here longer. Yet you're higher ranking than me."

"I'll put in a good word for management, if you just hurry up and tell me."

"Really?" Joshua asked, and then he sighed. "Fine, what the hell. I guess you'll find out one way or another. We put him through the garbage chute. I was told it was treason, and that I had to keep it under the wraps. We launched him out the back, so no one would know. You want to know what happened to him? He's dead."

Marcell was quiet. "You really are so nonchalant about it."

He shrugged. "It's a dog-eat-dog world, bro. Especially now that Lusky's our leader. Why are you acting so virtuous? I was just following orders, man."

"I'm not acting virtuous," Marcell stated. "Thank you for telling me."

Marcell walked away, holding his tongue from saying more and losing his cool. He hoped Alan Lusky was going to get his comeuppance with Maddie's plotting, or he'd have to do something drastic himself.

***

When Madison woke up again, her head was far clearer, and she felt much better. She groaned, stretched her arms. She looked at the clock nearby, which read that it was 9:36 p.m.

A whole day wasted, she thought.

Madison was, once again, extremely dehydrated and starving. Fortunately for her, the most recent (and final) drop off by Marcell had yielded them some snack bars, so she ate the last protein bar she had before going over to the sink and drinking what felt like half a liter of water. When her thirst was quenched, she moved back over to the nightstand.

Madison tried to turn on her phone, but found quickly that the phone was out of battery. Instead, she decided to plug it in. As the phone powered on, she got out of the sheets and headed into the bathroom, where she washed off, switched out of her clothes into a new comfortable outfit, slipping her crucifix necklace on before brushing her teeth. Manual toothbrushes had been encouraged from the very beginning, so she'd brought her own up to the ISH. As she manually scrubbed her own teeth, she felt like she was cleaning an alien. Did people seriously use to brush their teeth every day by hand? When she was finished, she clasped her crucifix necklace, grateful to be alive.

Her memory had been so spotty before, but now she remembered what had happened, what that needle contained: it had been morphine. It had been excellent at first. More excellent than she ever could have hoped. But it was clear that she hadn't known her limits and had injected more than was safe. That likely explained the adverse effects from earlier.

Stupid, stupid. I was showing symptoms of overdose. I could've died, Madison thought. *Never again, not until it's safe. Not until we deal with this.*

Madison knew she still had a duty to warn Graham and Skye about what was to come. She didn't see any solutions, but knew Graham was a smart cookie and Skye was a woman of action. They would figure it out, together. When Madison returned back at the bed, she checked her phone, figuring she would probably have a better chance at checking in with them tomorrow, given how late it was.

Then she gasped. Wednesday, July 5th, 2048. 9:50 p.m.

Madison hadn't slept for a day. It'd been two days.

Madison had ten minutes to reach their room before curfew was imposed, and the window of opportunity for saving them was closing quickly. She didn't know why, but she grabbed her phone, and the needle. She didn't fancy getting caught red-handed with a sharp needle in her hand by security, however, so she first packed it hurriedly, hoping the needle wouldn't pierce through the sides of the bag. It did.

Chapter 29

Madison pounded Skye's door like her life depended on it. Probably because she thought it did. She was fortunate that the hallway in the vicinity was empty, and there were no guards to assess her behavior or check her bag. Otherwise, she was certain she would've drawn a suspicion unlike any other.

"Skye! Skye!"

Skye answered the door quickly, flinging the door open.

"Maddie!" She gasped, her face rapidly changing, from worry, to surprise, to joy. "Oh, thank God! I haven't seen you at all in two days! You're all dressed up in pajamas already?"

She wrapped up Madison in a hug which Madison returned until breaking out of it a second later, remembering the urgency of the situation.

"Where's Graham!?" Madison asked.

"What? Next door!"

Madison ran out the door, veered to the side.

"Other way!" Skye called.

Madison switched back to the other room, Room 33, and Graham, luckily, also answered the door.

"Hey," Graham told her. "Skye was worried sick."

"Come on! We need to get in Skye's room! Quick!"

"What are you talking about?" Graham asked. "The curfew's in a couple minutes."

"Exactly! Just trust me!" Madison begged. "Please listen to me."

"I trust you," Graham offered, hurrying out as soon as he went and grabbed his phone. Skye was standing at the threshold of her room and, confused, was firing off questions to Madison, but Madison wasn't having any of it.

"Close the door," Madison said. "Now! And lock it!"

Skye listened, locking the door at Madison's behest. Madison just wished that there had also been a chain as well, but unlike all the hotel's she'd visited on Earth, there was not (for security purposes, or so they were told).

"Okay, okay," Madison said. "Now let's head over to the couch and away from the door. Hit the lights."

Even though Skye was still extremely confused, she listened.

The trio moved over to sit on the couch. Madison sat in the middle, which meant that her left arm was next to Skye, who grabbed it once she took a seat.

"My God, look at your arm," Skye said, examining her arm, which was lit in the dim light coming out of Graham's phone's flashlight.

"Stop," Madison complained. "You're inspecting me like you're a doctor. I'm the medical intern here, and I can tell you that I'm fine."

"Well, it looks like you got shot with a needle," Skye replied.

Graham looked aside in shame. "I told you it was a bad idea."

Skye whipped around to Graham. "The hell do you mean? You mean you knew about this!? Why wouldn't you tell me?"

"She told me to keep a secret!" Graham answered apprehensively.

"Jesus," Madison said. "Smooth, Graham, smooth."

"Well, it's in the open now," Graham said. "So, we may as well fess up to it."

"We have more important things to do than talk about my bad habits," Madison replied.

"But you're using, aren't you?" Skye asked. "Drugs? What type of drugs?"

"I'm okay," Madison promised. "Yes, Skye, that's why I was out for a couple of days. It was just morphine… But I took a little bit too much, so I might've not been feeling very well yesterday. I don't really remember yesterday at all, actually."

"How did you even obtain that to begin with?" Skye asked, her eyes widening.

"We lifted some stuff from the pharmacy," Graham answered. "A few weeks ago, right around the Red Day, I'd reckon."

Skye shook her head.

"You are addicted…" Skye grumbled. "You need rehab. But you, Graham, you're an asshole."

"She told me to keep a secret! She had me take an oath! That's sacred. Right?" Graham asked, second-guessing himself.

"Shut up," Madison interjected. "Shut up, please. Skye, don't be mad at Graham. I totally manipulated him into staying silent. Yes, I'm a junkie, I have issues. But I'm sober now. And we have bigger problems. Like everyone about to be forcibly removed off the ship tonight."

"What?" Skye questioned. "What do you mean, Maddie?"

"I mean, we're getting kicked out today, if we can't think of anything. Did Marcell make contact with you guys the past couple of days?"

"No," Graham said. "We tried getting in touch with Marcell the past day or so. Couldn't find him at all."

"Shit…" Madison replied. "What am I kidding? If he'd have made contact, you would both probably be in a lot worse moods, and you wouldn't be questioning me so much."

"You're scaring me," Graham commented. "Madison, what's going on?"

Madison pulled out the needle from the bag, using her light to illuminate it before setting it out on the nightstand.

"Woah," Graham exclaimed. "That's… sharp."

"I brought this as a weapon," Madison replied. "Damned thing almost poked me in the hand multiple times. But I brought it in case we needed it. I mean it's sharp, and with a well-placed strike to the brain or neck, it could kill someone."

"Kill…" Skye asked. In the dim light illuminated by the flashlight, Madison could read the fear in her eyes.

Madison explained the situation to Graham and Skye over the course of the next few minutes. How the plan was to lock their front doors, and then, room by room, clear out as many of the non-essential individuals as possible. How both herself and Skye were on the list, although Graham would be safe. How he had given her a master card to bypass security into rooms.

"They have some ethics about it," Madison explained at one point. "They'll at least send us down in escape pods, rather than eject us out the garbage chute. Probably to clear their consciences. So then, we might survive for at least a few days or weeks until we die of radiation sickness or being killed by some starving cannibals."

Then she told them about how Marcell had met her and said he would try to help them in any way he could. But that he had no idea how to solve the situation, and that he hoped they would find a way. That he put his faith in them.

"You really screwed us," Graham stated matter-of-factly once she had finished recapping everything that had happened a couple of days ago. "Royally. Madison, if what you're saying is true, then it's happening, tonight. Pardon my French, we're *fucked*. We're dead."

"No," Madison replied. "I'm dead, and Skye's dead. You're on the list to stay."

Graham fell silent.

"Hold on," Skye said. "There's one way to test if what you're saying is true."

Skye moved over to the front door, unlocking the door and tugging at the handle. Despite her best efforts, the door remained locked shut.

"Just as you predicted," Skye said. She turned on her phone to check the time, and the glow of light revealed her panicked expression. "The front door is locked. There's no way out of the room, even if we want."

"Oh, shit," Madison said. "Guys, what do we do? How do we get out of this?"

"I don't know," Graham responded. "That might've been a viable question with an answer if you'd asked it, I don't know, two days ago!"

"Jesus. Well, I'm sorry!"

"You really had to go and shoot yourself up," Graham groaned. "At such an important time. It was the most important time of your entire life to stay sober, and you didn't. I'm ashamed for you."

"Come on! We can think of something! I believe in us," Madison said, turning to Skye, who was sitting there, silently. "We can stop them."

"What? You think this is some kind of joke?" Graham asked. "Let's just stroll out there, magically knock out everyone with our force powers, and then take control of the ship? If only we could do that, because that's pretty much the only solution I can think of."

Madison's jaw dropped. "That's it… You genius."

"What? I'm a genius? How?" Graham asked, confused. "I was joking… I'm not Darth Scorsone, and I don't think taking control of the ship is a good idea."

"No," Madison clarified, shaking her head. "We knock them out. That's how we do it."

***

Madison remembered the Noxium from her interaction with Sarah, and explained how they stored it in the pharmacy, with the keys from the same location that Graham had seen her take from the back of the room when she'd raided the cabinet.

"There's also this," she added, taking out the master card. "This master key allows access to pretty much any room, according to Marcell. We can use this to our advantage."

"That… might work," Graham admitted. "If we can get that and plug it through the system from the Oxygen Center, then it would diffuse through and knock out all the guards. Allow us to take control of the ship."

"It's a slim chance," Skye replied. "But you're telling me that they just leave knockout gas sitting there, in a pharmacy? Wouldn't that be in the armory or barracks, whatever you call it?"

"I know," Madison answered. "It seems like that. It has a medical purpose, though. I'm pretty sure it can knock people out to conserve oxygen."

"There's a far bigger problem," Skye said. "How are we even supposed to get out there in the first place? The door to the hallway is locked."

"You need to hide," Graham said, standing. "Oh, no… We should've gone in my room. Darnit!"

"Why?" Skye asked.

"Because they might not check my room," Graham said. "Now that we're in your room, they'll be coming here to take you out. We could've all just hidden in my room and possibly gotten away without them exploring it at all. They're guaranteed to go in here."

"Fuck…" Madison groaned. "You're right. But we can use this to our advantage… We just need to concoct the right plan."

"How?" Skye asked.

"We gotta think of something, and quick," Graham insisted.

***

"You ready guys?"

Marcell directed the question towards the other security guards: Joshua, Audrey, and Sylvester. Tonight was the night of reckoning, and Marcell knew that there was a distinct possibility that something unpleasant awaited on the other side. They were entering Room 33, which was Skye's room. Marcell hoped that the plan Madison and her friends had devised did not involve indiscriminately attacking them.

"Yessir," Audrey affirmed, and then, with another directed nod, she tapped the keycard onto the card reader, automatically unlocking the door and allowing passage inside as the four rushed inside.

The lights were out, and Sylvester flipped them on all the way as they called in for them to get up and exit the room, Joshua and Audrey pointing their tasers out into the room.

Marcell felt his heart race at the sight of Graham sleeping underneath Skye's covers.

What the hell is he doing? Marcell asked internally. *What kind of boneheaded plan was this?*

Joshua, Audrey, and Sylvester rushed forward to detain him, seize him in their grip. He woke with a start, shouting and flailing in their grip and landing a kick that smacked Joshua in the head before he got his hands around his leg and pulled him out. Graham was still fully clothed, which indicated to Marcell that he must've been planning something. Either that, or he was potentially overthinking things vastly and they hadn't planned for anything at all.

"This isn't the person we're looking for!" Sylvester remarked, while Audrey saw amidst the commotion, movement from underneath the bed and pointed under it.

"Look! Look!" Audrey shouted.

There was a commotion, a struggle, a scream, and Audrey had tackled Madison, much to Marcell's chagrin, bringing her down from behind with perfect form, like a linebacker tackling a slow running back. Madison had tried hiding, and had failed.

"Oh my God! Stop!" Madison shouted. "Stop! Stop! Help!"

"Are we sure this is her?"

"That's her!" Marcell lied. "It's gotta be, I checked the records."

"Is there anyone else hiding out?" Sylvester asked. "We can't be sure, after finding this guy."

"Don't you touch my girlfriend!" Graham called out aggressively. "Just leave her be! Take me instead!"

Marcell was satisfied by Graham's acting skills.

"I'll scope out the bathroom," Marcell said, knowing that there was a non-zero chance that Skye was hiding inside (they hadn't yet checked her room).

Madison and Graham. Come on, Skye. Come on.

Marcell flicked on the lights to the bathroom, stepping inside and closing the door slightly behind him. He pulled back the shower curtain and almost screamed, his heart pounding like a snare drum.

Skye stood there, a needle in hand, raised high in the air, like she was ready to arc it down and plunge it into his heart: but she saw him and stopped, covering her mouth and preventing her from saying anything or letting out a cry. Her eyes were red as if they were full of tears, and Marcell tried his best to let her know things would work out.

"It's okay," Marcell tried mouthing to Skye, but then he knew he had other matters to attend to, and he flicked off the lights, but not before re-adjusting the shower curtains to conceal Skye's presence.

"I got this guy's keycard," Sylvester said, and Marcell scanned it. It was a match in the system, as he expected. Graham Scorsone.

"Should we take him in?" Audrey asked.

"No witnesses," Joshua said. "I say we do."

"No," Marcell said. "He's on the list. He stays."

"But-"

"I'm the lead here. We do as I say," Marcell asserted. "Unless any of you take issue with my decision?"

But the other three guards didn't, and they shook their heads, and clicked the handcuffs onto Madison. One of them would escort her back to the prison; while the remaining three would move onto the next designated room, hopefully with another person having returned from dropping off their individual into the holding cell.

"No! *Graham*! Please don't take me! *Please*!"

"Maddie! No! Take me instead…"

The four dragged her out in handcuffs. Graham sank to the ground in defeat, crying, and Marcell felt his heart melt a little bit, because he knew now that Madison and Graham weren't acting anymore. He just wished he could tell Graham that he had a chance, however slim it was; but he wasn't about to blow his cover.

So instead, Marcell looked back one last time to see Graham. Graham was sitting upright on his knees, his face rather blank apart from his mouth which was formed in a grimace, and his eyes looked like they were welling with tears. He hurriedly propped the door open by nudging his shoe on the door prop, setting it down to keep the door open just a smidge.

Then Marcell walked away, using all of his collective willpower to not break down into tears on the spot. He didn't know why he cared so much, and figured it was perhaps because of how helpless he was to stop his superiors; but maybe it was because, finally, he had started to grow out of the shell that he'd been encased in for so long. The shell of self-centeredness and mistrust that had plagued him for so long, like a chronic, festering illness, finally, no longer controlled him.

Godspeed kids, Marcell thought, *my hopes rest with you.*

Marcell knew he was pathetic for his own inaction, yet he clung to these hopes all the same.

Chapter 30

"Graham! Graham!"

Skye shook Graham for a few moments until he stirred and climbed back onto his feet.

"Are you ready?" She asked.

"Yes…" He said, nodding. His face was a visage of darkness that, despite the bleakness of it all, was more determined than she'd ever seen. "We have to do this. For Maddie."

"We need to go out… But how do we know what to do first? Where to go?"

"The pharmacy, first," Graham said. "I've looked at a lot of schematics and layout of the ship, as well as walked a lot around it for my job. It's in the center of the ship, equidistant from both ends. That's where we go, first. Then we go to the oxygen center. That's in the back of the ship, with most of the other utilities."

"Okay…" Skye said quietly, before pointing to the door. "Look at that, Marcell even propped the door open for us."

"Thank God," Graham said.

"I wish I could thank Marcell for this. If the door had been closed, there would've been nothing we could do."

"We'll thank him by saving Maddie."

"Amen to that."

***

They first opened the door by Skye pushing it a few inches, just enough for her to sneak her hand with the master card through the crack of the door and bypass the card reader. It unlocked with a small click, allowing them to exit the room. They checked whether the coast was clear, and when they saw that it was, they then closed the door behind them and ran as fast as they could. Graham now had the master card, and Skye had the needle, which she held down and off to the side, hoping she wouldn't trip and accidentally kill herself.

The hallways were dim, and the lights were turned down to almost their bare minimum. The flat escalators were turned off, no doubt to conserve energy while security patrolled at night, and the hallways were eerily quiet apart from the slapping of their feet. But at one point, Graham stopped in his tracks, and Skye followed suit, deeply exhaling for a few moments as she caught her breath.

If anyone was actively watching the cameras and monitoring the screen, it was probably already too late. There was nothing they could do to hide from the cameras. All they could do was move, making Graham's pause all the weirder.

"Let me test something," Graham said, and then he yanked the fire alarm he had located in the hallway. Nothing happened at all.

"Just as I suspected," he murmured.

"What?" Skye asked. "Why?"

"They didn't want anyone raising the alarm," Graham explained, before taking off once again, Skye following "I… they planned this out. A couple of days ago, I saw a lot of people out and about… I guess they were preparing. I should've seen this coming."

Within the course of a couple of minutes they reached the pharmacy. The front gate had been lowered, and, for a few moments, Skye was certain that they were doomed. But the master card was clutch and delivered results, as a little scanner near the handle of the gate of the meant that the entire gate rolled up. When they were inside, they lowered the gate again behind them.

Skye set down the needle when they were inside, using her phone to illuminate the drawer that Graham slid open as he dug through it.

"Are you sure it's in there?" Skye asked after what seemed like a minute of rummaging through the drawer.

"It has to be," Graham replied, until he finally pulled out a ring of keys. "I mean, surely… Thank God!"

"Great," Skye commented.

They walked up to the cabinet, where a metal keyhole separated both of them from the inside. Graham tapped the keycard to the hole, and, of course, nothing happened.

Despite the seriousness of the situation, Skye snorted in laughter, and Graham shrugged.

"Hey, I just had to try, you know."

Graham didn't know which key to insert into the keyhole, but he was lucky. On his second attempt, the door clicked open, revealing a plethora of various prescription medications lining the shelves.

"Wow," Skye said. "There's a lot of this stuff."

"Here," Graham said, pointing to a crack he spotted.

Skye adjusted the light so that it shone through. Sure enough, there was a line of metal canisters behind a metal grate.

"Noxium," she read off the label. "That's the stuff we're looking for, right?"

"Yeah," Graham answered.

"Look at that," Skye said, shaking her head. "We need to bypass another damn lock."

This time, Graham didn't have nearly as much luck finding the key. He tried one, and it didn't fit. Another one fit, but didn't turn the lock. Soon enough, he had gone through a dozen keys, with no luck at all of getting inside.

"Shit," Graham cursed, slamming his fist down on the open metal door before rubbing his sensitive knuckles. "This isn't working!"

"Focus," Skye said. "One of these keys is going to work."

"I don't know," Graham said. "None of them are."

"One of them is going to," Skye replied. "It *has* to."

And sure enough, it did. It took a while—it wasn't until the third to last of the twenty or so keys looped around the key ring that the door locked—but when the lock finally clicked open, both Skye and Graham exhaled loudly in relief before high-fiving each other. They knew they had to remain upbeat if they wanted to prevail.

"We got this," Skye said. "Never doubted for a second."

"How much of these do you think we're going to need?"

"I don't know," Skye said. "You're the smart one here."

"I think, better to be safe than sorry," Graham said, hefting several canisters of Noxium from the inside of the cabinet.

When he pulled them out, he was able to read the label far more closely. He was able to see a skull and crossbones on each canister, which warned that the gas could be lethal in some cases, and was only to be used in the event of an emergency.

"It can be lethal," Skye said, hesitating.

"Yes," Graham replied. "You didn't think that knock-out gas was perfect, did you? I think it has something like a 5% fatality rate. There is a good chance people are going to die tonight."

Skye was silent.

"But we have to try," Graham replied. "Better for one villain and one innocent to die than dozens of innocents, right?"

"Yes," Skye answered. "Right."

It would be difficult, if not impossible, to carry around several canisters of Noxium, especially if they wanted to make good time, so Graham came up with a solution to their transportation problem by rolling a cart over from the corner of the building (almost every store had a few shopping carts for guests) and folding his arms. Skye sighed.

"God, waltzing around with a shopping cart like a pair of idiots," Skye murmured. "What has this world come to?"

"It's the most practical thing I can think of to move them," Graham replied. "Unless you can think of something better?"

But Skye shook her head. Graham agreed to push the cart, and Skye took the needle again before they both ran back into the hallway.

In a brief moment, it occurred to Graham that they could check out the adjacent area, the infirmary, which was gated off just like the pharmacy. Perhaps they could have found some tools that would have made much better weapons, such as a scalpel or a hammer, if they had bothered to check. He could even use the master key card to head to the armory and arm themselves in case they needed to fend off any opponents with guns. But that plan was probably too dangerous, and neither Graham nor Skye had any experience with firearms.

But that wasn't the only alternative. For a brief moment, a different idea flashed in Graham's mind, before he wrote it off. They could use their master card to access some of the other hotel rooms, the guests and employees who hadn't been taken away to be kicked off. They could recruit them to the cause. Surely working together, they would quickly raise an unstoppable force that could take down the security guards, especially if they caught them when they were spread out. But that idea faced some big logistical problems: first, Graham had no idea which rooms were occupied or unoccupied, making the process tedious. Furthermore, he had no idea how cooperative anyone would be to agree to their plans, let alone to take any sort of violent action against the guards. Then there was the issue that Skye and Graham had no idea whether Marcell and the others were working to clear out rooms in any sort of set pattern or order, and, if so, how they were doing it, meaning that there was a chance they would be caught completely off guard while they moved in the hallways with no chance of retribution. No, that was far too big of a gamble for them, especially since it likely would compromise their situation. His only hope rested with the metal canisters of gas in the shopping cart. Skye and Graham beelined straight for the back of the hotel. To the oxygen center.

***

While their rush to the pharmacy had not led to any encounter so far, their luck would not last forever.

Everything was looking up at first. As they approached the oxygen center, there was not a single soul in sight in any of the dim hallways that they rushed through, or the dark windows that they passed. But they would not go unseen forever. Somehow, as they reached the T intersection near the back, things would take a turn for the worst.

"We're almost there," Graham was saying, and then they could hear it. The shout.

It was from behind them, at a decent distance, but it was certainly directed towards them, calling for them to stop.

Skye craned her neck behind herself and spotted two figures. Although she couldn't make out many of their details at all from their distance, their lighter skin color let Skye know that whoever it was, it wasn't Marcell.

"Oh my God!" She cried. "There's two of them!"

"Oh no!" Graham exclaimed. "We're so close!"

"What do we do?" Skye asked. "You said it's up ahead!"

"We turn," Graham said, grabbing the cart and yanking it to the side.

"*Wha!?*"

"We're improvising," Graham replied, panicking. He ran down to the nearest door and tried the handle. It was locked, of course, and he fumbled through his pockets to whip out the master card and press it to the card reader.

The door opened to reveal nothing except a janitor's closet, where despite the near pitch black it was clear that there was nothing stored inside but cleaning supplies and a deactivated line of androids.

"No, no," Skye said, pulling her hair. "Do we go in?"

The panic of the situation had clouded Graham's judgment, and he realized that the next room over was one that he'd spent plenty of time in, one that he knew almost as well as the back of his hand. The electrical room. That would be a great place to hide. Between all of the generators and engines spread throughout the massive room, and all of the various hiding spots, there would be no way that they would find them.

There was another shout, from much closer this time. It was clear that they were closing in, and probably less than a half minute away. They had to act, and quickly, if they wanted to see their plan through.

Graham sprinted over to the next door, Skye not far behind, and practically slammed the master card in front of the card reader. Nothing happened for a second, and Graham felt his heart flutter;

and then the light turned green and the door unlocked, and he threw it open, letting Skye rush inside first before she looked to him for guidance, confused.

"Where do we go?" Skye asked. "I've never been here!"

"I know the perfect place," Graham said, motioning for Skye to follow him. They were lucky - Graham knew that a lot of the lights were disabled during the night on the ship, but this room, critical in its functionality, had a few dimly activated lights on the side walls, making their path at least somewhat straightforward.

He hurried over to the back corner of the room, rushing past the familiar structures of the generators, their metal mounds always roaring and crackling, with Skye following close behind. The large circular transfluxor of each generator on each side captured the line of electricity connecting between two points, looking like a contraption straight out of a science fiction franchise, especially with the new spider-like Generation Conservation Machines attached to them. But Graham was worried that, despite their self-containment, the generators would somehow arc to the shopping cart and set off the Noxium in a chemical reaction that would kill them all. Still, he knew the equipment posed less of a threat than their pursuers.

Graham reached the door he was aiming for, which led to a crawl space underneath much of the machinery. He went to pull the handle before discovering what he dreaded most.

"Shoot," he said. "It's locked."

Why was it locked? He thought. *There's no reason to lock this shut. Stupid. Stupid!*

There was no time to mope, and Graham pulled out the ring of keys, trying the first one and trying to cram it into the lock. It didn't even get close to fitting, and it was apparent that there would be no forcing it during his first try.

"There's no way that works," Skye said. "I mean, the entire thing."

"I have to try," Graham said. Ideally, he'd have a key ring from his work, from Mr. Xiong, but he didn't have that luxury right now, so he'd try. If he'd had the time, he'd have explained that the keyholes for most of the electrical rooms were identical, but he was far too concentrated on the task at hand. He tried the next key, and it didn't work. Another. And yet another.

It was only after this next attempt that the door opened, and a voice called out from across the room.

"Trespassers!" A voice called. The voice, feminine sounding, was practically a scream. It had to be in order to exceed the roar of the machinery in the room. "Come out with your hands up! We can work out an arrangement! No one has to get hurt!"

Graham tried the next key, and the door finally clicked open, revealing a substantially large crawlspace. It was so large, in fact, that the shopping cart was just short enough to be able to fit inside, and that's what the pair did first, lifting the cart an inch off the ground before rolling it in. Skye hurriedly ducked inside. Then Graham. The space was uncomfortably tight with Graham, Skye, and the shopping cart inside, but they fit, and that was what mattered. Graham just hoped that in the corner of the large room, with enough columns blocking views from the entryway, that they hadn't been spotted.

"Come on!" A voice shouted. "Show yourself!"

The voice might've been twenty paces away, and Graham only had a couple of seconds to cram the door shut. He grabbed at the handle, holding the door closed; and he prayed, with all of his heart and soul, that they wouldn't try the handle, or it would all be for nothing.

But their pursuer didn't try the door at all. They could hear footsteps walking by for a couple of seconds, and another voice calling out. But after that, there was nothing but the crackling of the generators. Both of them panted for a couple of minutes to catch up on their breathing, until Skye spoke once again.

"How did you know?" Skye asked quietly.

"I didn't," Graham whispered. "I just hoped it would work, and it did."

The pair waited a couple of more minutes until Graham finally exited out of the space and went to check the surrounding room. The guard, or guards, Graham had no idea how many people had been in the room, were gone, and the door to the hallway shut.

They went over to the front of the room with the Noxium gas. For a few moments, Graham hesitated before leaving the room. Some part of him thought that he was being lured out into a trap, and that the two guards were simply waiting for them. But eventually, Graham remembered time was off the essence, and he cracked the door open to look down the hallway towards the right. There was no one there, so then he opened it further and checked to the left. Again, there was nobody. With that, he stepped out into the hallway, and broke out into a run once more, Skye right behind with the cart.

Chapter 31

There was one last stop before the oxygen center, and that stop was extremely close to it. Graham knew where they could find some gas masks, and that was in the engineering facility.

The master card granted them access without difficulty, and they quickly grabbed a handful of masks, more than they would need, and tossed them on top of the shopping cart. Graham also dug through the various schematics that he had looked through recently, hoping to find some valuable information. He had seen a strange sight about a giant weapon in the schematics before, but now it was missing. However, he did find a detailed layout of the oxygen center, including where all of the vents led.

"Jackpot," Graham celebrated as he snagged the piece of paper and added it to the growing pile of goods on the shopping cart. He also grabbed a toolbox before they left the room.

"I'm glad you knew what to look for," Skye said. "I'm next to worthless. I don't know where any of this stuff was, or even how we can do this at all."

"Nonsense," Graham replied. "I couldn't do any of this without you."

But Skye shook her head, knowing that Graham was simply being nice. If she had a chance to go back to Earth, to college, she knew she'd switch her major to something more practical. But that was all wishful thinking: there was only the International Space Hotel to think of, and even then, that would only be the case if she and Graham succeeded in their goals. Skye made an active effort to set aside her emotions and pushed forwards.

Skye and Graham were only a stone's throw from the oxygen center, and the last leg of the journey happened quickly.

Inside, there was the assembly of cylindrical metal, where the oxygen was generated; and then, snaking through in multiple directions, were vents. Using the blueprints, Graham was able to deduce quickly which ones led straight to the spots which he believed they needed to target.

"You see, we want to get them near the lobby over here, and the cells over at this hold," Graham explained. "We go for that, and this swath of the hotel, and that should be real good coverage."

Graham screwed off the grates and positioned the Noxium in the entrance.

"This doesn't make too much sense to me," Skye said as he readied the cans in their position and started putting on his own gas mask. "Please explain the situation."

"What's up?" He asked.

"I mean, won't the gas just spread through to the other vents? How is this going to work? I don't get it."

"When you consider the porosity and design of this system, no, I don't think so," he replied. "Any effect will be marginal… But yes, we're putting on our gas masks, because we're bound to get some blowback. Besides that, we control the circulation from here. I'll go over to the control board and crank up the wind speed to the maximum."

Graham leaned forward to one of the cans, gripping it by the valve at the end and twisting it. All of a sudden there was a hiss as the can started to depressurize. But before the gas could really spill out, and the two could execute the plan, there was the sound of a throat being cleared, and both Graham and Skye whipped around, but not until Skye deftly slid her needle in between the crossbars in the vent.

"Put your hands up where we can see them clearly."

Sure enough, the two guards who had been pursuing them earlier had caught up to them. They sported assault rifles, like they were members of the armed forces, and not the security for a space resort for the rich, that were wrapped around their bodies in slings. And they were clearly there to stop them, no matter what it took.

***

Their name tags were still attached to their uniforms, allowing Skye to, despite the dimmed lights, read off their own names to appeal to them.

"Joshua… Audrey…" Skye said, reading off their names in the light. During this expedition with Graham, she had felt like she had been more of a hindrance than a help. Not anymore. Now it was her time to shine. "I'm Skye, and this is Graham."

"Now listen up. Both of you. Step away from the vents. Slowly approach us," Joshua commanded. Skye perceived the earpiece he, as well as Audrey, wore. The way he collected himself and paused, it looked like he was receiving orders and repeating them.

"Surely we can talk about this," Skye negotiated.

"There's nothing to talk about," Audrey replied. "Follow our orders, and no one has to get hurt."

"You're rounding up people to their deaths," Skye countered. "Surely you can't just go along with this. Think about how wrong it is, what you're doing. And help us."

"Nonsense," Joshua replied. "If we all stay on board too long, we'll be running out of food, and we'll all slowly die. At least this way, there's a chance. A chance for everyone. You'll have a new beginning on Earth."

He stopped for a few moments. "Yes, sir. I will no longer engage these two individuals in conversation."

"You're receiving orders through your earpiece?" Skye speculated. "Come on, you can't see the cruelty and injustice in this? In whatever *he* is saying?"

Skye made contact with Joshua; his glare was unwavering, and his face was narrowed into a frown that showed a resolve and determination that she knew meant he was committed to the plan. But the woman was folding. She could see the look of concern, the slouch in her stance, and clearly was feeling something rising up deep inside her. A thought, an objection. It was all Skye could hope for. Her last appeal to her humanity.

"If we're all expendable, do you think they'll stop at us?" Skye questioned. "Getting rid of us. Who do you think they're going to dispose of next? Management will look at you, able-bodied security guards with guns, and recognize that you're a threat. They'll stop at nothing to protect themselves, and, panicking, they'll decide that you're next."

"Shut up," Joshua commanded through gritted teeth. "Shut the *hell* up! You don't speak for management."

But Audrey froze in her tracks.

"We can't do this," she said. "I can't do this anymore."

Joshua looked at her, aghast, turning around. "You can't give up now."

"We can say that we've caught them. We can say we're done."

"They're listening in to my fucking earpiece, Audrey. What do you want me to do, throw the earpiece away and go on my merry way?"

She nodded, mouthing that he could play along.

"No," Joshua said. "We're halfway through the night. We're going to do this and finish this for the good of everyone on board."

Graham looked at Skye. He was looking to her for guidance; perhaps if Skye wielded the needle, and Graham used one of the nearby metal Noxium canisters like a baseball bat, they would be able to get the jump on the two quarreling guards. But Skye doubted it. By the time they retrieved their weapons, Skye surmised they'd be taking bullets to the torso. She shook her head, silently conveying her skepticism, and Graham sighed in frustration, conceding to her judgment to hold off.

"You don't have to listen to them anymore," Skye pleaded. "You're not on their payroll. The world, it's gone. You can do what's right. *You* have guns, and you know how to use them."

Joshua leaned over, whispered in Audrey's ear. She shook her head. It looked like where she had been faltering before, she was regaining her willpower. Joshua now let his gun rest down on his sling as he pulled out a pair of handcuffs.

"I'm now going to place both of you under arrest," he stated matter-of-factly. "Do not run away, or my colleague will be forced to pull the trigger of that gun. That gun isn't firing blanks, let me warn you. It's not worth dying over this."

Joshua and Audrey started walking towards them. Both Skye and Graham raised their hands even higher into the air.

"Think of all the equipment around us," Skye begged, trying one last plead to change their mind. "We're in the oxygen center. If you damage or destroy any of this equipment around us, we could *all* die. Nothing's worth doing that."

They were unfazed by Skye's plea. Graham took a step back, and Audrey slowly trained her gun over at him. Skye's heart raced, but her jaw clenched when she saw what was behind them. She tried her best to focus on them instead of the background, but in a split second after processing what she'd seen, she knew that wasn't going to be an option for much longer.

It wasn't a matter of what was behind Audrey and Joshua, but who. It was Marcell, and he had a gun aimed in their direction. A gun which, before Joshua could get too close to Skye to detain her, sprayed bullets in their direction.

*****

Skye dove to the ground, covering her head and praying that, caught in the crossfire, she wouldn't catch a stray bullet. She could hear the clanging of metal nearby, as bullets slammed into the vicinity, and the sound of intense screaming. She opened her eyes to the chaos because the noise was so loud, she thought she was going to go deaf. Within only a few seconds, the gunfire had subsided. Marcell must've not been the best marksman on Earth, and had been recruited to the International Space Hotel for his other talents, because both Joshua and Audrey were left standing, appearing perfectly unscathed, at least physically. Their emotional state was a completely different matter.

Both had turned around, their assault rifles turned towards the space Marcell had opened fire from. To say they were startled was an understatement.

"Shit!" Audrey was screaming.

"Did you see that? What the hell! Who the hell was that?" Joshua yelled.

The barrel of the gun poked out from behind the right wall at the previous T-intersection of hallways once again, and a couple of more gunshots rapidly resounded.

This time, Skye gasped as Audrey collapsed backwards onto the metal platform onto the ground. There were dull eyes, a blank expression, and a bloody mark slightly to the left on her forehead. And the blood. The blood pooled around her already. There was a piece of something gray. The body was oddly serene; it reminded

Skye of that one painting she'd seen, of the pale woman entering eternal sleep immersed partially in a lily pond.

"Oh my God," Graham exclaimed, eyes widening. "She's dead. She's dead!"

Skye felt a wave of adrenaline surging into her body, breaking out of her stupor as she climbed up onto her knees. Joshua was screaming at the top of his lungs, and shooting rapidly and sporadically in the direction the gunfire had come from, so much so that it was likely only a matter of time before his magazine ran out of bullets.

"Oh Jesus! You killed her! You fucking bastard! Die! Die!" Joshua yelled.

Skye looked back at Graham, who was crouched against the back wall, mortified, and knew that she was the only hope of helping Marcell. Simultaneously, as she gathered the strength to act, Joshua's magazine clicked empty, but not before there was a scream of pain and a thud as Marcell slid behind cover in the intersecting hallway up ahead, ducking just out of sight.

"Got you, *bitch*!" Joshua shouted. "Ha!"

He stepped forwards, about to discover the identity of the marksman, but it was too late for him. His fate was sealed. Skye seized the needle in her hand by grabbing the back of it from where she'd left in the vent and lunged forwards some paces, stabbing the needle straight through the back of Joshua's neck before he even could turn around. He collapsed face-first onto the ground, convulsing. Skye looked down at her hands, and saw that they were now slick with his blood, blood that was now spurting onto the floor.

I killed him. I killed him.

Skye was wrong. He was still alive, but fading quickly, and Skye stood back, fearing she might fall into shock, until she remembered Marcell, how he'd been shot, and before she could truly dwell on what she had done, she rushed over to his position, pushing aside the disgust she felt in the situation.

***

Marcell was hurt. He looked to have been shot on the side of his torso, slightly down below the midpoint. Skye was no expert on gunshots, or wounds, in any sort of manner, but she knew that, depending on what organs may have been hit, the wound could have been either unlucky or very unlucky for him.

"Marcell," Skye said. It wasn't a statement, or a question. It was a statement of sadness, and wishing things hadn't turned out this way.

"Get the earpiece from him," Marcell whispered, his face flushed with pain.

Skye nodded, running back and plucking it out of Joshua's ear, but not before first wiping the blood off of her hands onto the walls. By now, Joshua rested, still, and Skye couldn't tell whether or not he was breathing. Skye trembled in fear and disgust but pulled it out without any major difficulties. She saw Graham was still sitting in the corner, a blank expression plastered on his face. She wanted to help him, but knew that Marcell's situation was more urgent, so she returned back to the hallway. All the while, she could faintly hear what sounded like someone yelling through the earpiece.

Marcell grabbed the earpiece, briefly hitting the mute button to mute their end of the line.

"So, what's your plan?" Marcell asked.

"What?" Skye asked.

"You had a plan, right? Or are you just running around without a plan?"

"Noxium the vents, put them to sleep," Skye hurriedly explained. "We want to make sure they're in the right area… Uh… Lobby, the executive officers, Lusky's quarters. Maybe some of the hallways, we just don't want to kill any bystanders."

Marcell nodded. "I'm on it." With that he pressed the mute button again and slipped the earpiece into his ear.

"Hey, hey, can you hear me?" Marcell asked.

"Marcell!" The voice called. "What are you doing on this? Where's Joshua?"

"He's dead, Fritz," Marcell responded. "I heard you talking, so I went over and retrieved his earpiece."

"Jesus… We'll switch over back to your line."

With that, Marcell dropped the earpiece, now talking over his own personal earpiece. Skye opened her mouth in confusion, but Marcell shook his head and Skye shut up before any words could escape her mouth.

"What the hell happened?" Fritz asked. "I heard gunfire."

"A couple of interns appeared to have gotten their hands on guns."

"That's impossible… How could they have accessed them?"

"I don't know," Marcell replied. "I don't know! Now that I think about it, my master key is missing. It's possible they swiped it out and went to the armory."

"What about Audrey…? You didn't tell me about her status."

"Listen," Marcell said. He had to pause for a moment, grimacing and gingerly touching his wound, which seemed to throb in sync with his heart. "They're dead. Joshua and Audrey. But I got them. I avenged them."

"Oh, God," Fritz replied. "Oh my God. Do you need help? Reinforcements?"

"No," Marcell coughed. "No, listen. I took care of them. They're dead."

"Where's your location?"

"O-oxygen center."

"Oxygen center? How did that happen?"

"I don't know. There was a chase of some kind, I think."

"You sound like you're in pain," Fritz remarked.

"I took a bullet. It's only a flesh wound. Trust me, I'm good."

"Are you sure? We can wake up Dr. Silva or Dr. Chetana for you."

"Dr. Chetana never agreed to this plan. The doctors never would have agreed to this plan. No, that's not a good idea."

"Who? Who was it? The culprits? I heard the names, Skye and Graham. Is that true? Just who was it?"

"I don't know who they are," Marcell replied. "You're not watching the cameras?"

"Me? No, none of us are. Security had their hands full with the removal process, and management's… uh… recalibrating, but I'll get on them immediately. See if there's any more of those rogues running about. Mark my words, I'll kill them all with my bare hands if I have to."

Shit, Marcell thought. *That would be bad.*

"N-no! There's no good at this point. They're dead. We have a more pressing need than that."

"What's that?"

Marcell felt like gears were churning behind his brain. "I need to let the others know. The crew… Give them that extra motivation to complete this night as fast as possible."

"Okay," Fritz relented. "Look, I know we didn't set a strict time limit to this mission, but the sooner we can complete it, the better. I'm going to head out to the cameras in the surveillance room, and make sure I help catch any stragglers. First things first, the boss wants to talk to you."

"Uh… Okay."

"Marcell," Alan Lusky said. "I've heard this whole conversation. What a tragedy."

"Yes, sir." Beyond Alan Lusky's calm tone, Marcell swore he could make out the quiet tune of a piano and the low din of chatter.

"I trust you."

"Thank you."

"That trust was well placed?"

"Pardon?"

"I mean, you're not betraying my trust, right?"

"No sir. Why would you ask that?"

"I've had doubts. If you do betray me, it will be the biggest regret of your life. If not, then go finish the job."

"I will, sir… I will."

"Good luck with the rest of the night."

"Thank you, sir."

Marcell pressed the mute button at his end, and then he sighed.

"Do it… Hurry!" Marcell called to Skye. "They're sending someone out to the cameras soon… Act now! Before it's too late."

***

There was likely only a couple of minutes until reinforcements arrived. Skye operated at double time as she hurried over to Graham, trying to shake him from his strange crouched position.

Graham didn't rouse at Skye's words, nor when she literally tried shaking him in his hands. It took a full direct slap to the face for him to break out of his stupor.

"Ow!" He cried, rubbing his now lightly red cheek. "You didn't have to slap me!"

"Hurry the fuck up!" Skye said, shaking him. "We have minutes to spare until our cover is blown! Please!"

"Right… Right!" Graham said, jumping on to his feet.

This time, he quickly put on the gas mask over his mouth within seconds, and he ran over to Marcell leaning against the wall some distance away, and helped cover him with a mask of his own. He had to be careful, as on the way running back, he slipped a little bit on the red, slick puddle that had formed in the middle of the room, and he almost tumbled to the ground before catching himself on the beam of the edge of one of the intermittent airlocks, pushing himself back onto his feet.

Despite the odds against them, Skye and Graham had been fortunate. If they had been caught in the act of putting on their gas masks, or after they had put it on, their plan would have been compromised. The guards would have reported their activities to the management, and the entire security team would be on their trail. However, it seemed that Joshua and Audrey had been too preoccupied with handling other matters to notice the duo's activities or pay attention to the shopping cart filled with gas canisters and masks in the background.

"Put it on," Graham told her, waving at her to hurry up.

"Okay," Skye said. With trembling hands, she started putting on the gas mask over herself. But she was struggling, and Graham noticed.

"Here," he said, adjusting her mask slightly. "You need to make sure the straps are tighter. Like this."

Graham tugged on the straps behind her, and Skye muttered a thank you.

"You good?" He asked, gently.

Skye nodded. Graham and Skye could feel something in that moment, but they were too flustered and stressed to acknowledge it.

Graham appeared to remember the time crunch of the situation, because then he was running off, pressing a couple of buttons to adjust the wind's velocity before screwing off the proper Noxium canisters and letting them loose. When each canister was opened, yellow gas would spread around from where it released, exactly how Skye would've imagined tear gas canisters launched their contents, except the wind would quickly catch the gas and suck it down the proper vent before it could spread too far or blow back into the room.

They didn't know how long it would take exactly, for the gas to have their effects and to knock out everyone needed. But they waited until every last droplet of gas had been expelled from the canisters, and the room had fallen into relative silence apart from the whirs of the oxygen generators, which were far quieter than the roars of the electrical engines. Then they waited a couple of minutes, until everything was silent, and moved over to Marcell, whose chest was rising and more slowly now.

"Marcell? Are you okay?"

"No…" He said, wheezing for each breath. "I don't think I'm handling this well. I think I need a doctor, or better yet, a surgeon."

"Fuck," Skye said. "We need to help him *now*. This doesn't look good."

"Do you know where we can get help?" Graham asked. "Where we can find where any of the doctors live?"

"No… There should be a registry… There's a lot," Marcell sputtered. "You can get one in Lusky's quarters, in the security office, in the control room… Find where Dr. Silva is… Get his help, and bring their guns, just in case."

He gestured in the direction of the fallen guards. Skye and Graham looked at each other.

"Well…" Skye started, "what are we waiting for?"

Chapter 32

There was so much to do, and yet so little time.

At this point, Graham and Skye weren't even sure if their plan had worked. If it hadn't, and guards were still roaming the ISH's hotel looking for them, then they were doomed. Even with their assault rifles, they wouldn't stand a chance. Graham knew that Joshua's gun was out of ammunition, but he didn't have the heart to tell Skye.

In addition to rescuing everyone from the jail cells and escape pods, they also had to find a way to secure the knocked-out guards. If they didn't act quickly, the effects of the knockout gas would wear off in a couple of hours, and the guards would wake up armed and ready to apprehend them. But worrying about these things would only slow them down. Among those in the cells was Madison, someone both Graham and Skye were determined to help.

The problem was that they didn't know where the armory was located, and they didn't want to risk going to Lusky's quarters either. Even though it wasn't too far away, there were too many uncertainties there, and the thought of confronting a possibly conscious and furious CEO was too much for Skye to handle.

That left the single possibility of fetching the registry from the control room. Skye had been in there once shortly after Grace Elliott had been assassinated—it was unbelievable how long ago that felt now, even though it had only been weeks—and Graham had been there a few times over the course of working his internship.

Neither Graham nor Skye took off their gas masks in the process of running to find the registry, as Graham had warned it would take likely an hour for the gas to naturally dispel and become harmless. They also brought another gas mask with them, since they were bringing a doctor out into a potentially hazardous situation. However, despite feeling clunky and stressed, so much so that she hadn't hardly thought about the fact that she had taken a life minutes before, Skye did spot something strange that got some clarity on their questions about their success as they ran to the front of the ship. She saw it amongst the cushioned seats, and strewn out in front of the stage like some discarded wrappers.

Bodies.

"Oh my God," Skye said as they reached the lobby. "Look."

She pointed over to some of the front seats of the main lobby, in front of the stage, where, slumped over seats, and the floor were a handful of the security guards, presumably unconscious, or so Skye hoped. There also looked to be someone in handcuffs, some sort of client, who also had passed out likewise lying across the seats. Overall, there must've been five or six security guards in the area.

"Marcell said there were ten of them, right?" Graham asked as they reached the control room, Skye swiping the master card to unlock the door and grant them passage.

"I think so," Skye answered.

"Well, I think there were six of them, plus the two guards back there, plus Marcell… That's got to be almost all of them, except for maybe one?"

"Sounds about right."

The two entered into the front cabin, relieved to find that there was no one in the area before turning their attention to scoping out the room.

The control room was quite large, with all sorts of different stations spread out among the walls, all with a myriad of buttons resembling something from you'd have seen from a classic space opera. A giant window covered the front wall. In the back area, there were a few seats arranged near computers. Skye had remembered how she had been brought here shortly after Elliott's assassination, and found it strange to acknowledge how that had been a less stressful time than now.

Graham and Skye agreed to both check out this back section first, as it looked like it had a higher chance of containing their object of interest. Skye stepped over to the thin screen of the nearest computer.

"Do we have to go through the computers?"

"No," Graham responded. "Let's look for paper. I'd think they'd have had this printed out the old-fashioned way in the 3D printing room. Maybe more portable and definitely immune from mechanical or power issues."

Skye and Graham dug around the room for a couple of minutes, opening various drawers and digging through stacks of papers, before finding the untouched registry. It clearly hadn't been adjusted for those who were being removed from the ship, because Skye found her own name on the list almost immediately. They flipped through by surname alphabetically and came across a doctor's name.

"Dr. Miguel Silva," Skye read. "He's a doctor, fifty-five years old. Is it him?"

"It has to be," Graham replied.

"Room 225," Skye answered.

And both of them nodded at each other, springing up from the ground before running as if they were track athletes sprinting on the final stretch to reach the finish line.

****

The soundproofing of the room must've worked, because in Room 225, Dr. Silva had been fast asleep.

Room 225 had been plenty different from Graham's room insofar as when they entered, they weren't even in the bedroom, which pretty much made up his whole hotel room, but rather they entered into a half-kitchen, half-living room.

"Lucky," Skye blurted out when they entered the room. "I wish our rooms had come with a living room."

How Skye could have been thinking about the living arrangements, in a moment where Marcell lie bleeding on the ground, Graham did not know. But Graham stopped for a moment, staring over the room and processing what she had said. Somehow, in the tense moment, it seemed to help him regain his cool.

"Me too. That must be the perk of being a big shot. I hope we can get a room like this, someday," Graham whispered, before coughing awkwardly. "By we, I mean, each have our own room obviously. I don't mean to insinuate anything."

"Yeah, I don't think we're going to be here that long," Skye answered, but she smiled before pointing at the closed door in the wall over to the right. "I'm guessing his room must be through that door, right there."

"Yes," Graham agreed. "Let's go in on the count of three. One… Two… Three!"

Skye and Graham opened the door on the right and flicked on the lights. What followed was Dr. Silva and a woman who must've been his wife, perking up from behind their covers, screaming. It would be less than a second before they jumped out of their covers, half-nude, begging for mercy.

"It's okay! It's okay!" Graham pleaded, but it wasn't okay, and it was clear that this part had been a grand oversight in their objective.

***

It wasn't easy convincing Dr. Silva to come along with them, especially considering both had broken into their room in the middle of the night wielding assault rifles that were pointed in the couple's direction. But, after a couple of minutes of conversation, Skye was able to persuade him about the plan, how the management on board had decided to forcibly remove dozens and dozens of people and send them back down to Earth in a likely deadly journey.

"There's no way, there's no way," Dr. Silva had replied incredulously, until Skye and Graham's insistence had proven, in fact, there had been a way.

Even though Dr. Silva eventually agreed to go and help them, his wife appeared much more opposed and distrustful of what they were saying. Not that Skye faulted her at all. She spoke quietly in his ear in what sounded, and from a distance, it sounded like Spanish. Skye hadn't taken a Spanish class in years but it sounded like she was evidently warning him about going off with these teenagers or young adults with guns.

"If we wanted to hurt you," Skye interrupted at one point. "We already would have. That's not our angle. Obviously."

Dr. Silva's wife eventually released him, and after giving him a gas mask, they headed out. Skye wasn't thrilled with the way they convinced Dr. Silva to wear the gas mask. Graham lied and said that it could be dangerous outside and that there seemed to be a sleeping gas. Skye decided to go along with it since it would be more challenging to get his help if he knew about the gas attack.

While en route to the oxygen center, Dr. Silva stopped at the infirmary to gather some supplies. The infirmary was well-stocked, much like the pharmacy, with items like stitches, painkillers, gauze, bandages, and tools. Luckily, Silva was able to carry the supplies in their own bags, allowing Graham and Skye to keep their guns at the ready the entire time. Although they were both inept with guns, it made them feel more secure.

"These hallways are eerily empty," Dr. Silva commented at one point as they jogged through the hallways. "Are you sure that there are these people you talked about? Exiling people from this ship?"

"Yeah, about that," Skye replied. "We can't be entirely sure whether or not there's anyone standing in our way. We need to help Marcell. That's all that matters. Then we'll help the… others."

Dr. Silva didn't like the sound of that judging by his grunt of displeasure, but he kept up with them. Unfortunately, there was yet another obstacle standing in their way before they could reach the oxygen center. They hadn't taken out everyone, because a figure stood in their path, wearing a gas mask over his face. Skye felt like she was going to faint but knew that they had to confront this man. They had to get through, no matter what, if they wanted Marcell to survive.

Chapter 33

This time, they had more warning about their opponent, so that they could try to assess ahead of time who it was up in front of them. He blocked their path from a distance, and, much like Joshua and Audrey, had an assault rifle slung over his chest. From this distance, Skye couldn't make out the individual's name, and she wasn't about to step close to him to find out, although she could tell by his build and tall stature that he was a man.

"Sir," Skye greeted him.

"It's Fritz," Dr. Silva mumbled under his breath. "Fritz Nussbaum."

"What the hell?" Fritz asked. "So, he was lying?"

"Pardon?" Skye asked.

"I talked to Marcell. He said that you were dead," the man explained. "He said that he'd killed a couple of interns, but here you are, alive, and with a doctor, nonetheless. Wow. Color. Me. Impressed."

"Who are you?"

"It doesn't matter," he said, training his rifle in between Graham and Skye, who raised their rifles back at him, and the man laughed.

"You two aren't even holding the guns right," he laughed. "Do you think I'm afraid that you're going to shoot me?"

"I don't know," Graham countered. "Why don't you mess around and find out?"

"Hush," Skye managed, shaking her head before calling out more loudly. "We don't want any more trouble. Please let us pass through. Marcell's bleeding, bad."

"Well, if you want, I can escort you there, and then I can ask him a couple of questions. And if I find out that he was in on your plan, well, then I'll kill him. And I'll kill you too."

"I don't think that's a good idea," Skye responded. "I think there's been enough unnecessary bloodshed tonight."

"Bastards," the man sputtered. Despite his distance, Skye could see his eyes flicking around rapidly underneath his gas mask, and knew that he was unhinged. "Did you, or did you not kill Joshua and Audrey? I saw their bodies on the cameras. I saw what you'd done with the gas attack, and I was able to get a gas mask before accidentally wandering and getting myself killed too. And then I saw you running down the hallways, and I knew, oh I *knew*, that I had to stop you."

"What's going on?" Dr. Silva asked. "I thought you guys said that there was a gas attack."

"Yes," Graham sighed. "We did."

"We had to," Skye insisted. "They were going to kill all of us. The Noxium gas isn't lethal. We knocked them unconscious. Its…We had to, in order to stop over a hundred people from dying tonight. They aren't dead. We hope."

"My God," Dr. Silva murmured under his breath.

"That's fucking bullshit," Fritz growled. "What are you talking about? Sending people back down to Earth. So what? So fucking what? You gunned them down. You gunned them down, slaughtered them like *animals*. I heard their final words over the radio call. They were going to arrest you, and you killed them."

"You weren't there!" Skye asked. "Ask Marcell: he was a witness to what we'd heard. The Earth isn't safe! We didn't want to kill them! They were the ones who opened fire. We were defending ourselves."

"You really are cool with this?" Graham added, trying his best not to falter, knowing that Skye had lied about their engagement in gunfire. Perhaps it was better that way, than to let this man know that his fellow employee, Marcell, had killed them. "You really are cool with purging all of us? Just what, so you and management can eat well, let us slowly get ill and die of radiation sickness? You're really cool with that?"

"That wasn't me!" Fritz said. "I was following orders. That's different."

"Doesn't matter who was the mastermind," Skye spat. "You all did this! You! Just because you were sitting on your ass doesn't make you any less culpable for everyone who would die."

Fritz looked down, looked back up. He shook his head. Then he chuckled. Skye and Graham glanced at each other, hesitating, having not expected this reaction, of all possible responses.

"You're telling me," Fritz said, laughing. "You're telling me that Alan Lusky, one of the richest business magnates of the entire world, and that all ten of our security team, were overthrown, by two bumbling interns? Oh my. Oh my God."

Then he dropped the gun, his laughs fading away until they were a faint whisper, and his smile had been wiped clean from his face. Within only a couple of seconds he was screaming at the top of his lungs. He stepped over to the wall, punching it, once, twice. There was a snap of bone, and he shouted in pain. Then he grabbed his wrist, his face contorted in pain.

"You know what?" Fritz asked, grimacing. "What am I going to do? Stand in your way? Kill some kids? Go. Just go. I checked back on Lusky's quarters. They're unconscious. Management. All of them. The plan's off. You win. You want this? You want a Lord of the Flies, except it's the real-life version? Be my *fucking* guest. I don't care anymore."

The three slowly approached him, nervous about his erratic behavior and whether he would change his mind about peaceful surrender. Graham picked up his assault rifle, handed it to Skye, who was extra careful when handling it, as if she was carrying an heirloom. The whole time, Fritz hardly batted a glance, pacing around in a circle. Then the three were only a short walk away from the oxygen center, where they found Marcell, barely conscious. Dr. Silva got to work.

***

Fritz had been a man of his word. He stepped back, watching as Dr. Silva tended to the prone Marcell for a minute, before he paid respects to the deceased two security members over closer to the vents, where the Noxium canisters still rested inside. After only a couple of minutes, Graham and Skye bid farewell, explaining they had other matters to attend to.

Their first part of the plan involved seizing the guns from all of the unconscious security guards in the lobby. They did so, before deciding to stash them in Marcell's old empty room, which had been vacated now. They didn't know where else to put it, and it was the room they were familiar with that was the closest to the lobby, so that it was only a couple of minutes' walk each way.

From there, they made their walk towards where Marcell had directed them. Graham theorized that, the way they had used the Noxium canisters in the various hallways, anyone in the particular hallway of interest, near the jail cells, hadn't been affected.

"But what if you're wrong?" Skye asked him at one point. "What if the gas hit all of them? If there are dozens of people exposed to the gas, and this thing has a fatality of like 5-10%... Then there could be several deaths."

"I-I can't be," Graham answered, pale. The way his voice shook didn't provide Skye with confidence.

Skye checked her phone as they neared the hallway, only a few minutes away. It was 1:24 a.m. In the last hour, they'd released Noxium, she had killed someone, and they'd gotten a surgeon to try to save Marcell's life. It had been a roller coaster, and she prayed that finally, it would be easy coasting.

As it turns out, she was in luck: the main jail cell was packed full of various people, probably around thirty or so total, shoulder to shoulder. All of them perked up, awake, when they saw them arriving through the slits of windows on the wall. They surely hadn't been knocked out, not with the response they were receiving.

"Oh my God!" Skye replied, jumping for joy. The reaction seemed to have confused the people in the jail cells, who noticed that they each carried one assault rifle (Skye had put the other one with the ones she'd confiscated from the unconscious guards. Despite her offer, Dr. Silva had not been interested in keeping a firearm).

Skye swiped the master card, opened the door. All at once, there was a flight towards the door. No fewer than ten people stepped closer. As soon as it unlocked, most of the group rushed towards it, but Skye and Graham stood their ground, ready to block their path. The sight of the guns in their hands was enough to deter them from making any sudden moves, but Skye could tell that they were considering their options based on the way they looked at each other. Despite this, Skye and Graham remained vigilant, keeping their weapons at their sides.

"Hold it!" Skye screeched. "Don't stampede...!"

"Graham!?" Madison asked. She pushed through the crowd of a couple of people who stared at her, running forwards and wrapping both Skye in an embrace that defused even the boldest captives who seconds before were ready to throw hands at their presumed captors.

"Maddie," Graham grinned. "I'm so glad to see you!"

"Right back at you, Graham," Madison grinned.

"There's toxic gas out there!" Skye explained, ripping off her gas mask. When those in the crowd saw her exposed face, they appeared to loosen up a little bit. A good amount of them appeared to recognize Skye as one of the interns, or at the very least as someone who was not a member of security. Some of them sighed in relief, others even broke into grins.

"Who are you?" Someone asked in the crowd.

"We're your saviors, and today's your lucky day," Graham replied. "We've come to bust you out. But you need to wait. There's toxic gas out in the hallways, and if you all scramble out recklessly like it looked you wanted to, you might walk yourself into being knocked out, or worse yet, killed."

"There is?"

Skye looked to see that it was Lucas who had posed the question. Lucas lounged on one of the benches in the back of the room. A goofy grin stretched from almost ear to ear on his face, and it looked like he was about ready to slap himself in the back.

"I was right!" Lucas said, laughing, circling around the room. "I was right! I told you all."

"What…?" Graham asked, but Madison shook her head.

"Don't even bother…"

Look," Skye said. "All of you need to stay here. Graham and I are going to recover a few gas masks, and then we're going to need some of your help. We're going to round up the people responsible.

Alan Lusky. His executives. We're going to put them in this cell, and then we're going to straighten things out. They tried getting rid of all of us like pieces of trash, but it's time to show them that we're not disposable, and that we'll find a way to survive, and to thrive. All I ask of you now… is to patiently wait here for an hour."

Most of the people seemed moved by her words, or at the very least, motivated by her speech. And of course, Graham could see Drake and Minnie in the back of the room, smooching together so passionately that it seemed like their lips had been fused together. It was enough for him to almost facepalm.

***

It was only several minutes later and Skye and Graham had recovered the shopping cart from up in the oxygen center, and had filled them in with around ten (all that remained in the engineering facility) of the gas masks. Skye figured there would still be more in the armory, but Graham agreed with her that it wasn't worth the hassle. Ten people to help them with their task would be enough.

After returning with the masks, Graham and Skye handpicked ten reliable individuals to assist them in bringing the management to the jail cells and detaining them if they woke up. However, since there were more people in the cell than they could take, many had to be left behind, and some were unhappy about it.

"Come on!" Lucas moaned. "You're telling me that she gets to go with, and I don't get anything?"

"Sorry," Skye offered. "There's only so many gas masks to go around."

"You know what?" Lucas asked, huffing. "I think that this is all a bunch of *bullshit*. You're not even letting me help, and you really believe that those… those women can get that physical labor done better than me?"

292

"Hey," one of the women in the gas masks, whose name eluded Skye, protested. "I'm plenty capable, and, unlike you, I don't have one too many screws loose."

"I'm going," Lucas said, stepping forward to the door. Skye moved to block his path, but, despite Graham's pleading, Lucas sprinted out into the hallway, looping around Skye with ease.

"We need to stop him!" Graham called. "Idiot's going to get himself killed."

"It's too late," Skye replied. "He may be a headcase, but I think he's harmless. Besides, we have a more important goal right now."

"You're right," Madison replied. "Let's go."

Madison finished adjusting her own gas mask, and then Graham went around and made sure everyone else's gas mask was securely fastened to their faces. At one point, he had to switch out one of the men with another individual due to the man's thick facial hair preventing the mask from adequately sealing over his own face. He wasn't going to risk a loose mask killing someone: there had already been too many deaths as is.

Within a minute, however, the newly assembled group was heading towards Lusky's quarters, and it only took a few minutes further until they all had lined up in front of them. Skye warned them about their circumstances, how they were going to apprehend Lusky, any of the executives, and help move them back to the prison cells. Then, she swiped her master card to the door, raising her gun into the air, just in case. She'd warned everyone else to stand back away from the door in the event they were shot at.

Their plan, much like Fritz had told them, succeeded. Management and their families must have gathered into Lusky's quarters. Judging by a knocked over platter that had been covered with crackers and cheeses, and the placement of many empty and partially full glasses of alcohol, the families had been plying themselves with alcohol to numb the pain and guilt of sending the majority of the ISH down to an irradiated Earth. Their unconscious bodies were strewn all over the suite.

Closest to the door, practically leaning up against the door itself, was Lusky, his face forming a grimace which showed that he appeared to have known something foul was happening. There was not only the people Skye recognized, but their families, their wives or husbands, their children. All of them limply lying out on the ground.

"It's kind of sad," Madison commented.

"What?" Skye and Graham asked in tandem. A few people stepped forward, pulled Lusky out. Despite the hands over him, he didn't wake up. The gas seemed to have done its job, and perhaps the gas effects were still potent enough that he could not wake up. That would have been ideal for all of their sakes.

"There are a couple of young people," Graham said after a short pause, as one by one, people filled in, dragging their bodies out back towards jail cells.

"Yes, there's that," Madison agreed. "But, I mean, the whole thing. This elaborate party, or gathering, whatever you call it. Like they had to throw one thing just to convince themselves that they were doing the right thing. And instead of helping, or dealing with the fallout, they locked themselves in the room. No harm done, if they were never around to see it."

"They got what they deserved," Skye mumbled. "Every last one of them. Except the kids. They were innocent bystanders."

"Look at that, though," Madison said, pointing over at the far side of the room, where a fancy woman with hoop earrings slumped across a bookshelf. "Is that Eva? My God, I think that's Eva."

"I think you might be right," Skye replied. "Geez, that's awful. She's with them."

"Day ruined," Madison groaned. "As if our last day hadn't been shitty enough, now one of my favorite celebrities had to go and do this."

"This is why you don't put celebrities on a pedestal," Graham replied. "They always find some way to stab you in the back. If they aren't secretly a pedophile, racist, transphobic, or homophobic, then they're all up and close with the corrupt. Case in point."

"Yeah, sounds like an excuse you use when you don't remember the most famous celebrity names," Madison countered, rolling her eyes. "Damn, this hurts, though."

Graham's eyes narrowed. Graham stepped forwards towards the closest body, a man on the sofa who leaned his head up against someone else. He couldn't make out his face until he stepped a bit closer, and when he did, he gasped a little bit.

"Ugh," Graham said. "I know that man. He's my boss."

Madison stepped forward, patting his shoulder.

"Do you think we leave him?" Madison questioned. "He's down for the count, that's for sure, so if you want, we can leave him."

"No," Graham replied, a little bit sadly. "If he's here with them, then I have no doubt. He goes in the cell."

Madison and Graham put their hands around his legs.

"One… Two… Three… Lift!" Graham said, heaving as he lifted Mr. Xiong off the sofa. The entire time, he pretended he was doing a heavy lift in the gym, and not carrying a man who he had trusted, a man who had forsaken him.

Chapter 34

The whole process of moving the unconscious bodies took around a half hour. In that time, none of the unconscious individuals in Lusky's quarters woke up. Not until they were in the holding cell, afterwards.

Unfortunately, Skye had to be reminded of Graham's earlier warning of the skull and crossbones on the Noxium canisters the hard way. It was one of the children. They weren't moving, and one of their helpers had discovered it the hard way, having broken down nearly into a panic attack when she thought that, by trying to carry the boy, she had killed him. Skye had calmed her down before the three friends stood over near the body, debating over what to do next.

"Oh my God," Skye said. She had to turn away to keep her composure. "He's just a kid. He can't be older than ten. That's so wrong."

"It's okay," Graham said, rubbing her back. Skye didn't pull away at all. "It's okay, Skye. This isn't… your fault. This was a group decision. It was me and Madison's plan."

"We couldn't have done anything different," Madison commented. "We had to do this, right? I didn't think I'd second guess myself, but… Look at him…"

"Yes," Graham replied. "We had no other option…"

"We can't just leave him," Skye mourned. "He deserves a proper sendoff."

"I know," Graham agreed. "There's also the issue of the bodies in the oxygen center."

"*What?*" Madison asked. "You said *what?*"

"Well," Skye explained. "Marcell saved us from a couple of guards… He killed one. The other one… he got taken care of. Marcell got hurt. He's being tended to right now by Dr. Silva. It's why he's not with us."

Madison nodded understandingly. "What a predicament. Shit."

***

After the job was complete, they got the several unconscious guards from the Lobby over into the holding cells. This time, they weren't quite as lucky as they had been extracting the other ones. One of the guards woke up and was quite tenacious in throwing off everyone carrying him and making a run for it. But in the end, they rounded him up with the rest and put him in the holding cell.

After that, they freed all of the previous captives from the remaining cells. There had been some individuals in there the entire time, but Skye had been too busy with helping establish control over the ship that she had neglected them.

Finally, once they had finished freeing the captives who'd been seized by the security team, as well as finished placing the rest of those in Lusky's quarters into the cells, it was clear that they had finally gained true control over the ship, and it was only 3:11 a.m.

Now there were a grand total of five security guards in the prison cells (Fritz was unaccounted for). There was also a grand total of twenty-four individuals between the management in Lusky's quarter, the allies of management (such as Mr. Xiong), and their families, all unconscious. There had been a child who was unresponsive, as well as another, an adult this time, who wasn't found to not be breathing until later, after the one security guard who had woken up had gone around checking their pulses and found that they weren't breathing. He was a middle-aged man who was the husband of one of the Vice Presidents also in captivity. Skye had the man dragged out. She dreaded having to have that conversation with the unconscious family members, because the VP was going to find out sooner than later, and so too were the family members of the boy who had died in his sleep.

If I even have to do that, Skye reminded herself. *We're not their friends anymore.*

Even though Skye had told herself that everything she had done was for her own survival, it still felt wrong for Skye, and it was a decision of how to deal with them that she had to grapple with over the next few minutes.

"We don't owe them anything," Madison told her at one point while they escorted many of the now freed captives back to the hotel rooms. By now, the fumes had dissipated, the air filters in the ISH doing their jobs to clean the air. "We can send them down to Earth, the sooner the better."

"How can you say that with a straight face?" Skye asked.

"Do you not remember what they did to us?" Madison inquired. "What they did to me? They were going to do that to you, and remember, Marcell said we're running out of food, anyway."

"Look, we have to deal with a lot," Graham said. "First things first, we need to make sure everything is running smoothly. Then we can deal with what to do with all of them."

"Who the hell even is going to be running this ship?" Skye asked. "Lusky and all of the managers are gone. We've probably got to go down like 10 spots if we're going by order of seniority."

"I don't know," Graham admitted. "What I do know is that you showed you have leadership qualities. Skye, you motivated darn everyone. You saved my life back in the oxygen center, when I… I choked. Skye, why don't you run things? I respect your opinion so much."

"I don't know how to properly cook spaghetti without A.I. assistance, and you're expecting me to run a spaceship of hundreds of people? Come on, Graham."

"For the record, I can't cook for shit either," Madison said, managing a smile. "But right now, we got a couple dozen people who were previously running things sitting in prison cells, and now we gotta figure a way to keep us all living."

Their captors, now turned captives, were indeed sitting in their cells. One by one, they began waking up, pounding on the door. But there was no help that would come for them. They were locked up tight, and Skye prepared to talk to Alan Lusky.

Before then, Skye and Graham managed to get control of the communications room as well, and were able to receive an update from Dr. Silva, who said that Marcell was in stable condition, now resting with Fritz watching over him. They checked on him at one point, and found him now recovering in the infirmary.

"I'm okay," Marcell said. "Hey, can you do me a favor?"

"Sure," Skye answered.

"Bring Lusky over to my room," Marcell said. "I want to have a chit chat with him."

The tone of his voice let them all know that whatever they were going to have, it wasn't going to be idle chit chat at all.

"We'll do that," Skye promised. "Soon as we get him out, we'll bring him to your room."

***

Skye went into the holding cell with Graham and retrieved Alan Lusky. Both of them used their assault rifles to deter anyone from doing anything brash. A few of the members of management

299

were firing questions off at her, but she didn't address them. Not now.

One of the men in the cell was furious, yelling at her and asking where his son was. Skye couldn't look him in the eye, and, as they left the room, closing the door shut behind themselves, the man angrily slammed his fists on the window over and over again. It seemed like he could sense something was terribly wrong by the way Skye and Graham had averted his eyes. That didn't inspire confidence in another woman, who repeatedly quietly asked if she could speak to her husband. Skye didn't have the heart to tell them, not now.

Despite the obstacles, Graham and Skye followed through with their promise to Marcell. They took him straight towards the infirmary, and Madison met them on the way.

"I don't know where you're taking me," Alan Lusky told them as Skye guided him by grabbing him roughly by the collar, "But I can tell you that you're making a terrible mistake. Ow! Careful on the collar. It's a vicuña wool, it's pricey."

"We're not going to play stupid with you," Skye said through gritted teeth. "In return, we expect that you don't take us for idiots."

"Look, we can talk this through," Alan Lusky pleaded. "This certainly is all some kind of misunderstanding. I mean, I was just throwing a little gala with Eva, having her play some piano for us and then, all of a sudden, out of nowhere, there was this gas… it was heavy, it knocked us out. And then I wake up in a holding cell. I promise, that's the truth, and the whole truth. I don't know what else to say."

No one acknowledged Lusky's story, but the three of them continued dragging him to the infirmary in a couple of minutes, where he was presented with a sight that shut him up instantly for a minute.

"Fritz. Marcell." Alan Lusky said quietly, as Skye pulled up a chair, which he accepted, sitting down, but not before evaluating the chair closely for a couple of seconds, as if he expected it to collapse under his own weight, or for a spike to protrude upwards at a moment's notice.

"Hello, Mr. Lusky," Marcell answered from his bed.

"What is this?" Lusky asked. He swiveled on his seat to look at Fritz. "You too?"

Fritz shrugged.

"You told me whether or not I could trust you," Marcell replied. "I think that question was a little bit rich, what with what happened to Franco and all."

"Franco?" Skye asked. "What about Franco?"

"The radio controller," Marcell explained quietly, wincing in pain. "You know him?"

"Yes," she replied. "I'm… I was a communications intern. I've worked mainly with him and Lex."

"Well, some days ago, he took me to have a conversation. It ended up with a fight with him. Now I know what was going on. You, Mr. Lusky, were getting him on your side to execute this plan. To thin out the ship, and have him act as your golden poster boy in the announcements, explain how everyone willingly left when they got the green light for Earth."

"Shit," Madison responded. "That's a whole new level of messed up."

"I overheard that he was d-disposed of," Marcell replied. "You gave him the same treatment that you give trash. You launched him into space, and he died quickly, I imagine."

Lusky sat up. Fritz seemed to stand up straighter too, his face animated in disbelief.

"That's… That's not true!"

"You don't need to lie to me about it," Marcell replied. "I had a conversation with the people responsible. Some of the other guards. They admitted to it, straight up. Said he'd stolen rations. You didn't even have the dignity to tell them the truth. You lied to your own foot soldiers. Finally, karma's a bitch."

"You…" Madison said, shaking her head. "You monster."

"This! This is absurd!" Lusky exclaimed. "I already told them what really happened today. There was nothing going on. I was just having a party in the late hours of the night, and you had to go and gas us all. Where are the others that are missing, by the way? Vice President Mosi's husband is missing, and so is Mr. Bertrand's child. I can only imagine what your move is."

Marcell looked at the others for guidance.

"I think you already know the answer," Skye replied quietly.

Lusky shook his head. "See, that's the thing. You villainize me for making the difficult decisions, and yet you use a weapon, a weapon which, if used upon a civilian population back during ordinary times, would've been considered a war crime, and you use it against us, against our wives, our children, who know absolutely nothing about our plans, and you kill some of them. Yet you think we're the bad guys?"

"There were no other options," Graham contested. "We didn't bring you to debate the morality of what we did. We came for answers."

"What is there to say? It's obvious you've already acted. What the hell do you want me to say? To answer for?"

"I was hoping to see you a little bit more… What's the word for it? Contrite?" Skye inquired. "I guess that's why I'm a little bit disappointed that you're pouting like a schoolboy who just got grounded and lost his video game privileges."

Lusky sighed. "Being a leader isn't easy. You know, in American culture, it's so ubiquitous and normalized to just dunk on every single successful human, post so many death threats online at a second's notice. You get banned? No problem, you can just set up another account because you're using a VPN. Sometimes, they even sent things over the mail. You think we don't see them, that we aren't affected by them. The rich and successful, like us. But we are. Because we're humans, too. It's the same thing here. I didn't want to eject all of you back to Earth. Which, for the record, would've been using our space pods, and as safe and ethical as possible. But we were out of food. Your odds were better on Earth than they were staying here. That's all I have to say about that."

"You knew about the state of the Earth, don't play dumb. I was in the room with you when we got that transmission," Skye countered. "You knew it wasn't safe, and yet you decided to try to get rid of a bunch of innocent people. That's disgusting."

"So what? What would you have done? Let them all starve to death? The skinniest would go first. You," Lusky said, pointing to Madison, who frowned. "You don't have a lot of meat on your bones. You'd probably be one of the earlier ones to go. They'd have to cannibalize your body to survive, and eat every single last organ. Because that's pretty much the only way you can sustain a population with everyone sticking around. Cannibalism. Are you okay with that?"

"Freak," Madison spat, before eyeing him down. "I think we'd start by eating the rich, and you seem to be rich in fats. And for the record, I am an organ donor. But I'm not giving my left kidney to an asshole like you."

"Hmph," Lusky harrumphed.

"Life isn't binary," Skye argued. "We didn't have to either launch all those people, or starve to death. It isn't that simple. You can reduce it down to that, but that's a false dichotomy."

"Well, let me know what other options there are," Lusky continued, staring at Skye. "Because me, and all of my managers, couldn't think of anything else. You, I bet you would choose to have everyone stay on board. But now, I'm assuming you're going to launch us, and all of our innocent families, back to Earth, just to lighten the load. You think that that would make you the good guys, but in reality, you'd be doing the exact same thing as us. Because there are no good guys or bad guys right now, now that everything is fubar. There are only survivors, and non-survivors, and I was going to be one of the survivors, *dammit*. So, what'll it be, Skye, hmm? Are you going to send me back down to Earth as a "lesson"?"

Skye stared for a few seconds at him. She could feel goosebumps running down the length of her spine.

"Don't listen to what he says," Graham said.

"You don't need to tell him anything," Marcell replied.

"I'm through talking to you," Skye said. "There's always another way. You were looking out for yourself above all. It might be natural. But at the expense of innocents… That's not right. I'm not going to do that. Maybe when people are on the verge of starving to death, but we're not even close; we've had rations, and we're not even out of food yet. No, I won't let your distractions dissuade me."

"How could you possibly run a spaceship by yourself?" Lusky asked. "What are you, twenty? When I was twenty, I was sitting around drinking, and hell, snorting coke. You've never even been in the real world at all. I helped build the real world. I started the most lucrative hotel in the world. You're nothing. You can't run a spaceship by yourself. You'd be a lost little lamb trying to steer a marvelous piece of technology that you wouldn't even begin to comprehend."

"You shouldn't underestimate her." The voice came from the back of the room, and Skye and everyone else did a 180 to look at Fritz who had spoken up. "This kid is less jaded, less broken down, than any single politician or businessman I've ever met. You included. I respect that. She's got morals, guts, and a brain. The brain's still developing, I would reckon, but if she's like this now, I can't imagine what a leader she'll be in five years when we're rebuilding the world."

"Fritz," Marcell mumbled gratefully. "I'm glad you're on our side."

"There are no sides, as Lusky explained," Fritz corrected him. "Only survivors and non-survivors. I think I'm going to go with the living."

"Fritz, how could you," Lusky whined. He looked up, this time with pleading eyes that almost reminded her of puppy eyes. "You should let me take control again. I've learned my lesson. I won't eject all of you. But if you really want to survive, then management, who understands everything and has all the knowledge to keep this hotel functioning, needs to be in charge."

"Gave me a chance? How in the world did you ever give me a chance?"

"Back in that meeting I set you up with Ron. I know, I know, you just think that we're these skeevy old dudes trying to exploit you. But remember, that man's wife and children were gone. He gave you an option to get on the list, and yet you declined it. I absolutely did give you a chance to stay. So how about it? Will you hear my counter-proposal for how to maneuver in these trying times?"

"No," Skye said. "Maddie, Graham, let's take him back. Unless you've got anything more to say, Marcell?"

"No," Marcell responded. "I've said my piece."

"Marcell?" Lusky said, turning to him. "Oh, you're the one who leaked everything? Of course, it was you… It could only be you."

Marcell's lips were pursed, but he didn't look away when Lusky stared at him as Madison and Graham escorted him back towards the jail cells, and Lusky walked slowly out of the room, not even bothering to fight or run, not with Skye and Graham's weapons. He did, however, have something to say.

"I trusted you," Alan Lusky repeated. "I trusted you, Marcell. And you broke that trust."

"Your trust means nothing to me," Marcell muttered.

Something about the conversation did shake Skye. Lusky did have a point. She couldn't help but acknowledge that by sending the group to Earth, she would be employing the same tactics as Lusky. Moreover, if she were to include Lusky and his family in the group, it would extend beyond the realm of justice and into the territory of revenge, which was not something she was comfortable with. After all, Lusk's wife and child had nothing to do with Operation Exodus, which was the work of only a handful of people, she guessed. But there was a time and a place to experience emotions and weigh moral conundrums, and now wasn't the time, because the fatigue was seriously starting to set in. It was almost 4:30 in the morning once Lusky had been whisked back to his cell.

Chapter 35

"We, er, need to think about leadership soon, Skye…"

"I know, Marcell."

Skye and Marcell were now together in the infirmary, staring out over the devastated Earth. While Skye was standing in front of the window, its parted curtains flung off to the side, Marcell was in a bed on one of the hospital beds. He had received some strong painkillers (it appeared that Madison hadn't raided *all* of them), but was somehow still lucid. Surgery was to be performed in the coming hours, and Skye had visited him to wish him good luck. He was hooked into a patient monitor, which beeped quietly with his heartrate and gave comprehensive information on his vitals. Skye never remembered being around one before in real life, but she didn't like it. The knowledge, and accompanying bleep, of his heart's rhythm on the monitor creeped her out.

"You shouldn't talk so much," Skye advised.

"Nonsense…"

Currently, the ISH was orbiting over the Pacific Ocean, hovering above some Southeastern Asian islands that Skye wasn't quite familiar with, and she and Marcell observed in awe. Skye vaguely recalled this region of the world being situated on the so-called 'ring of fire,' and as she gazed down at the planet below, she was tempted to refer to the whole Earth as the 'sphere of fire' now. Despite the devastation of the Red Day, she was relieved to see that parts of the planet still flourished with patches of green, a welcome respite amidst the splotches of black, brown, and gray.

It was almost five a.m., and Skye was exhausted, and ready to head off to bed. But something kept her here.

"I think, we need to take a stance far different from Lusky," Marcell continued. "One that looks a lot less authoritarian."

"Yes," Skye agreed. "I think we should have a council of five of us running things. I think transparency's important after everything that happened with the previous regime."

"Good idea," Marcell said. His face looked drained, and now he spoke in a quiet tone, a loud whisper. Despite that, he had no intentions of refraining from talking. "Maybe Fritz can operate things as the head, or figure-head if he doesn't want to. We just need a qualified group of five members."

"Yes. You, me, Fritz… Who else?" Skye asked, before apologizing. "Sorry. I shouldn't be asking you all these questions when you're literally with a bullet in your side."

"No, it's a good point," Marcell rasped. "I don't know. We'd have to think about that."

Skye tried thinking aloud, but she was too tired. Even in her exhausted state, she thought appointing any of her friends, or anyone else her age, in a leadership position was probably a bad look. But she didn't know many of the older adults on board.

"You look fatigued," Marcell observed, smiling. "I will be too, once all the drugs I was prescribed wears off. That is, if I even survive."

"Don't say that. You'll survive this, and come back stronger than ever. I know it."

"Maybe you should sleep on this," Marcell replied. "God knows you've earned it."

Skye nodded, ready to return to her room, and she began crossing the room to exit. But before she could leave, Marcell called out her name quietly.

"Yeah?" Skye asked, turning around.

"It's still beautiful, isn't it?" Marcell asked, weakly lifting his finger and pointing over to the islands they looked at, which were relatively intact apart from what looked like a spattering of brown. As if the fires hadn't even spared this location entirely.

"Yeah. Yeah, it is. I hope one day we can set foot back down on the Earth again."

"Yes. I think we will be able to, if only we can get everything straightened out." Marcell thought deeply for a few moments. "I never got to thank you."

"For saving the ship? That was mainly Graham that did that. You should be thanking him, not me. *Hell*, I should be thanking you. You saved my life tonight."

"Nonsense," Marcell replied, his whisper growing fainter. "It was all of you. But that's not what I mean… Thank you for bringing me back."

"Excuse me?" Skye asked, raising her eyebrows.

"For so long, I was doing what I was doing, reporting to work, almost with a glaze over my eyes. I pretended that my life was fine even though it wasn't, and I hid my own demons instead of confronting them. I was so empty and emotionless; I was like one of those now-defunct service robots."

"I… That was never my intention, but I'm glad it helped."

"More than you would know. Now I remember… The importance of friends, of emotional vulnerability, of teamwork. It feels refreshing… The importance of deeper meaning in my life."

"You found deeper meaning?"

"Yes." Marcell stared at her intently.

Skye stood for a few moments silently. She never was so good at being emotionally vulnerable with people, but after quite literally catching a bullet for her, Skye figured Marcell definitely deserved it.

"I'm jealous. Right now, I have nothing," Skye answered with a stoic expression. "Yet I keep on going… Even though mom, dad, Em, Braydon, all dead… I don't know how I function. All of my hopes and dreams of living a regular yet successful life, gone out the window. Not to mention I killed a man just today. Somehow, I don't even barely feel anything anymore, like it's just some dream I'll wake up from now. All of my purpose, all of my family and friends, everything important to me, gone forever, just like that. Because some greedy old man somewhere pressed his nuclear launch button, everything's gone."

"Well, not everything's gone," Marcell countered.

Skye thought of Graham, of Maddie, and of everyone on board the ship, and she agreed.

"You're right," Skye said, managing a smile. "And, today's a new day, isn't it?"

"That's right. We'll lead a rebuild, re-organize the ship, and take care of management, one way or another."

"Alright," Skye said. "Sounds good. Now sleep."

There was nothing else that needed to be said. Marcell slunk back into his bed, his eyes closing all at once. For a few seconds, Skye felt her heart racing, certain that he was about to shudder as he rasped his last breath of air and that his heartrate would flatline to set off the monitor into a frenzy of beeping. But it didn't happen. His chest slowly rose up and down, and Skye sighed in relief as Dr. Silva returned to wave her away.

A new plan for survival was in the works, and Skye knew it was bound to be tough. And despite her expectations, running the ship and overcoming the ensuing obstacles would be much more complex, and arduous, than she ever could've imagined. But Skye knew that she would give it her all. Operation Exodus had failed. That marked an ultimate end to Lusky's International Space Hotel, and a new beginning in their journey. Skye slept well that night.

Author's Note

Book 2 is out now. Buy it on Amazon today! If you enjoyed, please feel free to review the book on Goodreads or Amazon. As an indie author, reviews are critical in promoting visibility for the series. Thank you for reading!